PRENTICE-HALL, INC.
A SPECTRUM BOOK Englewood Cliffs, New Jersey 07632

Charles J. Pecor

illustrations by Mike Fuller

The Craft of Magic

easy-to-learn illusions for spectacular performances

Library of Congress Cataloging in Publication Data

Pecor, Charles J (date)
  The craft of magic.

  (A Spectrum Book)
  Bibliography: p.
  Includes index.
  1. Conjuring.   2. Tricks.   I. Title.
GV1547.P38   793.8   79-632
ISBN 0-13-188847-1
ISBN 0-13188839-0 pbk.

A Spectrum Book

10 9 8 7 6 5 4 3 2 1

Printed in the United States of America

Editorial/production supervision by Eric Newman
Interior design by Jeannette Jacobs and Eric Newman
Cover design by Gayle Cadden
Manufacturing buyer: Cathie Lenard

Prentice-Hall International, Inc., *London*
Prentice-Hall of Australia Pty. Limited, *Sydney*
Prentice-Hall of Canada, Ltd., *Toronto*
Prentice-Hall of India Private Limited, *New Delhi*
Prentice-Hall of Japan, Inc., *Tokyo*
Prentice-Hall of Southeast Asia Pte. Ltd., *Singapore*
Whitehall Books Limited, *Wellington, New Zealand*

Charles J. Pecor has been performing magic for almost 30 years and is assistant professor of speech at Macon Junior College, Macon, Georgia, and a member of the International Brotherhood of Magicians and the Society of American Magicians.

This book is dedicated with affection and appreciation to my first three teachers in magic: Doyle Allen, Bob Carver, and J. C. Doty.

Contents

1 Magic with Cards 7

2 Magic with Coins 55

3 Magic with Ropes 97

4 Close-up Magic 139

5 Stage and Platform Magic 185

6 The Real Secrets 225

7 Conclusion: The Art of Magic 267

Index 271

Foreword

As I glance over the shelves of my own "magical" library, my eyes wander past the hundreds of books, pamphlets, and periodicals that have remained unopened over the years since that first reading at the time of purchase. They came to rest on a shelf of books much more worn and dog-eared than the others. This is my "working" shelf, containing books written by Fox, Vernon, Garcia, Ginn, Marshall, Annemann, Lorayne, and a few others . . . names that are household words to those of us who are immersed in the world of magic. These books are full of magical secrets and ideas for presentation, and they can teach one to be a magician. There is a space on that shelf reserved for Charlie Pecor's book, *The Craft of Magic;* that is how good it is!

The Craft of Magic is an outstanding book for those just beginning in magic. Too often the magic in beginner's books is little more than a collection of puzzles. Such is not the case here; every trick is in reality a routine fully and clearly explained. If the reader will study and practice, he can mystify an audience; if he carefully studies "The Real Secrets" and applies the principles found therein, he can also entertain an audience.

The intermediate and even the advanced magician can benefit from the book as well. The "Maximum Misdirection Card to Pocket," the "Mongolian Clock," the "Bionic Vampire," and the "Instant Cow" are routines that Charles has performed many times to the delight of many audiences, from those at Christmas banquets to those at magicians' conventions. They are worthy of our "in house" magic publications, distributed to magicians only. You will enjoy learning them and you will use them.

For the magic fraternity as a whole (which perhaps many of you are entering for the first time) the last chapter of this book, "The Real Secrets," is alone worth more than the cost of the book several times over. Charles Pecor, Ph.D., has a fine academic background in speech and drama that, when combined with his knowledge of and experience in magic and the stage, has resulted in a thorough treatment of the techniques of learning and presenting magic—techniques almost always treated in a cursory fashion elsewhere.

The Craft of Magic will be a welcome addition to the "working" shelves of many, many libraries; it is also an excellent book with which to begin one!

Dr. David R. Goodsell

Editor, *M-U-M* magazine
(published by the Society
of American Magicians)

Preface

In writing this book, it has been my intention to supply you with a means of entering the complex, fascinating, and rewarding world of magic. Although this book is basically designed with the "beginning" magician in mind, it will also prove useful to the more advanced conjurer because of its emphasis on the presentation of magic, an area that is sadly neglected in all but a few books on the craft of magic.

The tricks contained in this book have been chosen for their variety, ranging as they do from close-up magic with cards, coins, and other miscellaneous objects to stage and platform tricks using tubes, ropes, and boxes. The tricks have also been selected on the basis of the amount of skill required to perform them. In each chapter there are some tricks that can be performed with a minimum of skill, but, at the same time, other tricks will challenge you to extend your ability as a magician. A number of the "classics" of magic have been included in these pages, but you will also find a number of novel, off-beat tricks as well.

There are several features that make this book useful in learning how to perform and present magic. The tricks are taught through step-by-step instructions with numerous illustrations so that you may clearly understand *how* to do them. At various points in the book, you will be given "Bonus Times." These items show variations on the basic trick that you have been taught. At other points in the book, you will be faced with "Thinking Times" that call on you to employ some creative thinking about the trick that has just been described. Both of these features serve the function of stimulating you to "think magic."

A characteristic of this book that makes it valuable to magicians of all degrees of training and skill is that it stresses not just the mechanics of the tricks but the psychology behind the tricks as well. In addition to dealing with the "why" of magic in the chapters on tricks, the book includes a special chapter called "The Real Secrets," which examines the whole spectrum of presenting magic, from rehearsal and practice to suggestions on how to increase your knowledge and skill in the craft.

Several individuals are due my thanks because of their contributions to the preparation of this book. My fellow magician Mike Fuller spent many hours working from my demonstrations and rough sketches in drawing the illustrations. Nelson Miller, my colleague in the Humanities Division of Macon Junior College, worked diligently and tirelessly at the task of proofreading. In addition to being skilled at their work, they are both dear friends. My wife, Claudia, not only served as a proofreader but also became my "in-house" critic as well. I am sure that much of the clarity in this book came from her efforts to learn to perform the tricks on the basis of my written instructions and rough drawings. She also gave freely of her love and encouragement in this project.

Magic, when performed well, is fulfilling to the performer and delightful to the viewers. May the pages of this book teach and inspire you to weave the magic spell that leaves you satisfied and your audiences entertained.

Introduction
The Craft
of Magic

You may be asking yourself, "Why should I read *this* book?" My response is that I have attempted to create the kind of book that I wish I had read when I was beginning in magic. This book attempts to teach you not only the "how" of doing a magic trick but the "why" as well. If you have a magic set, a magic trick, or another book on magic, you may have discovered that the instructions from such sources often tell you how to do the trick without teaching you how to present it most effectively or without really explaining the magic principles involved. I not only explain many magic tricks, but I also point out to you why you do what you do in order to make the trick work. In addition to the chapters on tricks, you will find a chapter called "The Real Secrets," in which I discuss such topics as rehearsal, misdirection, and dealing with anxiety. These areas are seldom discussed in beginners' magic books, or even in more advanced texts on magic, yet they are of basic importance to a magician as opposed to "a person who does tricks."

In the title of this book, I have used the word *craft* in relation to magic because I think that is what magic is, a craft. I believe that, by mastering a certain body of skills, you can become a magician. I do not believe that it requires some sort of gift or supernormal talent. If you have even adequate coordination and are willing to work at it, you can become a magician. Can you become the "World's Greatest Magician"? This is not guaranteed, not from reading this book, not even from spending a lifetime studying and working at magic. For all the people who can play a musical instrument, how many great musicians are there? For all the men in this country who play football in high school and college, how many are successful in the pros? You may never become the World's Greatest Magician, but if you are willing to make the effort, you *can* learn to present entertaining magic.

I have decided to include what I call the "Ten Basic Rules of Magic." I have drawn these rules from years of studying, performing, and teaching magic.

1. Never tell anyone how a trick is done. It is, however, permissible to share the secret of a trick with another magician. One of the greatest temptations that a beginning magician faces is to show how a trick is done after he has fooled someone with it. This is a false ego trip because the beginning magician is really showing someone else's secret and not one that he has invented himself. You will discover as you study magic that most of the secrets are rather simple and that how you present the trick is more important than the secret itself, but part of the charm of magic is the mystery, the "how was it done?" If you take that quality away from magic by exposing the secrets, you deprive the audience of part of the entertainment value of the craft. It is, of course, necessary to share some of the secrets of magic in order to spread the growth of the craft, just as I am doing in this book, and you will discover that most magicians are happy to share their secrets with other magicians.

2. Never do a trick without sufficient practice. You should practice a trick a minimum of 50 or 60 times before doing it in public.

3. Never do the same trick twice for the same audience under the same conditions. Much of the success of any given magic trick depends on the element of surprise. The audience doesn't know in advance exactly what is going to happen, so they don't know what to look for; but, if you repeat the trick, they will know what to look for on the second showing. The element of surprise will be missing and the audience may be able to catch the trick. There are some tricks in which the magician apparently repeats the trick, but the ending is different or a different method is employed in order to throw the spectators off. Obviously, such tricks do not violate this rule.

4. Never force your magic on people. There is no quicker way to get the reputation of being a boring person than to always chase people around with the request to "take a card" or "look at this." There are some people who simply don't like magic, and even people who like magic, except for some magicians, can get enough of it. If you force people to watch your magic, they are likely to resist rather than cooperate, making your task of entertaining more difficult.

5. Never perform too many tricks at one time. This "rule" is closely related to number 4. You do have to learn when enough is enough. Sometimes one trick is enough. In most situations, three tricks are plenty. Even if you have been asked to perform in advance, on most occasions, a show that runs between 20 and 30 minutes is long enough. No matter how well your magic is being received, always keep in mind the old show-business saying "Leave them wanting more."

6. While watching another magician perform, never say to anyone else: "I can do that better"; "I know how that's done"; or "That's easy." You *may* be able to do the trick better, but the person who hears you say this may assume that you are jealous. You may know how the trick is done, but because you can't pass on the secret to a nonmagician, why even bring it up? The trick may be easy, as many apparently difficult magic feats are, but you don't want nonmagicians to know that, do you?

7. Never handle another magician's equipment without first getting his permission. Magic equipment is a very personal possession for most magicians and they tend to become anxious and agitated when other people handle their materials. You could damage some delicate mechanism or lose a piece of the apparatus.

8. Never ask another magician, directly, how to do a trick. While magicians are willing, many times, to share their secrets with other magicians, it is considered bad form to ask unless the other magician is a close friend. It is more appropriate to say something like, "That really fooled me. I'd sure like to know how it was done." Other magicians can then take the hint, and, if they wish, share the secret with you. If they do not wish to share, it is unwise to press.

9. Always compliment another magician when you sincerely think you have seen a good job. Magicians are just like other people in that they enjoy praise, and there is no praise quite so sweet as that from another magician. This does not mean that you should falsely praise a performer. Along these same lines, it is unwise to offer unsolicited advice to other magicians about how they might improve their acts. You might make an enemy or lose a friend.

10. Always remember that magic, effectively presented, will be warmly received by most people, giving pleasure to both the performer and the audience. This is not so much a "rule" as it is a general observation that you might reflect on as you study this book and work to become a magician.

In this book I have attempted to be as honest and direct with you as possible. This book does reflect, as any book must, the biases of the writer. You will, for example, find a good deal of magic that can be done close up because I believe that most magicians have more opportunities to do close-up magic than to do stage or platform magic. You will also discover that there are no large stage tricks in this book because I do not think that a beginning magician needs to attempt such feats until after having acquired a good deal of experience. You will note that many of the tricks employ humor and require assistance from the spectators. I have found that such tricks are useful in establishing rapport between the magician and his audience.

At this point, I think it is appropriate for me to comment on how you might most effectively use this book. I suggest that you read it from cover to cover before you start trying to do any of the magic. If you are so eager to get to the tricks that you can't wait until you read the entire book, I do recommend that you at least read "The Real Secrets" before you start attempting to do the magic. Throughout the text, in order to save time and space, I have used two abbreviations: RH means "right hand," and LH means "left hand." You will find both of these abbreviations used in the text and in the illustrations. To my female readers I must apologize for the use of "he," "him," and "his," but the English language does not yet have an acceptable neutral alternative for the third-person pronoun (except "it"), and I could not see writing "he/she" each time I intended to mean either. Nor could I refer to a spectator as "it." It should be understood, therefore, that when "he," "his," or "him" is used these words refer to either sex.

I hope that *The Craft of Magic* serves you well as your initiation into the world of magic.

1

Magic
with Cards

INTRODUCTION

When I began planning this book, it seemed only natural to deal with card magic in the first chapter. Of all of the props associated with magic, cards are the most prevalent. The total number of card tricks in existence outnumbers tricks done with any other object. There are hundreds of books written on card magic alone, and most general books on magic contain at least one chapter on card magic. Within the fraternity of magic, there are a number of magicians who do nothing but card tricks. (These magicians are known as "card men," and often clump together at magic meetings and conventions to show their latest tricks to others of their ilk. In spite of their devotion to the pasteboards, most of them are a good lot and can appreciate other kinds of magic.) You will even find many people who do not consider themselves magicians who know at least one card trick.

The popularity of card magic can be attributed to several factors. Cards are familiar objects to most people. Many people who have no interest in magic play games involving cards. Cards are easily transported; they take up little space and can be carried on the person. The variations of card tricks are almost, or seem to be, endless. Since I have been in magic, I have seen literally thousands of card tricks.

With these factors in mind, I think it is only fitting that your education should begin with this fascinating area of magic. You will note as you read this chapter that none of the tricks depend on a great deal of dexterity. There are, of course, card tricks that rely heavily on the ability of the performer to manipulate the cards; however, this is the realm for more advanced books on card magic. There are also many card tricks that rely on special cards or even special decks. As you pursue your interest in magic you will visit magic shops and see many examples of such cards and decks. These are referred to as gimmicked cards or decks. In magic, the word "gimmick" means the special preparation of some ordinary object or some hidden piece of apparatus that enables the trick to work. Tricks using gimmicked cards or decks will not be discussed in this chapter for two reasons. One is that beginning magicians (and too often magicians who cannot be considered beginners) often tend to use such cards as a crutch. Another reason is that these special cards and decks are sold by dealers who depend upon the sale of magic for their livelihood, and it would be unethical for me to expose these items. All of the tricks in this chapter have been selected because of their impact and their ease of execution. This does not mean that you will be able to do a trick the first time that you attempt it. Each of these tricks requires practice, but they are within the range of the ability of almost anyone who is willing to make the effort to learn them.

A final word on cards before we begin the tricks themselves. The kind of cards that you use has some importance. Most of the "card men" that I know prefer to use poker-width cards and they argue about which brand of cards is best. I do not feel that for most magicians (especially beginning magicians) poker-width cards are necessarily best. You should obtain both a poker-width and a bridge-width deck and try them out. Many people discover that the bridge-width deck, because it is narrower than the poker-width deck, is easier to use. For the time being, I suggest that you use the deck that best fits your hand. It is also wise to use a deck that has a white border rather than a deck with a back design that covers the entire back of the card. If you need to reverse a card in this deck, this reversed card is not as obvious if the deck has a white border, but the reversed card could be very obvious if the deck has a back design that covers the entire card. It is also wise for you to learn how to handle a deck of cards. Get a deck of cards and shuffle them, deal them, get the feel of the cards.

FORCING A CARD

Forcing a card means, literally, what it says. The magician causes the spectator to select the card that the magician wants him to take; but, at the same time, the spectator must think that the choice is freely made. Many card tricks depend on the ability of the magician to force a card. Three methods for doing this are given below.

method A

This method is simple and direct, and, if properly done, convincing. The card to be forced should be on the top of the deck. You may even shuffle the deck as long as the top card remains on top of the deck. When the time comes to force the card, do as follows.

1. Place the deck in front of the spectator and request that the deck be cut, but ask him not to complete the cut. This means that he will remove the top half of the deck (approximately) and place it to the side of the remainder of the deck.

2. Ask him to place the bottom half of the deck across the top half of the deck thus marking the point at which the deck was cut. This is called "Xing" the cut. (See Figure 1-1.)

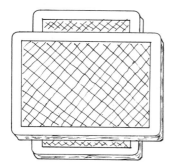

Figure 1-1.

3. You must now briefly break the spectator's train of thought by making some comment. This serves to momentarily distract his attention from what has happened. The comments that you make while performing a magic trick are known as "patter," and the patter that you use should, in some manner, relate to the trick.

4. Now pick up all of the cards in the top half of the X and point to the top (face down) card on remaining "arm" of the X, saying "Let's see which card you cut to," or "Take a look at the card that you cut to." In reality the spectator is going to look at the card that was on the top of the deck originally, but, if you properly distracted his attention in step 3, he will have forgotten which half of the deck was the original top half of the deck and will assume that this was the card that he cut to. This force should be done casually, boldly, and directly. (Later in this

10

chapter, I cover several methods for revealing a card that has been forced.)

method B This method can be called "the diagonal shift" and is more difficult than Method A, but it can be learned and executed smoothly with practice.

1. As in Method A, the card to be forced is on the top of the deck. The deck should be held down in the LH with your middle, ring, and little fingers curling around one long side of the deck. The index finger is near or rests on the upper right corner of the deck. The thumb rests on the upper left corner of the deck. (See Figure 1-2.)

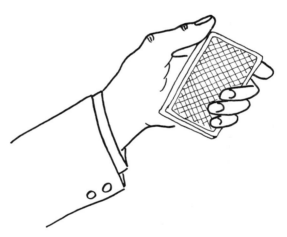

Figure 1-2.

2. Turn slightly to your right while, at the same time, rotating your LH, the hand holding the deck, so that the *bottom* of the deck faces the spectator.

3. Riffle the corner of the deck nearest the left thumb with the left thumb while the left index finger folds over and applies pressure to the bottom of the deck. You riffle the cards by running your thumb down the corner beneath the thumb. As you do this, say to the spectator, "Tell me to stop at any point." This riffling should be done at a moderate speed.

4. When the spectator says, "Stop!" you should stop. You will usually be stopped between one-fourth of the way from the top of the deck to three-fourths of the way from the top. The left thumb holds a break in the deck at this point by putting pressure on the portion of the deck below the thumb. (See Figure 1-3.)

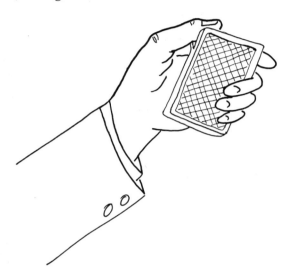

Figure 1-3.

5. The RH now approaches the deck. The middle and ring fingers of the RH grasp the upper short side of the deck while the right thumb grasps the lower short side of the deck. Both the middle finger, the ring finger, and the thumb of the RH should contact only the portion of the deck *above* the break. (See Figure 1-4.)

6. Now comes the most difficult sequence of moves in the force. The RH moves somewhat up and away from the LH in a diagonal direction away from your body, taking with it all of the cards *above the break* with the exception of the *top* card of the deck. The top card does not move because the pressure of the middle, ring, and little fingers of the LH hold it in place. The top card of the deck will, therefore, "slip" off the top portion of the deck and will end up on the bottom portion of the deck. As

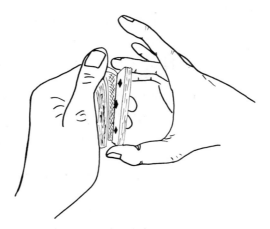

Figure 1-4.

the RH moves, the LH is also in motion. The LH turns palm
down as the RH is turning palm up. Study Figure 1-5 with care.
The movement of the two hands should be synchronized so
that both hands are moving at the same time.

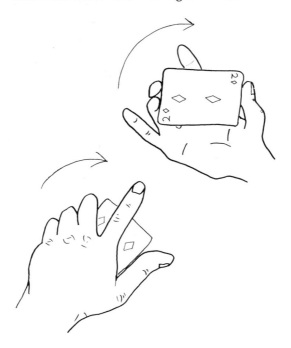

Figure 1-5.

7. The LH turns palm down at the same time that the RH turns palm up, and the index finger of the LH should be extended to point at the bottom card on the portion of the deck held in the RH, as shown in Figure 1-5, as you say, "We won't use this card because I can see it." If the moves have been executed properly, you will be looking directly at this card.

8. Turn the LH palm up and, at the same time, turn the RH palm down, while extending the index finger of the RH to tap the back of the top card on the part of the deck held in the LH as you say, "We'll use this card because I can't see the face of the card. This is the card at which you stopped me." If you have been following these instructions with care, you will recognize that this is the original top card of the deck, the card you already know.

9. Have the spectator look at this card. You have now forced a card! If you practice this method until you can perform it smoothly, you will have a force that is almost angleproof. You should take care to make sure that there are no spectators to your immediate right or to your right rear because they may see the move. Most magicians working close-up learn to adjust the position of their hands or bodies to cover any awkward angles.

method C   This is the most difficult of the three methods taught in this chapter because I am now going to deal with the method called the Classic Force. In this force you openly and boldly give the spectator the card that you want him to take and yet the selection appears to be very fair. This force depends on boldness and timing and each magician has his own favorite technique for doing it. I do think that you should be able to master the following one.

1. The card that you desire to force should be on the top of the deck. Hold the deck face down in your LH. As you approach the spectator who is going to select the card, you should cut the deck, placing the bottom half of the deck above what was

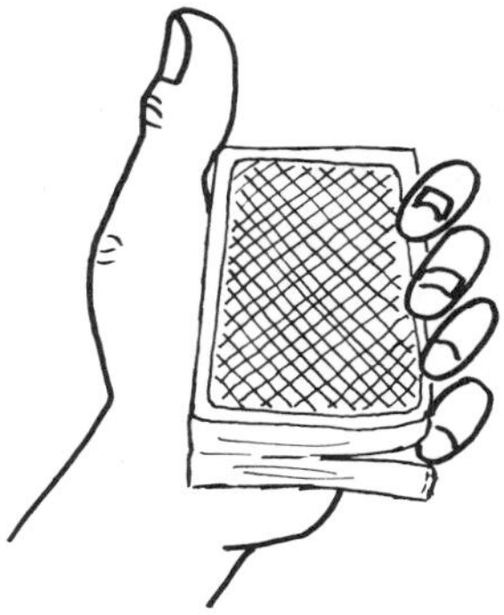

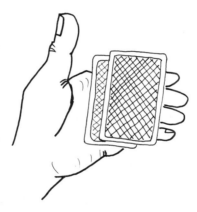

Figure 1-6.

the original top half of the deck. You should keep the two halves separate, unknown to the audience, by holding a little-finger break between them. (See Figure 1-6.)

The little-finger break can be made by inserting the tip of the little finger between the two halves of the deck, but as you become more experienced you will discover that the break can be held with the fleshy pad at the tip of the finger.

2. Gently push the top of the deck (the original bottom of the deck) to the right and release the little finger break. This will give the deck a slightly stepped arrangement and you will be able to maintain visual contact with the card that you are going to force. (See Figure 1-7.)

Figure 1-7.

3. Ask the spectator to extend his right index finger as you begin to move the cards on the top of the deck in the LH into the RH by pushing them over with the left thumb. (See Figure 1-8.)

The rate of movement should be moderate.

4. As you get to within nine or ten cards of the card that you want the spectator to select, you should say, "I just want you to drop your finger on any card." You should time your words so that you are within three or four cards of the selected card when you finish this statement.

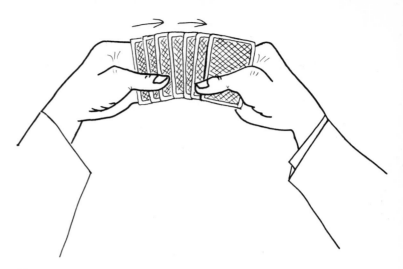

Figure 1-8.

5. Keep the cards moving from left to right and when you reach the card that you want him to take, push it slightly forward with the left thumb. In almost every case, especially after you learn to perform the steps smoothly, the spectator's finger will drop on the forced card. If this happens, ask the spectator to remove the card from the deck.

6. At this point, you are probably asking yourself, "What will I do if he doesn't take the card that I want him to take?" If this should happen (and it may happen many times when you are first learning this force), you should keep the cards moving and allow the spectator to take any card. (Later in this chapter I will teach you how to control a selected card and you can use one of the controls to get out of the situation.) Believe it or not, the Classic Force is "sure-fire" in the hands of someone who can do it; this is why it is worth your while to attempt to learn it and use it. Remember that it depends on your being casual, direct, and bold.

REVEALING A FORCED CARD

I have given you several methods of forcing a card because I feel that a magician should have more than one method for accomplishing a feat of magic, but the apparent results of the trick are more important than the method. That is, if you have only one method of forcing a card and six methods of revealing this forced card then, as far as the audience is concerned, you have six different tricks. On the other hand, if you have six methods of forcing a card but only one way of revealing it, as far as the audience is concerned, you have only one trick. Therefore, you should know a number of simple ways to reveal a card that has been forced.

telepathy

1. After you have forced a card on a spectator (for example, the Seven of Hearts), have the spectator return the card to the deck and place the deck aside.

2. Ask the spectator to concentrate on the value and suit of the card.

3. You should now appear to concentrate. Close your eyes. Wrinkle your brow. Make it appear that you are having difficulty in getting the "image" of the card.

4. After concentrating for a few seconds, you should say, "The card is a red card, correct?" Get the spectator to openly agree that the card is a red card.

5. You should next say, "That means that your card is either a heart or a diamond. I get the impression that your card is a heart. Am I right?" Once again, you should get the spectator to agree with you before moving on.

6. You have now come to the point of determining the value of the card. This should seem to cause you more difficulty and you might say something like the following: "Please concentrate on the value of the card. It's not a face card. It's higher than a five. It's the eight . . . no . . . the seven, the Seven of Hearts." This is a very simple revelation, yet if you have any acting ability at all, it can make a strong impression on the audience.

the psychological revelation

In this revelation you apparently do a psychological profile of the spectator to learn the identity of the card.

1. Force a card on the spectator and have it returned to the deck. For this example, let's say that you have forced the Ten of Clubs. Place the deck aside.

2. Get a pen and note pad or piece of paper as you patter about how the things that we like or dislike tell a great deal about our personalities.

3. Now ask the spectator a series of questions, such as his favorite color, food, month, day, sport, and so on. You can vary this by asking him to name things that he likes least.

4. As the spectator answers your questions, you should jot these items down on the note pad, assigning a number and a letter or series of letters to each answer. These numbers and letters have no meaning, although you should give the impression that they do.

5. After you have finished the questions, you should apparently make a series of calculations based on the numbers and the letters. Again, these calculations have no real meaning, but you should act as if they do.

6. When you have calculated for a few moments, you should say, "According to my system of analysis, if the information you have given me is accurate, you have a strong affinity for one card and the chances are that you have selected . . . the Ten of Clubs."

muscle control   In this revelation you apparently allow the spectator's muscles, controlled by his subconscious mind, to find the card.

1. Force the card on the spectator. Have him return it to the deck and shuffle the deck. Then have him spread the deck *face up* on the table so that all the faces of the cards are showing.

2. Spot the position of the force card as you talk of how the subconscious can control the body without the conscious mind being aware of it or, in some cases, even against the will of the conscious mind.

3. Offer to demonstrate this for the spectator and ask him to make a fist with his RH and to extend his right index finger.

4. Grasp the spectator's right wrist with both of your hands and ask him to point his index finger down toward the top of the table.

5. You should now move his hand over the face up cards on the table. Don't hurry this process, but pass his hand several times above the cards. Each time you should come closer to the selected card.

6. When you decide that you have given sufficient buildup to the trick, dramatically push the spectator's finger down until it touches the selected card.

the prediction   In this revelation you apparently tell the future by predicting the selected card.

1. Before your performance, seal a duplicate of the force card or a written prediction saying, "I predict that you will select the (whatever)" in an envelope. For example, let's say that you are going to force the Jack of Spades. Place a Jack of Spades from another deck or your written prediction in the envelope.

2. Place the envelope in full view of the audience before the card is selected but without telling them what you are going to do. This will protect you in case, for some reason, the force fails, and you have to do another trick to extricate yourself from the situation.

3. Force the card on the spectator. Have him retain the card and place the remainder of the deck aside.

4. Say to the spectator, "Earlier today I got an impression that a specific card would be selected by a member of my audience. I made a prediction and sealed it in this envelope. Now, for the first time, please show us the card that you selected."

5. The spectator shows the card and then you ask him to open the envelope. If you have written a prediction, you may have him read it aloud. If you have placed a duplicate card in the envelope, he can simply show it to the rest of the audience.

the strange thing

In this revelation you use a "strange thing" and a simple principle of psychology to find the selected card. In order to construct the strange thing, you will need a small marble, some plastic wood, and a piece of string about eighteen inches long. You will also need some cake coloring for decoration and a small container (a cuff-link box will do nicely) to be used as a case for the strange thing. You build the strange thing by forming a ball of plastic wood around the small marble and imbedding one end of the string in the ball. (See Figure 1-9.)

Allow the plastic wood to sit until it is hard and then color it by rubbing cake coloring over it. (The cake coloring will wash off your hands; avoid getting it on your clothing or any other item of value.) You will discover that you have indeed constructed a strange thing.

The strange thing is used in the following manner.

1. Force a card on the spectator (in this example, the Five of Diamonds).

2. After the card has been forced, ask the spectator to take four or five more cards from the deck, without showing you the faces of these cards or the face of the selected card, and mix them with the selected card.

3. Wrap the free end of the string around either your right or left index finger. Then place your elbow on the table and continue to wrap the string around your finger until the strange thing is suspended about an inch above the table. (See Figure 1-10.)

4. Ask the spectator to place the cards, one at a time, face up, beneath the strange thing.

5. When the selected card is placed beneath the strange thing, it will begin to swing, and neither your hand nor arm will appear to move. How does this work? It works because

Figure 1-9.

Figure 1-10.

you "will" the strange thing to move! This is true. If you concentrate on moving the strange thing, your muscles will respond subtly to this desire and they will cause it to swing without showing any external evidence. You may even allow the spectator to hold your wrist. Don't try to make the strange thing move. Simply will it to move. You can even control the direction of the swing by concentrating on the direction in which you want it to swing.

bonus time Would you like to be able to use the strange thing with the cards placed face down instead of face up? You can, by simply marking the back of the card to be forced. The marking should be subtle so that it does not call attention to itself. By taking a sharp instrument (a knife or pin, for example) and making a slight scratch near the corner of the back of the card, you can remove enough of the back design so that you can spot the card although the spectator will not notice it. You should make a similar scratch at the opposite diagonal corner so that you will have a mark at each end. (See Figure 1-11.)

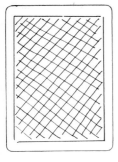

Figure 1-11.

Remember, the mark should be small so that only a person looking for it is likely to find it. Once you have marked the

21

card, all you need do is to follow the procedure for performing with the strange thing, but the cards are placed face down rather than face up. There is one more note of caution: never have more than one marked card in a deck, unless you vary the markings, because you might end up with two marked cards in the small packet of the spectator. If this happens, the chance of identifying the selected card will be diminished.

CARD LOCATIONS

In the preceding sections, you have learned several methods for forcing a card and several ways of revealing a forced card. Here are two methods of locating a freely selected card.

the crimp

Take a card from the deck and bend one of the corners down *slightly*. Replace the card in the deck and shuffle the deck. Can you locate the crimped card? You should be able to locate it since a crimped card will cause a slight break in the deck at the corner that is crimped. (See Figure 1-12.)

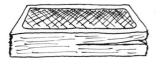

Figure 1-12.

This card can be used us a locator card by using the following procedure.

1. Allow the spectator to shuffle the deck containing the crimped card.

2. Take the deck from the spectator and cut the crimped card to the bottom of the deck.

3. Spread the cards from hand to hand, as in the Classic Force, but in this case you really do allow the spectator to freely select any card.

4. While the spectator is holding the selected card and looking at it, you should square up the deck. The crimped card is still on the bottom of the deck.

5. Cut the deck and place the top half on the table. Ask the spectator to replace his card on this half of the deck.

6. Now place the remaining cards, the bottom half of the original deck, on top of the spectator's card. At this point his

card is approximately in the center of the deck, and, immediately above it is the crimped card.

7. In order to reveal the selected card, all you need do is to cut the crimped card to the bottom of the deck. This places the selected card on the top of the deck. You can now command the card to rise to the top of the deck. Then turn over the top card and there it is.

8. If you prefer, you could conclude the trick in another manner. After having cut the selected card to the top of the deck, you could move it to the bottom of the deck by using the overhand shuffle. (For controlling a card by the use of the overhand shuffle, see the section on card controls in this chapter.) This shuffle transfers the top card (selected card) to the bottom. As you are placing the deck on the table after having used this shuffle, you can get a glimpse of the bottom card, now the selected card. Do this casually and do not be obvious about it. With this information, it would be a simple matter to reveal the card by using the "Telepathy," or "Psychological" revelation.

An advantage in using the crimped card as a locator is that it can be used with a borrowed deck. You borrow a deck, have it shuffled, and have a card selected by spreading the cards from hand to hand as in the Classic Force. Once the spectator removes the card, you square up the deck and allow it to rest in the LH. While the spectator is looking at the card and showing it to others, your RH rests on the top of the pack. (See Figure 1-13.)

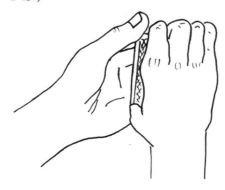

Figure 1-13.

At this moment, your left little finger puts a crimp in the lower right corner of the bottom card of the deck. You now use this card as a locator. Before returning the deck to the spectator, you should secretly straighten the crimp, thus removing the evidence. It is also advisable to remove the crimp from the card in your own deck between performances so that the corner does not become broken by keeping it in the bent position.

the Will De Sieve Locator

Over the last ten years or so, I have had a great deal of success, and a great deal of fun, with this particular card locator. It is more suitable for use with your own pack than with a borrowed deck because some advance preparation is necessary. To prepare the card that you are going to use as a locator, remove any face card from your deck. Place a quarter in the center of the *back* of the card and hold it in place with your thumbs. (See Figure 1-14.)

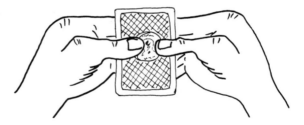

Figure 1-14.

With your fingers press on the *face* of the card. You should press around the edges of the quarter until a slight ridge is formed on the face of the card. You may now remove the quarter. What you have is a card with a slight depression in the center. The reason for using the face card is so that this depression will be camouflaged by the pattern on the face card. Obviously, a spectator would notice something strange *if* you allowed him to examine the card, but in normal use, the secret will never be discovered. The Will De Sieve Locator can be used as a locator card in the same manner as the Crimped Card Locator.

CONTROLLING A CARD

There are a number of card tricks in which you will be called on to control a card, that is, to move a card secretly to the top or bottom of the deck.

controlling the card with the crimp or the Will De Sieve locator

If the selected card has been returned to the deck, using the instructions for the Crimp or the Will De Sieve Locator, it is a simple matter to move the card to the top of the deck. This is accomplished by simply cutting the crimped card or the Will De Sieve card, and all the cards above it, to the bottom of the deck. This will automatically place the selected card on top of the deck. If you need to move the card to the bottom of the deck, this can be done by cutting one card past the crimped card or the Will De Sieve card and moving all these cards to the bottom of the deck; this will automatically place the selected card on the bottom of the deck. This will take a bit more practice since you must pick up one card past the crimped card or Will De Sieve card.

controlling the card to the bottom of the deck with the overhand shuffle

Let us say that the selected card is on the top of the deck and you want to move it to the bottom of the deck. This can be done in the process of apparently shuffling the deck.

1. Hold the deck in preparation for the overhand shuffle. The deck is held in the RH by its ends at the tips of the right fingers and right thumb. The selected card is on the top of the deck.

2. The LH approaches the deck; the left fingers go beneath the deck and the left thumb goes above the deck in order to pull cards from the top of the deck into the LH. Both the positions of the RH and the LH are shown in Figure 1-15.

3. The left thumb should peel off the top card allowing it to drop onto the left fingers; it should drop face down on the left fingers so that the audience does not get a glimpse of it.

4. The left thumb then immediately begins to pull more cards from the top of the deck onto the selected card. These cards can

25

Figure 1-15.

be pulled off in batches of two or three or more cards at a time. You are giving the impression that you are simply shuffling the deck. You will find it natural for the RH to move slightly up and down as the left thumb pulls the cards away.

5. After you have shuffled away from one-fourth to one-half of the cards from the RH into the LH, the remainder of the cards in the RH should be placed on the cards in the LH. This will cause the selected card to be the card on the bottom of the deck.

controlling the card
by the use
of the Hindoo Shuffle

By mastering a shuffle that is frequently used by magicians, although seldom used by others, you can control a card to the top of the deck in a most deceptive manner. In order to use this control, you must first learn to do the Hindoo Shuffle. In this shuffle the cards are held face down near one end by the fingers and thumb of the RH. (See Figure 1-16.)

The LH, held palm up, approaches the deck from the left. (See Figure 1-17.)

As the LH comes in contact with the deck, a small packet of cards is pulled from the top of the deck by the left fingers and allowed to fall on the palm of the LH. (See Figure 1-18.)

This process is repeated until all of the cards in the RH have been transferred to the LH. As it stands, this is a legitimate

26

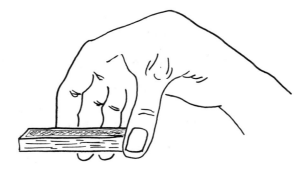

Figure 1-16.

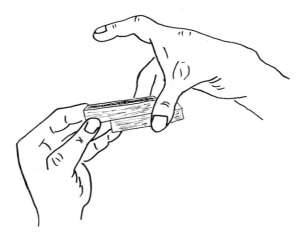

Figure 1-17.

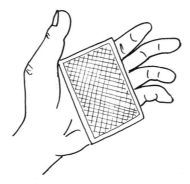

Figure 1-18.

shuffle and can be used as such. Here is how this shuffle may be used to control a card.

1. A card has been selected by the spectator. This card may be a forced card or a freely selected card.

2. Begin the Hindoo Shuffle and, after you have shuffled some of the cards from the RH into the LH (between one-fourth and one-half), ask the spectator to drop his selected card face down onto the cards in the LH.

3. You apparently continue to shuffle the cards, but what really happens is this: After the spectator has placed his card on the cards in the LH, the next time that the RH and LH come together for the shuffle, the thumb tip and the tips of the middle and ring fingers of the RH grip the top card in the LH packet and some of the cards beneath it. There should be a slight break between the remainder of the deck held in the RH and the cards picked up by the right thumb, middle, and ring fingers. (See Figure 1-19.)

LEFT HAND OMITTED FOR CLARITY.

Figure 1-19.

4. You now continue the Hindoo Shuffle until you reach the point of break that is being held with the RH. At this point all of the cards in the RH, the packet that has the selected card on top of it, are placed on top of the cards in the LH. This places the selected card on the top of the deck when it has apparently been lost in the shuffle. This control will require a good deal of practice on your part since you want to be able to do it smoothly and casually. One point that you will need to work

on is the proper grip to be taken on the deck with the RH. The thumb tip and the finger tips of the middle and ring fingers of the RH must extend past the pack far enough so that the pickup can be made without fumbling.

bonus time The Hindoo Shuffle, in addition to controlling a selected card, can also be used to force a card.

1. Have the card that you wish to force on the bottom of the deck.

2. Begin the Hindoo Shuffle, and, after you have shuffled off a bit over one-fourth of the deck, say to the spectator, "Tell me to stop at any time you wish."

3. Continue to shuffle until you are told to stop.

4. When the spectator says stop, you should hold up the packet of cards in the RH so that the spectator can see the bottom card (the force card) on the deck while telling him to "remember this card." The impression that you have given is that you have shuffled the cards to the point at which the spectator stopped you and that his card has been freely selected. This is a simple and useful force, but it should not be overused. If you need to force several cards during one performance, you should vary the method of your force.

So far we have covered some of the basics of card magic, and you have been taught some card tricks in the process. Now it is time to learn some specific card tricks. You should read this section and then select one trick you would like to do and master it before moving on to the others.

KARATE CHOP

I have used this routine for many years since the basic effect was taught to me by Doyle Allen, one of my first teachers in magic. I have had the pleasure of not only fooling non-magicians with it but also some rather knowledgable card men as well, and it is a part of my first lecture for magicians, "Off

The Wall With The Wizard." I pass it on to you for the entertainment of your audiences. In this trick the spectator selects a card, and it is returned to the deck. The magician then gives the deck a karate chop with the edge of his hand, and the deck is cut at the selected card. Another card is selected by the spectator, or by another spectator, and returned to the deck. This time the deck is placed on the floor, and the magician hits the deck with the edge of his foot causing the deck to once again cut at the selected card. An alternate ending is to place the deck on the table and stand on a chair to strike the deck with the edge of the foot. If you use the alternate ending, please be careful. You should make sure that the chair will support your weight. You will not impress anyone with your magic if you fall from the chair onto them, the floor, or the table. If the chair is not yours, you should get the permission of its owner before standing on it or before using the table; otherwise, you may discover that your magic is no longer welcome and neither are you.

method

This trick uses the Will De Sieve Locator card and it is almost self-working. You will need to practice a bit to develop the proper knack for striking the deck and making it cut at the selected card.

1. Use the deck containing the Will De Sieve card. The deck may be shuffled by the spectator before you begin if you wish.

2. Cut the Will De Sieve card to the bottom of the deck.

3. Spread the deck and permit the spectator to select a card. Since the Will De Sieve card is on the bottom of the deck, you should have little difficulty in preventing the spectator from selecting this card. He must not get this card.

4. After the spectator has selected a card, have him show it to several people nearby. (Spectators do forget cards at times and this is a wise precaution in most card tricks.)

5. Cut the deck and place the top half on the table or extend it toward the spectator. Have the spectator place his card on the top of this half of the deck.

6. Replace the original bottom half of the deck on the original top half of the deck. This places the key card directly above the selected card.

7. Square the deck and place it on the table or floor.

8. A sharp blow to the side of the deck with the foot or the edge of the hand will cause the deck to cut at the selected card. You should attempt to strike the deck near the point at which the selected card and the Will De Sieve card are located. (This should be near the center of the deck.) As I indicated above, it will require some practice to get the proper knack for striking the deck. When using your hand, place the back of the hand parallel to the table top and strike with the edge of the hand. (See Figure 1-20.)

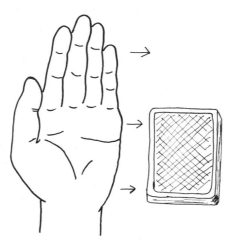

Figure 1-20.

When using your foot, strike with the inside edge of the foot.

patter and presentation

1. "Although many of you may not know it, I have spent many years studying the martial arts. I am a master of kung fu, judo, and karate, and I'd like to give you a demonstration of my skill." At this point you may allow the spectator to shuffle the deck. Then take the deck and cut the Will De Sieve card to the bottom of the deck. Spread the cards for selection as you say, "Would you please select a card and show it to a few people near you."

2. "Please return your card to the deck." Place the original bottom half of the deck on the original top half of the deck, trapping the selected card beneath the Will De Sieve card.

3. "In order to locate your card I must estimate its exact position in the deck and strike the deck with the proper amount of force at that point." This is not a total lie; a half-truth in magic is not a bad thing. "I think your card is located about 25th from the top of the deck. Now, with this hand, which can break boards, bricks, or bones, I will strike the deck causing it to cut at your card."

4. After the proper buildup, strike the deck, ask the spectator to name his selected card, and then turn over the selected card, revealing it to the audience.

5. Go through the same procedure of having another card selected and returned to the deck. Once again, be sure that the Will De Sieve card goes above the selected card.

6. Place the deck on the table or floor.

7. "Karate experts are also skilled in fighting with their feet. I am now going to attempt to locate your card with my foot. It will be easier for me to do this if I remove my shoe, but some audiences have told me that this gives an air to the demonstration that they don't care for, so I'll leave my shoe on, although this will make it more difficult for me."

8. Strike the deck sharply with the inside of either foot and go through the same procedure of revealing the card as in step 4 above.

THE TWO-CARD REVERSE

The magical reversal of one or more cards in a deck is a staple of card magic, and the method given in this trick makes it simple for you to present this classic of card magic. In this trick the magician uses one-half of the deck and the spectator uses the other half. The spectator buries a card from his half of the deck in the magician's half of the deck. The magician then buries a card from his half of the deck in the spectator's half of the deck. The spectator's half of the deck is then turned face up and divided in half. The magician's half of the deck is sandwiched, face down, between the two face up packets held by the spectator. The deck is then cut and the halves are shuffled together, thus leaving about half of the cards in the deck face up and about half of the cards face down. A bit of magic on the part of the performer causes all of the cards to face in the same direction—except for the two cards selected by the magician and the spectator. Sounds impossible? Read on.

method   The basis of this trick rests on a piece of information unknown to the spectator: the bottom card on the deck is reversed at the beginning of the trick, that is, it is placed *face up* on the bottom of the deck. This means, of course, that if the deck were to be turned over, the bottom of the deck would look just like the top of the deck since the spectator would see the back of a card in either case. It is important that the spectator does not realize the set-up of the deck. You will find it much easier to do the trick successfully *if* you use a deck that has a border on the back of the cards rather than using one with an over-all back design.

presentation   1.   Place a card face up on the bottom of the deck and *remember this card*. For our example, we will use the Five of Spades. The Five of Spades is face up on the bottom of the deck and the deck is in its case. You could, of course, reverse a card and place it on the bottom of the deck at some point in a program of card magic; however, until you acquire a fair amount of skill, it might be best to use this trick as an opening effect, the setup having been done in advance.

2.   Remove the deck from its case and hold it *face down* in your LH. This should conceal the reversed card on the bottom of the deck from the view of the spectators. The deck should be

removed from the case casually, but you must take great care not to show the reversed card to the spectators; even a glimpse can mar the trick.

3. Hand the spectator the top half of the deck and retain the bottom half of the deck for your own use.

4. Tell the spectator that you are going to remove a card from your half of the deck and memorize it. Remove a card from somewhere near the center of your half of the deck. You *do not* memorize this card. Later in the trick you are going to say that the card that you selected was the Five of Spades, the card that is reversed on the bottom of your half of the deck.

5. You now request that the spectator remove a card from his half of the deck and remember it. This is a critical point in the trick. When the spectator looks down to remove his card, you should allow the hand holding your half of the deck to drop to your side, and, at this point you simply turn your hand over. This action will cause the packet that you are holding to turn over so that all of the cards in the packet are facing up except for the reversed card. Since it is face down on the bottom of the packet, it will give the impression that all of the cards that you hold are face down. It is important that you do this casually and with the proper timing. You must do the turnover while the spectator is involved with selecting his card. If he is looking for a card and memorizing it, he will not be paying attention to what you are doing.

6. Without showing the spectator the face of the card that you have taken from your half of the deck, push the card face down into his half of the deck at about the center of the half that he is holding.

7. Ask the spectator to do the same with the card that he is holding, to push it face down into the center of the half of the deck that you are holding without allowing you to see the face of the card. You will want to make sure that you have a firm grip on your half of the deck so that he does not accidentally see that all of the cards in your packet are face up except for the top card.

8. Ask the spectator to hand you half of his packet *face up*. Place these cards face up on the bottom of the packet that you are holding.

9. Ask the spectator for the remainder of the cards that he is holding. Place these cards *face up* on top of the cards in your hand. What you apparently have now is a deck composed of one-fourth face-up cards, one-half face-down cards, and one-fourth face-up cards. What you really have is a deck composed of all face up cards except for the card that began face up on the bottom of the deck, the Five of Spades, and the card that the spectator selected, which he placed face down in your face up half of the deck. (He thought that he was placing it face down in a face down packet.)

10. Turn the entire deck over, cut the deck and give it a quick riffle shuffle, taking care not to reveal the true composition of the deck to the spectator.

11. Now you should recap what has happened for the benefit of your audience. You selected a card and placed it in the spectator's half of the deck. He selected a card and placed it in your half of the deck. Your face-down half of the deck was then sandwiched between the two face-up quarters of his half of the deck and the entire deck was then shuffled. You should point out that this means that the deck is mixed with about half of the deck face up and half of the deck face down. Point out how impossible it would be to locate the selected cards.

12. Now ask the spectator to reveal the name of his card. Let's say that it was the Queen of Hearts. You then name your card, but the card that you really name is the card that started on the bottom of the deck, the Five of Spades.

13. Snap your fingers, make a magic pass, or say a magic word, and spread the deck. All of the cards will be seen now to be face down with the exception of the two selected cards; they will be face up.

thinking time   Develop a patter story for this trick.

Years ago I wanted to do a card-to-pocket, but I did not have a great deal of confidence in my ability to steal the card from the deck and get it into my pocket. Because of this, I developed this trick so that I could perform this classic of card magic without the pressure of having to do a perfect steal of the card under the direct stare of the spectators.

method and presentation

1. Have a card selected and returned to the deck.

2. Control the card to the bottom of the deck, using one of the methods given in this chapter or by using any other method that you might know.

3. Cut the cards into three nearly equal piles in the following manner: starting on your right, allow the bottom third of the deck to rest on the table; move your hand to the left and allow the middle third of the deck to make up the center pile; to the left of the center pile place the top third of the deck. The piles will now be called the left pile, the center pile, and the right pile. The selected card is on the bottom of the right pile, but the audience should not be aware of this.

4. You now point out to the audience that the odds against the selected card's being on the bottom of one of the piles is roughly 1 in 17.5, but that you are going to show them the bottom card on each pile. Ask them not to say anything if their card happens to be on the bottom of one of the piles.

5. Using the fingers and thumb of the LH, pick up the left pile, show the face of the pile to the audience, look at it yourself, and call off the name of the card. (See Figure 1-21.)

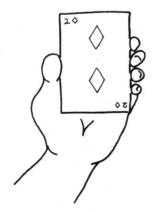

Figure 1-21.

For example, you might say, "The odds are against the Four of Hearts (or whatever card happens to be on the bottom of this pile) being your card."

6. The LH then turns palm down and the thumb and middle finger of the RH pull off the bottom card of the pile and place it face down on the table. (See Figure 1-22.)

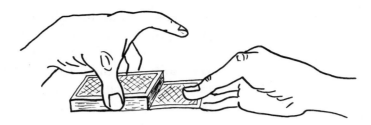

Figure 1-22.

The packet must be held as in the illustration so that when the proper time comes, when you show the bottom card on the right pile, you can use a sleight known as the "glide" to deal not the bottom card, but the second card from the bottom onto the table.

7. After the bottom card from the left pile has been dealt face down on the table, place the packet to the rear of the card, and with your RH reach into your right jacket or pants pocket and take out a quarter as you say, "I'm even willing to bet an entire quarter that this is not your card." Place the quarter on the back of the face down card that has just been dealt from the left pile.

8. Repeat the same procedure with the center pile: showing the card on the bottom of the packet, dealing it down, placing a quarter on it.

9. Now you come to the right pile, and, while you apparently do the same thing with this pile as you did with the left and center piles, actually something quite different happens.

10. When you show the bottom card of the right pile, the spectator will, of course, see his card. But, since you have instructed him not to tell you if he happens to see his card on the bottom of any pile, he will remain silent and he will think that you have made a mistake.

11. When the LH turns palm down and the RH comes over to pull off the bottom card, the following takes place: The middle finger of the LH, which is resting on the bottom card of the packet, pulls this card slightly toward the end of the deck that is nearest the palm of the hand. (See Figure 1-23.)

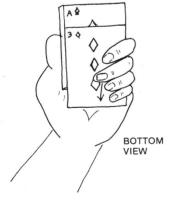

BOTTOM VIEW

Figure 1-23.

This move is called the glide. It should move the card no more than about one-fourth of an inch. This should enable the middle finger of the RH to pull off not the bottom card but the next card above the bottom card. It is, therefore, the second card from the bottom in the right pile that is placed face down on the table, and not the selected card. The selected card is still on the bottom of the right pile.

12. You should go through the business of placing a quarter on this card. The spectator now believes that his card is on the table with a quarter on top of it.

13. At this point in the trick there are three cards, face down, on the table with a quarter on each card. To the rear of each card is a packet of cards, each packet containing about one-third of the deck. (See Figure 1-24.)

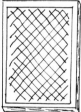
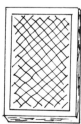
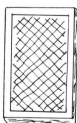

Figure 1-24.

14. Reassemble the deck by picking up each packet, starting from your left and working to your right. The left pile becomes the top packet on the deck and the right pile the bottom packet. This will place the selected card on the bottom of the deck.

15. The bottom card must now be controlled to the top of the deck. One method of doing this is by a reverse overhand shuffle. Hold the deck in the RH with the backs of the cards facing the spectators, just as in the overhand shuffle. (See Figure 1-25.)

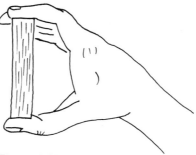

Figure 1-25.

Approach the deck with the LH as though you were going to do the standard overhand shuffle, but, instead of pulling off cards with your left thumb, start pulling off cards with the left fingers from the bottom of the deck. (See Figure 1-26.)

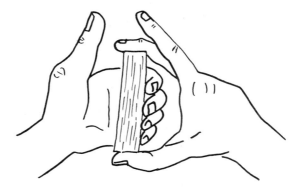

Figure 1-26.

This should cause the first card into the LH to be the bottom card of the deck, in this case the selected card. This card must be kept against the palm of the LH as you continue the shuffle, so that it will be the top card in the LH packet. Continue the shuffle until one-fourth to one-third of the deck has been shuffled into the LH. Remeber that the selected card must now be the top card of this packet. This shuffle should be done as rapidly as possible without losing control of the cards. After shuffling, place the packet of cards in the LH onto the remainder of the deck. The selected card is now on the top of the deck.

16. Hold the deck in the LH and say to the spectator, "The odds against my being able to locate your card in this deck by sound alone are 1 in 49, but I will attempt it." The spectator may smile at this point because he thinks that his card is on the table.

17. Hold the deck near your left ear and riffle the corner of the deck with your left thumb. Do this a few times and say, "Now, I've got it."

18. Take a card from near the center of the deck and place it face down on the table without letting the spectators see the face of the card as you say, "That's it."

19. You now state, "I'm so sure that this is your card that I'm going to bet two quarters on it." Put your RH in your pocket and get two quarters and place them on the back of this card.

20. Remove the quarter from the back of the left card and turn it face up as you say, "I knew that this wasn't your card."

21. Remove the quarter from the back of the center card and turn it face up as you say, "And I knew this wasn't your card."

22. Point to the right card as you say, "From the look on your face a few moments ago, I know that you think that this is your card, but it's not." Point to the card that you found by "listening" to the deck and comment, "I'm sure that *this* is your card."

23. At this point the deck is held face down in the LH. Your RH should casually approach the deck. As the RH approaches the deck, direct the spectator to remove the coin from the card that he thought was his selected card and turn it over.

24. As he is removing the coin and turning over the card, you have plenty of time to palm and steal the top card (selected card) from the deck. The misdirection is maximum because attention is focused on the card the spectator is turning over or on the remaining face down card on the table. The palming of the top card of the deck should be accomplished in the following manner: As the RH approaches the deck held in the LH, the left thumb pushes the top card about one-fourth of an inch toward the end of the deck and then moves away from the top of the deck. (See Figure 1-27.)

The RH comes over the deck, temporarily covering the top of the deck, and the four fingers of the RH, at about the point of the first joints of each finger, push down gently on the projecting end of the top card of the deck. (See Figure 1-28.)

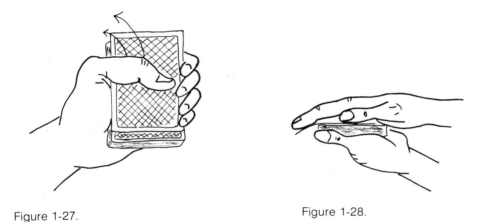

Figure 1-27.

Figure 1-28.

This action will cause the card to pivot into the RH where it can be held by the pressure of the right fingers and right palm. (See Figure 1-29 A and B.)

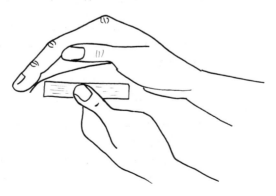

Figure 1-29 A.

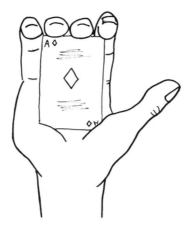

Figure 1-29 B.

25. As soon as you have executed the palm, move the RH away from the deck and at the same time move the LH and the deck toward your left. As you do this say, "In fact, I feel so confident that I have found your card that I'm going to up my bet."

26. The RH moves casually to the right pocket. Once it enters the pocket, the palmed card is left behind and the hand emerges with two more quarters.

27. The two additional quarters are placed on the remaining face down card. By this time the spectator should have turned over the card that he believed to be his card and once he discovers that this is not his card, he should be surprised.

28. You should now play up the idea that you found the selected card in the deck by sound alone, an impossible feat, and so on. After a few seconds of buildup, ask the spectator to remove the coins on the card and turn it over. It will not be the selected card, and he will be sure to point this out to you.

29. Be shocked, dismayed, upset! Say things like "Are you sure that this isn't your card?" After you have carried on in this vein for a few seconds, ask the spectator, "Just what card did you select?"

42

30. Let's say that his card was the King of Clubs. You then state, "That's impossible! It could have been any card *but* the King of Clubs. I put the King of Clubs in my pocket before I started this trick." Show that your RH is obviously and unmistakably empty and then reach into your pocket and bring out the selected card.

thinking time   Make up a story to serve as the introduction to this trick. You might consider a story involving gamblers, gambling games, and odds.

THE CARD IN THE BALLOON

There are a number of mechanical tricks on the market that can be used for the card in the balloon; however, this version requires only a deck of cards, a card case, some balloons, and a long pin. In this trick a card is freely chosen by a spectator and returned to the deck. The deck is placed in its case and a balloon is inflated and tied off. The magician then thrusts a pin into the balloon. The balloon bursts and the selected card appears. In this trick you may even have the spectator sign the face of the card if you wish.

method and presentation

1. Have a card freely selected by a spectator and returned to the deck. Control the card to the top of the deck by using the Hindoo Shuffle. If you are going to have the spectator sign the card, this should be done before it is returned to the deck.

2. Place the deck in its case. You will need the kind of card case shown in Figure 1-30.

As you can see, this is a case with a flap at one end and a semicircle cut out of the case proper to make the flap easier to open. Most cards are sold in cases of this type. The deck should be placed in the case with the top of the deck facing the

Figure 1-30.

semicircle.

3. Close the case by inserting the flap into the case. This is a critical point in the trick. The flap must be inserted so that it goes between the top card (selected card) on the deck and the remainder of the cards in the deck. This can be accomplished by squeezing the sides of the case with the fingers and thumb of the LH while closing the flap with the RH. The pressure of squeezing the sides of the case will cause the top card to bend or bridge slightly, making it easier to insert the flap between this card and the other cards. (See Figure 1-31.)

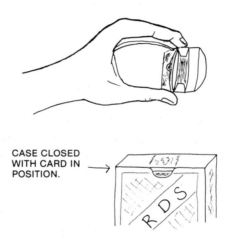

CASE CLOSED
WITH CARD IN →
POSITION.

Figure 1-31.

This will take practice because you need to be able to do it smoothly and casually. You should not give the appearance that you are doing anything other than closing the case. If at first you discover that the squeeze causes more than one card to bridge, this means that you are squeezing too hard. Keep working on it and you will soon learn the proper amount of pressure to apply.

4. Now show the case on both sides by holding your right thumb over the semicircle, thus concealing the portion of the selected card that would otherwise be seen by the audience, and by turning your hand to show the front and back of the case. (See Figure 1-32.)

5. Place the case, flap side *down,* on the table and bring out several balloons.

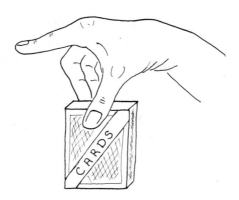

Figure 1-32.

Figure 1-33

6. Have one of the balloons selected by a spectator. (You might even have the balloon examined if you wish, although this strikes me as unnecessary and adds to the running time of the trick.) Inflate the balloon and tie it off.

7. Pick up the card case and hold it in the LH. (See Figure 1-33.)

You will note that the semicircle side of the case faces you. This means that you can see a small portion of the back of the selected card.

8. While calling attention to the inflated balloon in the RH, with your left thumb push the selected card up out of the case about a quarter of an inch. (See Figure 1-34.)

Figure 1-34.

This will allow the left thumb and the index finger an opportunity to grip the end of the selected card. Obviously, you would not want to show the palm side of your LH to the audience at this point.

45

9. Insert the knot and the neck of the balloon between the index and middle fingers of the LH. This means that a small portion of the balloon (the neck and the knot) are behind the fingers of the LH while the bulk of the inflated balloon is in front of and above the fingers of the LH.

10. At this point the left thumb should press the projecting end of the selected card against the portion of the balloon that is behind the left fingers; then the left thumb presses both the balloon and the card against the index finger. (See Figure 1-35.)

Figure 1-35.

11. With your RH, produce the pin. The best place to carry the pin is to have it thrust through the material on the inside left lapel of your jacket.

12. Hold the pin in your dramatically raised RH while you recap what has happened.

13. Thrust the pin into the balloon. At the moment that the balloon breaks, release your pressure on the card case in the LH while retaining your grip (with the left thumb and index finger of the LH) on the selected card and the neck of the balloon. The case will fall to the table and you will be left holding the selected card and a piece of the balloon. You have apparently caused the card to leave the case and appear in the balloon. This part of the trick will require some practice in order to get the proper timing. You may need to break a number of balloons before you are happy with the timing. I have found that the most natural timing can be gained by letting the sound of the breaking balloon serve as the cue for dropping the case. In fact, there is an almost natural reflex involved since most people give a slight start at a loud noise.

THE MONGOLIAN CLOCK

This trick is based on an old mathematical principle that has been used in a number of "clock" tricks, and I have enjoyed presenting it for a number of years. It has also been used by many magicians and has served one of my "card men" friends in magic, John Miller, as an opening effect for his card routine for several years. It proved so popular, in fact, that I released it to the magic fraternity through another friend in magic, Dan Garrett, a popular performer and demonstrator of magic. Since neither John nor Dan uses the exact handling or patter that I use in the trick, I am including it in this book.

The magician shuffles a deck of cards (winds the clock) and has a spectator mentally select an hour from one o'clock through twelve o'clock. While the magician's back is turned, the spectator removes the corresponding number of cards from the top of the deck and places them in his pocket. The magician then "ribbon spreads" the deck, face up, and uses the top 15 cards to form the face of a clock—hands and numbers. The spectator is then asked to concentrate on the card at the position corresponding to the number of cards that he removed from the top of the deck. The performer then proceeds to turn all of the cards face down except the card that the spectator is concentrating on. This is the first revelation. The performer then turns the selected card face down, and it is revealed that the selected card is different in back color or back design from the rest of the cards in the deck, the second revelation.

method

1. Take a deck of cards and discard the Two of Diamonds. Remove the Two of Diamonds from a deck having a contrast-

ing color of back or a contrasting back design. The two decks must be of the same size. For the purposes of illustration, let's assume that we are using a blue-backed deck for our basic deck; therefore, discard the Two of Diamonds from the blue-backed deck; then take the Two of Diamonds from the red-backed deck and place it *sixteenth* from the *top* of the blue-backed deck. (Obviously, you could use any card. The Two of Diamonds is simply being used for the purposes of illustration.) Be sure that you do discard the blue-backed Two of Diamonds so that you will not run the risk of having two Two of Diamonds appear while performing the trick.

2. Place the deck face down on the table and remove from one to twelve cards from the top of the deck and place them aside or in your pocket. Let's assume that you have removed five cards.

3. Ribbon spread the deck *face up* from your *left to your right*. (See Figure 1-36.)

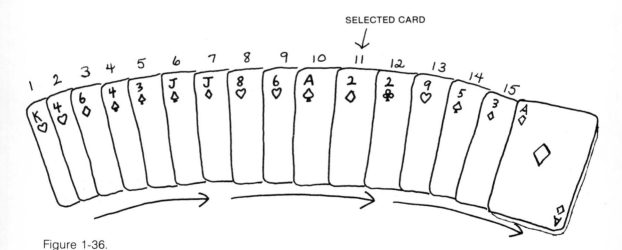

Figure 1-36.

4. Remove the *first three* cards from the *left* end of the spread. These three cards are used as the "hands" of the clock. The first of these cards becomes your imaginary hour hand, the second and third cards become your imaginary minute hand. (See Figure 1-37.)

Figure 1-37.

5. Count from the *left* end of the spread to the twelfth card. Scoop up these twelve cards from *left to right without disturbing their order*.

6. Hold the packet of twelve cards *face up* in the LH, and, starting with the one o'clock position on an imaginary clock, deal the twelve cards *clockwise* until the last card is dealt at the twelve o'clock position. (See Figure 1-38.)

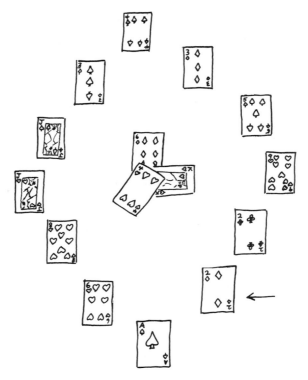

Figure 1-38.

If the above instructions have been followed correctly, the Two of Diamonds should be at the five o'clock position. This card, the one with the dissimilar back, now lies at the position corresponding to the number of cards originally removed from the top of the deck. You are now prepared for the double climax, but since you know how the effect works, you are not likely to be impressed by doing it for yourself. So, read the patter and presentation section, practice the trick, and try it on an audience. *Note:* Always make sure that the card with the dissimilar back is sixteenth from the top of the deck *before* starting the routine.

patter and presentation

1. Hold up the deck in its case. "What does this appear to be to you? A deck of cards? It's not. It's actually a Mongolian Clock. Would you like to see it in operation?" (If you wish, you can draw a few Chinese characters on the card case and point out that they say that this is a Mongolian Clock.)

2. Remove the deck from the case. If you wish you can do a false shuffle at this point. The following is a useful false shuffle that can be used in this trick as well as others. Hold the deck in the LH, as shown in the Figure 1-39.

Figure 1-39.

With the RH, cut away the bottom half of the deck. The RH approaches the LH and the left thumb pulls the top card from the half of the deck held in the RH so that it falls on the cards held in the LH. (See Figure 1-40.)

This card should not fall neatly on the cards held in the LH but should overlap the end of the deck. (See Figure 1-41.)

The remainder of the cards in the RH should now be shuffled onto the cards in the LH in a somewhat casual and careless manner. When the stock of the cards in the RH has been exhausted, the RH goes *beneath* the LH and, using the over-

Figure 1-40.

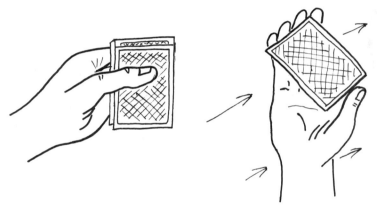

Figure 1-41.

lapped card as a guide, picks it up and all the cards *above* it and takes them to the bottom of the deck. Although this shuffle mixes the bottom half of the deck, it leaves the original top half of the deck (and the 16 cards on the top) undisturbed. This is a good false shuffle for keeping the top half of the deck intact. Of course, you do not have to shuffle the deck at this point, but it might serve to make the trick even more impressive. If you do use the false shuffle, refer to it as "winding the clock."

3. "I'll show you how the clock works. I want you to mentally select an hour from one through twelve. I am going to turn my back, and I want you to remove the number of cards from the *top* of the clock (deck) that corresponds to the number of the hour that you selected. For example, if you mentally selected

three o'clock, remove three cards from the top of the clock; if you selected eight o'clock remove eight cards from the top of the clock. After you have removed the cards, place them in your pocket or somewhere out of sight. Please don't sit on them since this tends to warp the cards."

4. Turn away from the spectator so that he can carry out your instructions. Give him a few seconds to do this, and then ask him if he has done so.

5. Turn back to the spectator. Take the deck and spread it *face up* from your *left* to your *right*. "Now I'll show you how Mongolians tell time. What do you see when you look at the face of a clock?" If you persist with this question, the spectator will, sooner or later, say, "hands and numbers."

6. Remove the *first three cards* from the *left* end of the spread; use one of them for the hour hand on the imaginary clock; use the other two for the minute hand. "Right! You see hands and numbers on a clock. We'll use this card for the hour hand and these will be the minute hand."

7. Count off twelve cards from the *left* end of the spread and scoop them up *without disturbing their order*. "We'll also need twelve numbers for our clock."

8. Hold the packet of twelve cards, *face up*, in the LH. Starting with one o'clock, deal out the twelve cards, clockwise, on the table in order to make the clock. "Here we have one o'clock, two o'clock . . . twelve o'clock."

9. "Now concentrate on the card that corresponds to the hour you selected. For example, if you removed six cards from the clock, concentrate on the card at six o'clock."

10. Remove the two cards that represent the minute hand on the clock. "The Mongolians don't care what minute it is, so we don't need the minute hand."

11. Remove the card representing the hour hand. "The Mongolians have their own way of telling the hour, so we won't need the hour hand on our clock."

12. Turn over (face down) all of the cards that represent the hours, except the Two of Diamonds. It should, unless you have made a mistake or the spectator has failed to follow your instructions, lie at the position that corresponds to the number of cards removed by the spectator.

13. "You are thinking of the Two of Diamonds; this means that you selected [name the hour] o'clock." Your audience will be amazed that you could know the hour.

14. Turn the Two of Diamonds face down; it has a different color back or a different back design. This will also startle the spectators. They have selected the only odd-backed card in the deck. "Of course, the Mongolians always want to make sure that they get the correct hour, so they always make a double check."

The effect is now over and the spectators will cheer wildly and acclaim you a great magician. At the very least, they will have been entertained by the trick.

CONCLUSION

In this chapter you have been taught some of the basic principles of card magic and a number of useful and entertaining card tricks. I have by no means exhausted the potential information on card magic, as you will discover if you pursue your study of magic, but if you master the material contained in this chapter, you will have made a significant beginning.

2

Magic with Coins

INTRODUCTION

Next to cards, coins are the most widely used magical props. The popularity of coin magic can be explained by the fact that coins are common objects and are, therefore, in theory at least, free of suspicion. It is also easy and logical for the magician to carry a number of coins. In addition, it is frequently possible to borrow coins from a spectator in order to perform a trick. This can add another element of mystery to the magic, the spectators later telling their friends of the impossible feats that were done with "their" coins. However, since many tricks call for specific coins, I recommend that you have your own coins ready for use in case you cannot borrow the proper number of specific coins from a spectator.

Just as there are a number of card tricks that use special decks or special cards, you will also discover, as you continue your study of the craft of magic, that there are many tricks that can be done with special or gimmicked coins. Many of these are excellent pieces of magic in the hands of a skilled performer. They are not dealt with in this chapter for the same reason that gimmicked cards and decks were not treated in the card chapter, that is, many of these trick coins are dealer items, which I feel obligated not to expose; I believe that a beginning magician should master the basics rather than use special props as a crutch. The sleights required to perform the tricks in this chapter can be mastered by anyone who possesses basic coordination skills and the willingness to practice.

THREE BASIC PALMS

The ability to palm a coin (to hold a coin concealed in the hand while giving the impression that the hand is empty) is essential to most coin magic. The ability to palm a coin can also be applied to other objects (as you will discover in later chapters), and if you master this skill with coins, you will find it useful in other areas of magic. Although there are a number of methods of palming a coin, the three basic and most frequently used methods are covered in this chapter. You should practice palming with both hands and with coins of different sizes.

the finger palm   This is by far the easiest of the palms to master.

1. Place a coin, a half-dollar or quarter, at the roots of the middle and ring fingers of the RH. (See Figure 2-1.)

2. Close the middle, ring, and little fingers of the RH over the palm of the hand while leaving the index finger extended. (See Figure 2-2.)

Figure 2-1.

Figure 2-2.

The coin is now palmed (concealed) and the RH can be used fairly freely and naturally. For example, the right index finger is in a natural position for pointing, and a magic wand, a pencil, or other similar objects can be handled quite freely with the thumb and index finger of the RH. Place a coin in the Finger Palm position and experiment to see how much freedom you have with it. Turn your hand to see if there are any angles from which the coin is visible. If it is visible from any direction, these are the angles that you will need to protect in performance. You should take care not to hold the coin too tightly with the fingers because this will make the hand look unnatural and will call attention to it. Although the audience may not be able to see the coin, they will become suspicious if your hand appears to be paralyzed or arthritic. In other words, you must strive for naturalness in your handling. You should practice this palm with both hands in order to give yourself flexibility. I am naturally left-handed, but, because most magic books are written for and by the right-handed, over the years I learned to use my right hand. I can now palm effectively with either hand.

the thumb palm

1. Clip a coin on its side between the tips of the index and middle fingers of the RH. (See Figure 2-3.)

Figure 2-3.

2. Close these fingers so that they come to the crotch formed by the thumb and edge of the RH. (See Figure 2-4.)

3. When the coin is placed in the thumb crotch, the index and middle fingers release their grip on the coin, and the thumb applies pressure so that the coin turns on its side. The coin is then clipped, on its side, between the inner edge of the thumb and the edge of the RH, and the index and middle fingers are extended. (See Figure 2-5.)

Figure 2-4.

Figure 2-5.

You will discover, with practice, that the coin can be held fairly securely in this position. You will also discover that the hand cannot be shown quite as freely as with the finger palm, because the coin would be exposed to the view of the spectators. This palm does have its uses, however, because the fingers of the hand can be held open, in a natural position, rather than held closed. Practice this palm until it can be done with both hands.

the classic palm

1. Balance a coin on the tips of the ring and middle fingers of the RH. (See Figure 2-6.)

2. Close the fingers until they contact the palm of the hand. Actually, they will probably bring the coin to a point slightly past the center of the palm; the coin will rest at a point nearer the heel of the hand. (See Figure 2-7.)

Figure 2-6.

Figure 2-7.

3. Press the coin into the hand with the fingers and, at the same time, attempt to grip the edges of the coin with the muscles from the thumb side of the hand and the little-finger side of the hand.

4. Straighten your fingers and then turn your hand over. The coin should be retained in the hand by the pressure of the

muscles on the edge of the coin. *Do not be discouraged if the coin falls from your hand.* The muscles will require some training before they "learn" to hold the coin in place; therefore, it will take days or weeks of practice to master this palm. Once you have mastered it, you will discover that it is very useful. You will discover that you can move your fingers and your thumb quite freely, and you can use the hand with the palmed coin naturally to pick up objects such as a pencil, a magic wand, or other coins. As with the two other palms, you should practice this palm with both hands, check it for angles, and practice holding and moving other objects while holding the palmed coin.

COIN VANISHES

It is now time to consider a number of methods of apparently placing a coin in one hand while retaining it in the other. This means, of course, that when you open the hand in which the audience believes the coin to be, it will have apparently vanished.

the finger–palm vanish

This is a very simple vanish, but it can be very deceptive with the proper timing.

1. Place the coin in the RH in position for the Finger–Palm; the fingers of the hand should be extended at this point.

2. Hold the LH palm up, with the fingers open about six inches to the left of the RH.

3. Move the RH toward the LH and begin turning the RH palm down as it moves. As the RH turns palm down, the ring, middle, and little fingers of the RH begin to close, thus trapping the coin in Finger–Palm position.

4. At the same time the RH approaches the LH and as the RH is in the act of turning palm down, the fingers of the LH begin to curl toward the left palm. The curling of the fingers masks the fact that the coin is being retained in the RH rather than being dropped into the LH. (See Figure 2-8.)

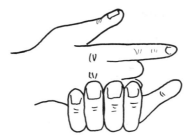

Figure 2-8.

5. The RH stops moving when it is completely over the LH. At this point the RH has been turned completely palm down and the fingers of the LH have closed over the left palm. The LH now apparently holds the coin.

6. The LH should now move up and away from its previous position until it is held shoulder height at about arm's length. The RH remains stationary with the index finger extended, pointing at the LH. *Your eyes should follow the passage of the LH; they should not look at the RH.* This is an important key to misdirection.

7. Lift the LH a bit more as you stare at it. At this point you should allow the RH to drop naturally to your side. Forget about your RH. Focus all of your attention on your LH. This will cause the audience to also focus on your LH.

8. Say a "magic word," make a squeezing motion with your LH, and slowly open it to show that the coin has vanished.

9. If you wish to reproduce the coin, simply reach under your left elbow with your RH and push the coin into view at the finger tips as you bring the hand away from the elbow. This can be varied by pretending to find the coin behind your knee, or inside your jacket, or reproducing it from a spectator's ear or hair.

Now go back to steps 3, 4, and 5. They are the keys to this sequence. You must give the impression that you are simply placing a coin that has been shown in the RH into the LH. It might be wise to actually place the coin there a few times to get the feeling of how it would look and feel if you were to really put the coin in the LH. You must practice the series of moves until they are smooth and look natural. As with any sleight in magic, the timing is the important element. The fingers of the LH must close neither too soon nor too late. The timing on the turning of the RH must be well coordinated with the closing of the fingers of the LH. By this point you may be tired of hearing about the need to practice, but I keep repeating it because I know from experience and observation that it is of prime importance in learning a magic sleight.

the pull-down vanish

Figure 2-9.

I discovered this vanish a few years ago when I started teaching a magic course for youngsters (10 through 16 years old). I wanted to give them a simple but deceptive vanish that they could use in their coin work. I feel sure that other magicians have independently "invented" this move, as often happens in magic, but I cannot recall having seen it in print.

1. The coin is displayed by holding it in the RH at the tips of the index and middle fingers, held in place with the thumb. (See Figure 2-9.)

You will note that a portion of the coin projects past the tips of the fingers and is visible, therefore, to the audience even though the back of your RH is facing them. You may, if you wish, rotate the hand showing both sides of the coin, but you should come back to the original position with the back of the hand facing the audience before attempting the vanish.

2. Hold the LH palm up with the fingers open about six inches to the left of the RH, just as in the Finger–Palm Vanish.

3. The RH moves toward the LH and begins to turn palm down at the same time.

4. As the RH turns palm down, the right thumb *pulls* the coin down behind the fingers into Finger–Palm position. (See Figure 2-10.)

Figure 2-10.

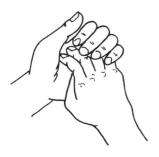

Figure 2-11.

5. By the time that the RH has turned palm down, it should have arrived at the LH. The RH pretends to place the coin on the palm of the LH and the fingers of the LH mask the fact that the coin is not being placed in the LH.

6. As the tips of the fingers of the RH touch the palm of the LH, the fingers of the LH begin to close. (See Figure 2-11.)

7. As the fingers of the LH touch the backs of the fingers of the RH, the fingers of the RH are withdrawn from the LH by sliding them out and to the right.

8. As the RH fingers clear the LH, the middle, ring, and little fingers close on the coin, trapping it in Finger–Palm position. The right thumb, which has been holding the coin in position, moves from beneath the RH to a natural position, and the right index finger remains extended, pointing at the LH. (See Figure 2-12.)

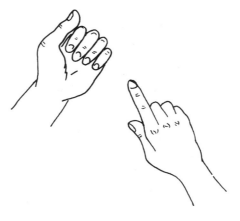

Figure 2-12.

9. You have apparently displayed a coin in the RH and placed it in the LH. You should now follow the procedures given in steps 6, 7, and 8 of The Finger–Palm Vanish. If you wish to reproduce the coin, see step 9 of the Finger–Palm Vanish.

the Stanfield vanish

This deceptive vanish was devised and taught to me by one of the most entertaining magicians that I have ever known, John Stanfield. I have taught it for years in my magic lecture as part of a longer coin routine. I include it in this book because I feel that the time you spend in mastering it will be well worth your while.

1. The display of the coin prior to the vanish is as follows: The edge of the coin is clipped between the right index and middle fingers near the tips of the fingers while the right thumb pushes the coin toward the index finger. The coin is held in its upright position by the pressure of the right thumb. (See Figure 2-13.)

Figure 2-13.

2. The LH is held palm up with the fingers open several inches from the RH.

3. The RH approaches the LH, and, as the tips of the left fingers touch the edge of the right little finger, move the right thumb. Removing the tension on the coin will cause it to fall near the first joint of the middle and ring fingers. (See Figure 2-14.)

The audience, viewing the action from the back side of your hand, will assume that the coin has fallen into the LH because, as the coin falls, the fingers of the LH should close and move to the left. The illusion is very strong because the audience *sees*

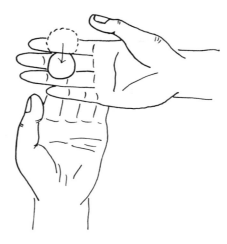

Figure 2-14.

the coin fall. The fact that it does not fall into the LH is masked by both the fingers of the RH and the closing fingers of the LH.

4. The coin is resting near the tips of the middle and ring fingers, and the closed LH is moving away to the left. You now have two options. If you curl the middle, ring, and little fingers of the RH, you can bring the coin to the Finger–Palm position. On the other hand, if you bring the tips of the middle and ring fingers to the palm of the hand, you can place the coin in Classic Palm position. You will want to practice doing both.

5. In order to complete the vanish of the coin and to reproduce it, see steps 6, 7, 8, and 9 of The Finger–Palm Vanish.

THE AMBITIOUS COIN

The following series of coin disappearances and reappearances can be done quickly and under a variety of circumstances. For this routine you will need two similar coins (for example, half-dollars), a small magic wand or "magic thing," and a handkerchief. You should be wearing a jacket with a handkerchief pocket. One of the coins should be in your left jacket pocket. The other coin should be in your right jacket pocket, with the small wand or magic thing. The bottom of the breast pocket of the jacket should have half of a paper table napkin folded and pushed into it. (The reason for this will become apparent as we proceed with the trick.) If you are not wearing a jacket, you can perform the trick in a shirt if the shirt has a breast pocket. In this case, the coins should be placed in your pants pockets and the folded napkin should be placed in the breast pocket of your shirt.

method and presentation

1. Remove the coin from your right jacket pocket. Flip it in the air and catch it in the RH.

2. Display the coin in the RH and then pretend to place it in the LH. Using the Pull–Down Vanish, retain the coin in the RH.

3. Lift the LH and make a squeezing motion with the left fingers. Open the hand to show that the coin has vanished.

4. Produce the coin from the left elbow with the RH.

5. Using the Stanfield Vanish, pretend to place the coin in the LH while retaining it in the RH.

6. Look the spectator in the eye as you say, "Why should I have all the fun? I'll let you use my magic wand [or magic thing] to make this coin disappear." As you finish this statement, reach into your right jacket pocket and remove the wand or magic thing, allowing the palmed coin to drop into the pocket. (Make sure that you do not allow the coin to clink against the wand or "thing" or any other object in the pocket. It is wise to remove, in advance, any extra objects in the pocket that could give you away by sound.)

7. Hand the wand to the spectator and allow him to wave the wand over your closed LH. In handing the wand to the spectator, it should be obvious that the RH is empty. Open the LH to show that the coin has vanished.

8. Reach into the left jacket pocket with the LH and remove the duplicate coin.

9. Display the duplicate coin at the tips of the left fingers. The coin is held in place by the left thumb. The fingers are pointing upward with the back of the hand toward the audience. (See Figure 2-15.)

10. With the RH, remove the handkerchief from your pocket and flip it open. Retain a grip on one corner of the handkerchief. Study Figure 2-16 to see the proper grip.

You will note that the thumb and index finger are on one side of the handkerchief and that the other three fingers are on the other side. The corner of the handkerchief should be well into the crotch formed by the index and middle fingers in order to hide the "dirty work" that is going to be carried out by the index finger and thumb.

Figure 2-15.

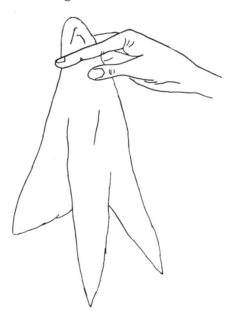

Figure 2-16.

11. You should now position the LH about fourteen inches in front of the breast pocket, with the tips of the fingers roughly in line with the top of the pocket.

12. Attempt to cover the coin and the LH with the handkerchief by pulling the handkerchief over the LH. You should "accidentally" pull the handkerchief too far, allowing it to slip off the LH. This is a very important feint. It serves as misdirection for what follows, and it should appear to be accidental. As the handkerchief slips off the LH you should say something like, "Sorry about that. I'll have to be more careful."

13. As you prepare to cover the LH again with the handkerchief, you should adjust the position of the LH *slightly.* Keeping it in line with the breast pocket, it should move about four inches closer to your body.

14. The handkerchief is now drawn over the LH again. This time it should be done fairly slowly and carefully. As the corner held in the RH passes over the coin held at the tips of the left fingers, the right thumb and index finger pick up the coin and carry it away with them. (See Figure 2-17.)

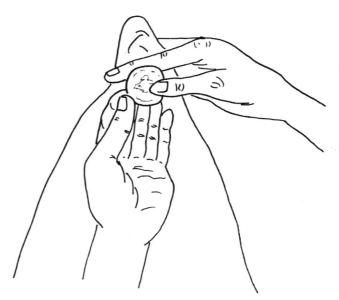

Figure 2-17.

The left fingers do not move from their previous position and the handkerchief masks the fact that the coin is missing.

15. The RH continues to move smoothly toward your body. By the time the center of the handkerchief is directly or almost directly over the left fingers, the RH with the corner of the handkerchief should be touching your jacket just above the opening of the pocket. (See Figure 2-18.)

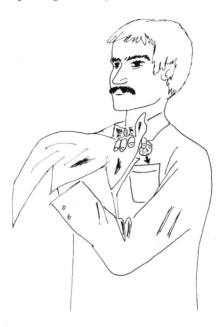

Figure 2-18.

The exact distance may vary depending on the size of the handkerchief used. You should experiment to learn exactly how far to hold the LH from the pocket. The important thing is that the RH and corner of the handkerchief (and the coin) should touch the jacket just about the time that the center of the handkerchief is over the left fingers. *Do not look at your RH during this move. Stare intently at the LH as if it were very important to make sure that the handkerchief is in the right spot.*

16. As the RH, holding the coin and the corner of the handkerchief, arrives at the breast pocket, release the coin from the right thumb and index finger and allow it to fall into the pocket. (Now you see the reason for the napkin in the pocket.

Not only will it deaden the sound of the falling coin, but it will also serve to help hold the pocket open.)

17. As soon as the coin drops, allow the corner of the handkerchief held by the RH to drop. It will fall to a natural position on the left forearm. Allow your RH to drop naturally to your side.

18. Now make a magic pass, or allow the spectator to do so, as he is still holding the wand or magic thing. Then dramatically whip the handkerchief away to show that the coin has vanished. The handkerchief can be examined if you wish. Your hands are empty. There is nothing "up your sleeve."

thinking time   You may decide that you do not wish to use the above routine as it is given here. You may want a series of coin effects that seem even more impromptu than this routine. See if you can modify the routine using what you have been taught about coin magic thus far. For example, can you modify the routine so that you use only one coin?

bonus time   Would you like to be able to do the above routine with a coin that has been marked with the spectator's initials? Would you like to be able to hand the spectator the initialed coin at the end of the routine, after it has been reproduced from an impossible place? If your answers are "yes," then read on, O apprentice wizard.

You should obtain some stick-on labels from an office-supply or stationery store. Stick a label on each half-dollar. Make sure that the labels go on the same side of each coin in the same position. With a pen write some initials on the label on one of the halves and place it in your left jacket pocket. Place the other half with its label in the right jacket pocket. At the beginning of the routine, allow the spectator to write his initials on the coin from the right jacket pocket and then proceed with the routine.

When you reach step 8 in the routine, the coin that you bring from your left jacket pocket is, of course, the duplicate coin. (The coin that the spectator initialed is in your right jacket pocket.) It would be a mistake to allow the spectator to get a close look at the coin at this point because he would discover that it is not the original coin. You may, however, give them a quick flash of the label, and the initials and then place the coin at the tips of the left fingers with the label facing you.

After step 18, take the wand from the spectator and place it in your right jacket pocket. As you do so, get the original coin in Finger–Palm position in the RH.

Sit down and begin to remove your left shoe. In the act of removing the shoe, place your fingers in the shoe as indicated in Figure 2-19.

Figure 2-19.

The coin is released from Finger–Palm position and allowed to slip into the shoe. Since your foot is still in the shoe, there should be no noise. Remove the shoe with the RH and in so doing lift the heel so that gravity will carry the coin toward the toe of the shoe. (See Figure 2-20.)

Figure 2-20.

Hold the shoe high in the LH and then turn it over so that the coin drops from the shoe to the table or floor. (You really should wear clean socks without holes if you plan to perform this version of the trick.)

COINS ACROSS

The "invisible" passage of a number of coins from one hand to another has been a staple of coin magic for many years. The routine offered here is similar to one that I have used and taught for a number of years. It will require practice on your part, but you will be rewarded by having a Coins Across routine that you can use under many conditions. For this trick you will need three similar coins, such as three half-dollars. The routine is usually performed while standing.

method and presentation

1. Display the three coins by placing them on the palm of the open RH. (See Figure 2-21.)

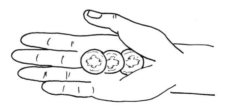

Figure 2-21.

You will note that one coin is in position for the Classic Palm and that the other two coins slightly overlap it.

2. Partially close the RH as you turn it palm down. Retain the half that is in Classic Palm position and allow the other two coins to fall onto the right fingers. (See Figure 2-22.)

The audience will not be able to tell from the sound if two or three coins are falling onto the right fingers.

3. Hold the LH open and several inches to the left of the RH. Toss the two coins held on the right fingers into the LH. The

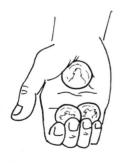

Figure 2-22.

LH should close so quickly that the audience does not get a chance to see that only two coins have been tossed from the RH to the LH. They certainly will not be able to count the coins in the air! You have retained the first coin in Classic Palm position in the RH. The RH is open and held palm down.

4. Lift the closed LH about eighteen inches and look at it. Make a slight up-and-down shaking motion with the LH, and, at the same time, close the RH.

5. Bring both hands to a position just above the table top, backs of the hands facing the table. The hands should be about 18 inches apart.

6. Open both hands to show that one coin has passed magically from the LH to the RH. After this point has registered with the audience, dump the coins from both hands onto the table.

7. Pick up one of the coins that has not "passed" with your RH as you say, "This coin has not passed." You display this coin in your RH in position for the Stanfield Vanish.

8. Execute the Stanfield Vanish as you apparently place the coin in your LH.

9. You then say, "This coin has not passed either." As you say this, your RH moves to point to the coin on the table. In the act of pointing, your right index finger presses on the coin on the table. You will find it natural for the other three fingers of the RH to curl in toward the palm of the hand. The curling fingers should press the coin concealed in these fingers into Classic Palm position in the RH. (See Figure 2-23.)

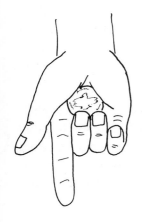

Figure 2-23.

You should have plenty of cover for this move because the larger motion of pointing to the coin on the table will mask the smaller move of pressing the coin into the Classic Palm.

10. Pick up the remaining coin on the left and display it at the tips of the right fingers. The back of the hand is held toward the audience so that the palmed coin is concealed from their view.

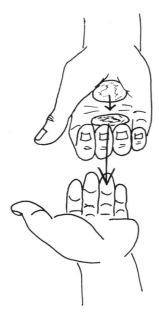

Figure 2-24.

11. You are now going to execute one of the versions of the Click Pass. At the end of this move, one coin will be in the LH and the other coin will be retained in the RH, but the audience will believe that both coins are in the LH. The Click Pass can be achieved by the following procedure. With the second coin held at the tips of the right index, middle, and ring fingers, rotate the RH so that it is palm down. The RH should be held just above the closed LH. Move your right thumb off the coin. Open the left fingers slightly, and, at the same time, allow the coin in Classic Palm position to drop from Classic Palm in the RH to the LH. As it passes the coin held on the tips of the right fingers, it should strike this coin, making a sound. (See Figure 2-24.)

This sound simulates the sound of a coin from the RH being dropped onto a coin in the LH. Since there is no coin in the LH at this time, you need the sound effect to convince the spectators that there is a coin in the LH. It is from this sound that the Click Pass gets its name. The left fingers should open and close quickly to admit the falling coin so that the audience does not get a chance to see into the LH. As you learn to perform this pass, you will note that the left fingers and the back of the RH serve to mask the action. It may take you some time to master this move, but it is well worth the effort.

12. At the end of the Click Pass, the closed LH moves slightly to the left, and the index finger of the RH extends to point toward it as you say, "Remember that these two coins have not 'passed.'" At the same time, the other three fingers curl in and press the coin that was on the tips of the right fingers into Classic Palm in the RH.

13. The LH moves up and to the left and the RH picks up the remaining coin (the first coin that passed) and displays it at the tips of the right fingers.

14. The RH closes into a loose fist and turns down; the knuckles rest on the table. One coin in the RH is in Classic Palm and the other coin is resting on the tips of the right fingers.

15. Tell the audience, "If you listen carefully, you will *hear* the second coin pass." Make the up-and-down motion with the LH and then release the coin held in Classic Palm in the RH. You will get a very nice sound effect as this coin falls on the other coin in the RH.

16. Open both hands to show that one more coin has "passed" from the LH to the RH; dump the coins from both hands onto the table. You now have one coin to your left and two coins to your right.

17. With your LH, position the two coins on your right on the palm up RH.

You will note from Figure 2-25 that one of these coins is in Classic Palm position. This is important for the final move in the trick.

Figure 2-25.

18. Place the remaining coin on the tips of the left fingers and hold the hands open, palm up, LH over the RH, as shown in Figure 2-26.

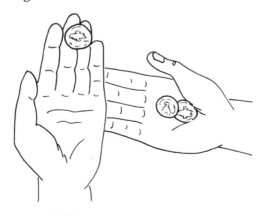

Figure 2-26.

Tell the audience, "If you watch carefully, you will actually see the last coin pass."

19. Quickly close both hands while turning them down and moving them a few inches apart. This should look suspicious. You want them to think that you have done "something" when, in fact, you have not. The LH coin is still in the LH and the RH coins are still in the RH. You should take care to make sure that the coin in Classic Palm in the RH does not shift during this move.

20. Ask the audience, "Did you see it go?" No matter what their reply, you say, "Well, it didn't go; I just do that to keep you honest." As you say this, open the LH to show that the coin has not "passed." Toss this coin on the table.

21. Pick up this coin and display it at the tips of the middle and ring fingers of the palm up LH. (See Figure 2-27.)

22. Now close the LH quickly while, at the same time, turning it palm down. In the act of closing the hand and turning it over, the coin should be trapped on its side between the tips of the fingers and the heel of the palm. (See Figure 2-28.)

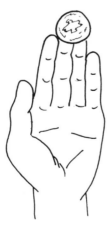

Figure 2-27.

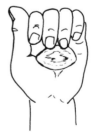

Figure 2-28.

With a bit of practice, the knack for trapping the coin in the proper position can be acquired. As you do this, you should say, "One coin in the left hand." The closed hand should be held directly in front of your body and several inches above the top of the table.

23. You immediately turn your attention to your RH as you say, "And two coins in the RH." Turn the RH palm up and open it so that the audience can clearly see that you have only two coins in the RH.

24. We now come to a very important move in this routine. It will require practice on your part in order to get the proper timing. The closed LH with its trapped coin is several inches above the table. The open, palm up RH should be several inches to the right of the LH and slightly above it. After you have displayed the two coins on the palm of the RH for a few seconds, you turn the RH palm down and to the left as though to toss the two coins on the table. You actually retain the coin in Classic Palm in the RH and yet two coins fall to the table. Where does the other coin come from? You guessed it! It comes from the LH. As the RH turns, allowing the coin that is *not* in Classic Palm to fall to the table, the fingers of the LH relax their pressure on the trapped coin and it falls along with the coin from the RH giving the illusion that the two coins have fallen from the RH. When you get the proper timing, the illusion is perfect. A helpful hint: Do not release the coin from the LH until the RH has almost completely turned palm down. Another hint: You may find it helpful to move the LH slightly to the left as the coins are falling. Practice the timing on this move. It should appear that you are simply tossing or dumping the two coins from the RH onto the table.

25. Move the closed LH up and to the left as you pick up the two coins on the table with the right fingers.

26. Say, "You will now see the last coin go." Open the LH as you make a throwing motion toward the audience; the LH will be seen to be empty. "It's going now; it's orbiting the room; it's coming to my right hand." Jerk your right hand sharply. "It's here." Allow the three coins to drop, one at a time, from the RH and then open it to show the hand empty.

By this point it is probably obvious to you that this routine will require a good deal of practice, but once you have mastered it, you can perform it almost anywhere. I have performed a slightly longer version of this routine (using four coins) from the close-up tables at magic conventions to the floor of a country store and it has always been warmly received.

THROUGH THE TABLE

In this trick four coins apparently pass, one at a time, through a solid table. This is another classic of coin magic, and the routine can be mastered with the proper amount of practice. It involves a technique called "lapping." Lapping is using your lap as a temporary servant, a place to conceal objects that have vanished or a place from which concealed objects can be obtained for production. Although you must be seated at a table to use the technique of lapping, its uses extend far beyond this trick. One of the first tricks that I learned involved lapping, but I was not impressed with it because it was so simple in method. (This is a common failing among young or beginning magicians; they tend to be more attracted to the method than to the effect.) Since it appeared to be so simple, I soon abandoned it. Years later, in 1968, I saw Tony Slydini, the master of lapping, perform. I had already read a few of his books, so I knew bascially what he was doing, but in spite of that *it looked like real magic.* I was so impressed that I took a lesson from him and plunged into a study of lapping. The time and effort I have spent in this area of magic have been amply rewarded.

To "pass" the coins through the table, you will need four similar coins (I use four half-dollars), a table, a chair, and a handkerchief. The height of the table and the height of the chair should be such that your lap is not too close to the edge of the table. If you are poorly positioned the audience might be able to see into your lap. A dining-room table and chair usually provide the right relationship.

Position yourself so that the edge of the table is about six to eight inches from your body. With your body facing the table, turn your legs slightly to the left. Cross your ankles and force your legs together as closely as possible. You may discover that there is still a slight gap between your inner thighs. This is where the handkerchief comes in. Either force the handkerchief into this gap or spread it over your lap. If you are female and wearing a dress or skirt rather than a pants suit, you may forget about the handkerchief because unless you are uncommonly thin the material of the dress or skirt should provide you with an automatic lap. You will need to practice assuming this position naturally, and you will need to train yourself to hold the position. You may well discover muscles that you didn't know that you had in the process of learning to hold this position. Once you are in position, you can proceed with the trick.

method and presentation

1. Display the four coins by placing them on the table. Allow the audience to see that your hands are empty.

2. With the LH, place the coins in a row on the RH. (See Figure 2-29.)

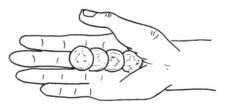

Figure 2-29.

You will note that one of the coins is in position for the Classic Palm just as in the passage of the first coin in the Coins Across routine. The RH is held over the table and should be in line with the center of your body.

3. Close the RH and turn it down, allowing three of the coins to fall to the fingers and retaining the fourth coin in Classic Palm. Once again this is similar to the first move in Coins Across, but, in this case, you are dealing with four coins rather than three.

4. Toss the three coins (the spectators think four) from the RH to the LH. Close the LH quickly so that they cannot tell how many coins are in the LH.

5. Raise your LH several feet above the table, *look at it,* and *at the same time,* allow your RH to drop naturally to the edge of the table. The RH should be on a line with the center of your body. The fingers of the RH should rest on the edge of the table with the thumb and palm of the hand dropping slightly below the edge of the table. At the point that the fingers of the RH touch the top of the table, you should release the coin that is in Classic Palm and allow it to fall into your lap. If you are in the proper position, the coin will land in your lap. As you look at the LH say, "Four coins." By the time you say this, the RH coin should be in your lap. Immediately lift your RH showing the palm to the audience and say, "Two hands." This action shows that your RH is empty without calling undue attention to the fact. Make a fist with the RH and rap the table and say, "A solid table."

6. Tell the audience that you are going to pass a coin through the table but that you must first locate the "soft spot" in the table. Do this by poking at the top of the table with your right forefinger. During this action, keep your LH well above the table and away from the edge of the table.

7. Having located the soft spot at a point about eighteen inches from your edge of the table on a line with the center of your body, say "Watch." Now place your right arm under the table and bend forward to position your LH over the soft spot. As this is happening, you should bend your right arm at the elbow so that your RH can reach into your lap to retrieve the coin that has been lapped. (See Figure 2-30.)

8. Bump your LH on the table and slap the coin in the RH on the bottom of the table so that the audience can "hear" the coin pass. You do not open the LH at this point.

9. Place both hands on the table about six inches from the edge. They should be about six inches apart, resting on their

Figure 2-30.

sides with the thumb side of each fist up as shown in Figure 2-31A.

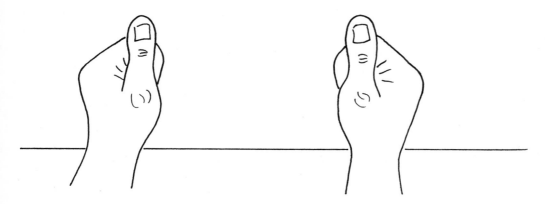

Figure 2-31 A.

10. The RH opens and slaps its coin down near the LH. (See Figure 2-31B.) The LH then quickly moves forward several inches, opens, and slaps its coins down on the table. (This is an important move because it sets up a key move that is going to be made later in the routine.) Remove your hands from the

81

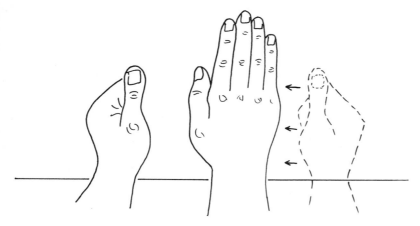

Figure 2-31 B.

coins showing one coin beneath the RH and three coins beneath the LH.

11. Position the coin that came from the RH about one inch from the edge of the table nearest you and on a line with the center of your body.

12. With the LH place the other three coins in a row on your RH just as in step 2. The only difference is that in this case you are dealing with three coins instead of four. The first coin placed in the RH should be placed in Classic Palm position.

13. Repeat steps 3 and 4. This will leave you with a coin in Classic Palm in the RH (unknown to the audience) and two coins in the LH (the audience believes three).

14. The RH starts to pick up the coin that is near the edge of the table. The right fingers cover the coin, an action that places the palm of the RH over your lap. At this point, the coin that is in Classic Palm in the RH is allowed to fall into your lap. (See Figure 2-32.)

15. Pick up the coin that is near the edge of the table with the RH and display it by holding it at the tips of the index and middle fingers and the thumb. Hold the hand so that the audience can see that it contains only the coin being displayed. Tell the audience that this coin will act as a magnet for the other coins.

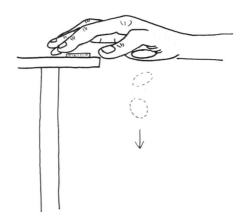

Figure 2-32.

16. Go through the process of locating the soft spot again. This time locate it to the right of the center of the table.

17. Go through the moves in steps 7 and 8. As the coin passes, allow the coin that has been retrieved from your lap to clink against the coin in the RH; this provides a nice sound effect. Now repeat steps 9 and 10. The RH should come very close to the LH when it slaps its coins down on the table. (Remember, you are setting them up for an important move.)

18. The situation is that you now have two coins that have passed and two coins that have not passed. Display two coins in each hand while pointing this out to the audience. The position of the coins in the RH is not critical, but the position of the coins in the LH is.

Figure 2-33.

In Figure 2-33 you will note that the coins are displayed in the LH so that one of the coins is resting on the index and middle fingers and the other coin is resting on the ring and little fingers. If you close your hand in this position, one of the coins will be above the other. This means that with the hand resting on edge on the table, the bottom coin could be released by simply relaxing the pressure of the ring and little fingers on the coin. (See Figure 2-34.)

If the LH were to move to the left, the coin would simply be left on the table. (You are going to use this move in a moment.)

83

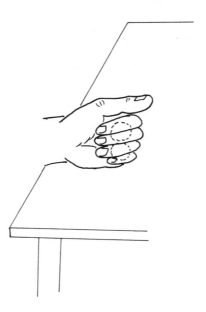

Figure 2-34.

19. Close both hands. Repeat steps 6 through 9. In this case you simply rattle the two coins in the RH beneath the table to simulate the passage of the third coin. There is no coin in your lap at this time; the coin that is going to pass is still in the LH.

20. Your hands should assume the position used in step 9. The left wrist should be *slightly* bent, turning the left fist *slightly* toward your body. The RH should be a bit closer to the LH than in the two previous sequences. Once the LH is in position, relax the pressure on the coin held by the ring and little fingers and allow the coin to slide down until it is resting on the top of the table.

21. Now comes the critical move. The RH is going to open and slap its coins down on the table, just as it has done on the two previous occasions. But this time, unknown to the audience, you are going to add a coin from the LH, the third coin that has apparently passed through the table. As the RH opens to slap its coins on the table, it should be close enough to the LH so that the fingers of the RH brush the knuckles of the LH. As soon as the fingers of the RH brush the knuckles of the LH, the LH rotates so that the back of the hand touches the table. At the same time, the LH moves several inches to the left, *leaving behind* the coin that has been resting on the top of the table. (See Figure 2-35 A and B.)

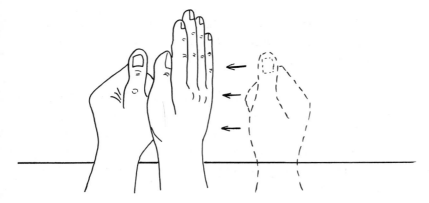

Figure 2-35 A.

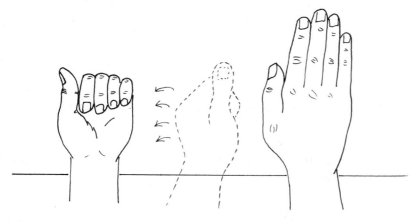

Figure 2-35 B.

This coin is now trapped beneath the RH. If the RH is now removed, the audience will see three coins. The impression that you want to give is that the RH was simply slapping its coins on the table and that the LH just moved out of the way so that everyone could see what was happening. Although this move must be carefully practiced many times in order to get the proper timing, it must appear to be casual in performance.

You must appear to be doing the same thing that you did the first two times that you slapped the coin(s) down with the RH. (This is, basically, a famous coin sleight, the "Han Ping Chien" Move.)

22. The RH moves away to display the three coins beneath it. The LH moves forward several inches, opens, and slaps its coin on the table.

23. You are now ready for the passage of the last coin. Place the three coins that have passed in your RH and close it. Pick up the remaining coin, display it at the tips of the left fingers, and close the LH. Position the LH on a line with the center of your body. It should be held directly over your lap; that is, it should be *past* the edge of the table, but it should be several inches *above* the plane of the table. Relax your grip on the coin and allow it to slide down until it is only held in the LH by the pressure of the little finger. If you were to drop the coin from your hand at this point, it would fall into your lap, *but* the audience would see it. What you have to do is to mask the action of the falling coin. With the RH closed, holding three coins, start looking for the soft spot again. On your first attempt to find the soft spot, you should move your right arm across your body to the left as you say, "Maybe it's over here this time." You should point far enough to the left so that the upper portion of the right forearm comes into contact with the little finger of the LH. (See Figure 2-36.)

At this moment the area between the LH and the edge of the table will be screened from the view of the audience. At this moment the little finger of the LH releases its pressure on the coin and the coin falls into the lap. This should take only a fraction of a second. As soon as the coin has been released, the RH should move to the center of the table, continuing its search for the soft spot as you say, "No, it's not there. Maybe it's here."

24. As the RH moves from the left to the center of the table, the LH should move forward and over the table.

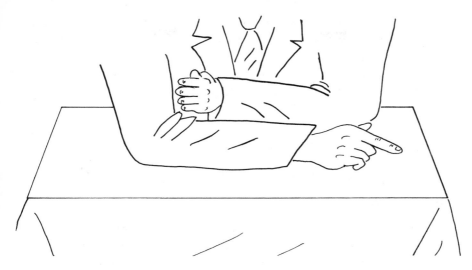

Figure 2-36.

25. After the RH locates the soft spot, you should place the right arm under the table and lean forward. (Don't forget to bend your arm at the elbow and retrieve the coin in your lap.)

26. Look at the soft spot and dramatically slam your LH down on the spot, opening the hand as you slam it down. Jingle the coins in the RH under the table to show that the coin has arrived. Turn the LH over to show it empty. Bring the RH from beneath the table to show that the fourth coin has indeed passed through a solid table, solid except for the magical soft spot.

Although it has taken several pages to describe this trick, just as it does to describe the Coins Across, you will find that both effects move very quickly in performance. The routines are not simple, but neither are they overly complicated. I urge you not to attempt them "in public" until you have put in many hours of practice and until you can do all of the moves without really having to think about what you are doing.

THE COIN IN THE BAG, IN THE BOX, IN THE SOCK

In the following trick a coin, marked for future identification, vanishes only to reappear in an impossible location. This is a small version of a stage trick that has been popular with magicians for centuries. The stage version was performed in France by Robert-Houdin in the nineteenth century, by Stanislas Surin in America in the same century, and by Houdini in America in the twentieth century. In order to do this trick, you will need several items that you can easily buy or make.

method   The first item that you will need is a coin slide. If you have one of the magic sets sold in department and toy stores, you may already have a coin slide, and it might serve for this trick. (See Figure 2-37.)

If you do not own one, however, one can be made rather easily from a cigar tube. More-expensive grades of cigars are packaged in aluminum tubes. You could either buy a cigar that comes in such a tube or obtain one from a cigar-smoking friend. Once you have the tube, throw away the cap from the tube and then cut off the bottom inch of the tube with tin snips. .(See Figure 2-38.)

Figure 2-37.

Figure 2-38.

This should leave you with a tube about five inches long, open at both ends. It is a simple matter to flatten the tube with your hands until you have a slide. Do not flatten the tube too much or the coin will not pass easily through it. This tube should take a penny, nickel, dime, or quarter; a half-dollar would be too large. Once you have the flat tube, you should attach it with tape to a rectangle of stiff cardboard (the kind used in making heavy-duty cardboard boxes) with electrician's tape. After this you will need to punch a hole in the cardboard and insert a medium-sized safety pin through the hole. This allows the apparatus to be pinned inside your coat. (See Figure 2-39.)

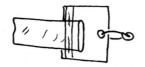

Figure 2-39.

The next items that you need are a series of containers to attach to the tube. First, you will need to make a small bag to fit over one end of the tube. It should be slightly larger than the coin that you are going to use in the trick. If you make one large enough for a quarter, it could also be used with smaller coins as well. It should be placed on the tube (as shown in Figure 2-40) and a rubber band should be wrapped around it to hold it on the tube.

The second item you need is a small match box, the kind that contains wooden matches. Remove all the matches and slip the end of the tube, already covered with the small bag, into the partially opened match box. Place rubber bands around it (as shown in Figure 2-41).

Figure 2-40.

Figure 2-41.

Figure 2-42.

The third item you need is a small sock. You will need a sock that is slightly larger than the match box. You will discover that a baby's sock or a small child's sock will work nicely. (Buy or borrow such a sock; do not steal it from a baby.) It is placed over the match box as shown in Figure 2-42.

You could, of course, use another cloth bag, but I think that the sock gives a more unusual and entertaining air to the trick. When you have this setup assembled (as in Figure 2-42), it is time to test it. Drop a quarter in the upper end of the tube. Pull the sock-box-bag off the tube. If you have made the apparatus properly, you will discover that the coin is now safely in the inner bag and that it will take several moments of removing rubber bands and opening containers to get to the coin.

You will also need to make a gimmick for the vanishing of the coin. First, obtain two bandana-type handkerchiefs. Carefully cut off one of the corners of one of the handkerchiefs. This should give you a piece of cloth slightly larger than the coin that you intend to make vanish. A quarter is a proper sized coin to use in this trick because it is likely to be the largest coin that can be used with the coin slide. Place a quarter near one of the corners of the uncut bandana and sew the corner that you cut from the other handkerchief carefully on top of it. (See Figure 2-43.)

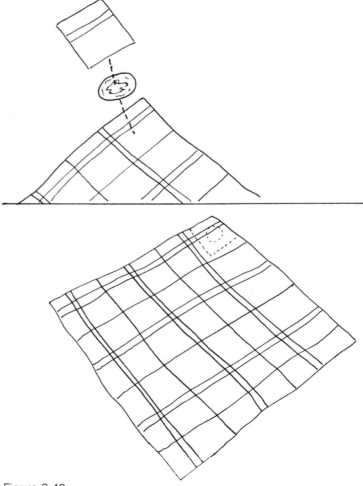

Figure 2-43.

You now have a handkerchief with a gimmicked corner, a coin concealed between two layers of fabric. The reason that I recommend the bandana is that the design on this type of handkerchief will hide the stitches used in sewing the small bit of cloth on the handkerchief.

With a few advance preparations you will be ready to perform the trick. Place the bag-box-sock setup on the coin slide and pin the slide inside your jacket on the left. The mouth of the slide should be near the opening of the inside jacket pocket. (See Figure 2-44.)

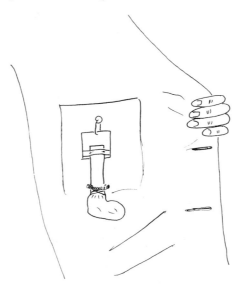

Figure 2-44.

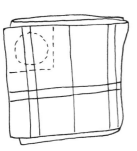

Figure 2-45.

Place a small magic wand in your inside left jacket pocket. Fold the handkerchief so that the gimmicked corner is toward the outside of the fold. (See Figure 2-45.)

Place this hankerchief in your outside left jacket pocket with the gimmicked corner *nearest* your body.

presentation   1. Place a gummed label on one side of a quarter and have it marked for future identification. Display the coin on the palm of the open RH.

2. With your LH, remove the handkerchief from the left jacket pocket. Holding the handkerchief by the gimmicked corner, snap it open, retaining and concealing the gimmicked corner in the fingers of the LH.

3. Place the gimmicked corner between the index and middle fingers of the RH. (See Figure 2-46.)

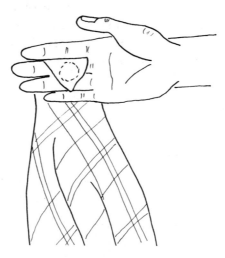

Figure 2-46.

Place your right thumb over the gimmicked corner to help conceal it from the audience. (See Figure 2-47.)

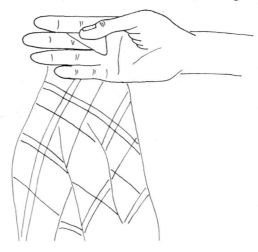

Figure 2-47.

4. Gather the hanging folds of the handkerchief with the LH and drape the handkerchief over the RH, covering the marked quarter.

5. With the LH, apparently pick up the marked quarter through the cloth of the handkerchief with the thumb and index and middle fingers of the LH. In reality you pick up the gimmicked corner. The marked quarter is allowed to slide into Finger–Palm position in the RH.

6. Hold the handkerchief up with the LH while pointing to it with the right index finger. The other fingers of the RH are curled to conceal the coin in Finger–Palm position in the RH. As you do this, say, "I'll need some trustworthy person to very carefully hold this large sum of money."

7. When a spectator volunteers, transfer the handkerchief with coin carefully to him. Make sure that he gets a good grip on the coin in the gimmicked corner *before* you release your grip on the coin. You do not want the coin to vanish prematurely! He should assume, of course, that he is holding the marked coin through the fabric of the handkerchief. During this process, your RH should drop naturally to your side.

8. Look around as you say, "I'll also need someone to hold my magic wand." Once you get a volunteer, reach inside your jacket with your RH, drop the coin into the coin slide, and immediately take the wand from your inside left jacket pocket and hand it to the spectator. In order to help you get the coin in the tube, you may discover that it helps to hold the jacket open slightly with the LH as you look in from above. You should turn your body slightly away from the spectators so that they don't get a glimpse of the bag-box-sock setup.

9. Now tell them, "I want to show you a strange gift that I received the other day." Allow the spectators to see that your RH is empty, and reach inside your jacket with this hand. Grasp the bag-box-sock setup, pull it off the coin slide, and toss it on the table.

10. Look at the spectator holding the wand: "You know, I always have such fun doing magic that I sometimes feel guilty about it. Why don't you do this trick for me? Just wave the wand toward the handkerchief."

11. Once the spectator has done this, you quickly grasp one of the corners of the handkerchief and quickly pull it from the spectator's hand. The coin will have apparently vanished. Grasp the handkerchief by the gimmicked corner to conceal the gimmick, and flip it a few times to show that it is empty.

12. Ball up the handkerchief and place it back in your pocket as you say to the spectator holding the wand, "That was very good! Now please bring it back." The spectator will protest that he cannot bring the coin back. Or he may try to bring it back and fail. In any case, the moment offers some possibilities for comedy. You could claim that the quarter was your life's savings. If it were a borrowed quarter, you could say to the spectator who loaned it, "It's not my fault! The one with the wand did it."

13. After a few moments of this byplay, ask the spectator with the wand to wave it over your "gift." Once he has done this, allow any spectator to open the gift. The marked coin will be found in the sock, in the box, in the bag.

14. Return the coin to its owner, and, as you take your wand from the spectator who acted as the magician, say to him, "You know, someday you are going to have to tell me how you did that."

REFLEX TEST

I think you will enjoy this next trick as much as I do because you don't have to make any props for it, you don't have to do any special setups for it, it can be done anywhere, and it really doesn't even require sleight of hand. All you need are seven pennies and the use of a little psychology. My good friend, fellow magician, and former student Dan Garrett performed this trick frequently when the TV show "Kung Fu" was popular. If you remember the show, I think you will be able to see how he was able to use the "Kung Fu" theme. Another feature of this trick is that it happens in the spectator's hand. This means that you will need to "borrow" a hand from someone in order to practice.

method and presentation

1. Have the spectator face you and hold out his RH, palm up. The seven pennies should be held on the palm of your open LH. Your LH should be several inches above the spectator's hand and slightly to the left of it.

2. Address the spectator: "Have you ever had your reflexes tested? Well, I'm going to give you a very simple reflex test. I'm going to count these pennies one at a time into your hand and when the last penny is counted into your hand, I want you to close it as fast as possible."

3. You proceed to do just that. Pick up the pennies, one at a time, with the index finger and thumb of the RH and count them into the spectator's open hand. Count aloud, "One, two, three . . ." as you do this. When you reach "seven," simply turn your LH and allow this last penny to fall into the spectator's hand. You should also allow each penny to clink against the others already in the hand as you are counting. (These two points are very important because they enable you to do the magic the next time you do the count.)

4. The spectator will close his hand as the seventh coin falls and you say, "Very good! Now let's try that again." Retrieve the coins and take the same position used in step 1.

5. Tell the spectator, "This time you are going to need to close your hand even more quickly because I am going to attempt to steal the last coin out of your hand before you can close it."

6. Go through the same process used in step 3. Make sure that you count the coins aloud and clink one coin against the others as you count. This time, when you reach the count of "six," simply clink this coin against the other coins in his hand, but *do not release it*. Retain it between the index finger and

thumb of the RH and move your RH under the spectator's RH. Immediately say "Seven" and turn the LH to drop the last coin into the spectator's hand.

7. The spectator will close his hand quickly and you should say, "You do have good reflexes. The only way I could get a coin from your hand would be by magic." As you say this, rub the back of the spectator's closed RH with the fingers of your RH. Then bring your RH into view holding the penny at the tips of the right fingers. The spectator may then open his hand and count the coins. He will discover only six coins.

As I pointed out earlier, it is not gimmicks or sleight of hand that makes this trick work, but psychology. The counting, the clinking of the coins during the count, and the spectator focusing on the *last* coin makes this trick possible.

CONCLUSION

As with card tricks, there are far more coin tricks than I have taught you in these pages, but I have made every attempt to give you a general selection of good coin magic. Some of these tricks require preparation prior to performance, but many of them can be done impromptu. Some are rather easy to learn, but others will require more practice and will hopefully stimulate and challenge you to learn the sleights and timing required for their proper execution.

3

Magic
with Ropes

INTRODUCTION

Tricks with ropes have been a favorite of magicians for many years because ropes are relatively compact and take up little space on the magic table, magic case, or even on the person of the magician. Although they are compact, they can be seen from a considerable distance when in use, so that they can be used as part of a close-up, parlor, platform, or stage show.

The type of rope that you use is important for the success of many tricks. For most tricks it is best to use soft, flexible rope that has a diameter of one-quarter or three-eighths of an inch. The proper type of rope can be purchased in hanks of fifty and one hundred feet, at a reasonable price, from most magic dealers. The rope sold by most dealers has an inner core composed of several string-like fibers. If you are going to do a trick that requires that the rope be cut, it is usually wise to remove the core of the rope. This can be easily done by holding the outer shell of the rope with one hand and pulling on the inner fibers until the core is free of the outer shell. "Decoring" a rope will make it much easier to cut.

If you are doing a trick that involves cutting a rope, it is important that you have scissors that will cut the rope with relative ease. You can buy special rope shears from magic dealers, but good scissors, like the kind used for cutting fabric, will do the job. Do not attempt to use children's scissors or any scissors that are lightweight or that have thin blades. If you do, you may eventually "worry" the rope apart, but this will not add much to your image as a magician and will produce only frustration on your part. A word of caution: the points of scissors can be very sharp; therefore, handle them with care and don't let small children handle them at all. You don't want to end up with bandages or lawsuits as a result of your magic act.

Many of the tricks in this chapter can be done with cord, string, or even ribbon. In some tricks, versions using items other than rope have been suggested. In other tricks, you will want to use your imagination, one of your most valuable assets in magic, to determine if a variation of the trick might be done with some other item.

THE CUT AND RESTORED ROPE

In magic there is an old saying: "If you give a magician enough rope, he'll cut and restore it." This statement indicates the popularity of the Cut and Restored Rope in the world of magic. Most magicians perform at least one version of this classic.

There are many methods by which a rope may be apparently cut and restored, and although I make no attempt to teach you all of them, I do offer three that are effective and fairly simple to use.

method A

In this method an extra loop of rope is used; therefore, this version of the trick requires some advance preparation.

The loop is made in the following fashion. Get a piece of rope about three or four inches in length; cut the ends in a diagonal fashion, as indicated in Figure 3-1.

Put rubber cement on the cut ends; allow the cement to dry and then stick the ends together. You now have a small loop of rope that can be concealed in your hand.

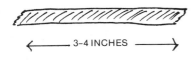
← 3–4 INCHES →

Figure 3-1.

1. Conceal the loop of rope in your LH. Remember to hold the hand naturally so that you don't call attention to it. You may find from experimentation that it is difficult to conceal the loop of rope. If this is the case, you should make a smaller loop. Keep experimenting until you find the right size loop for your hand.

2. With the loop concealed in your LH, display a piece of rope three or four feet in length between both hands. If you hold the rope by the thumb and index finger of each hand, the extra loop will be out of sight in your LH, concealed by the closed middle, ring, and little fingers of that hand.

3. Release the end of the rope held in the RH, at the same time raising the LH. This allows the rope to hang down from the LH.

4. Grasp the center of the rope with the RH, and then release the end held in the LH. This allows the rope to hang, by its center, from the fingers of your RH. (See Figure 3-2.)

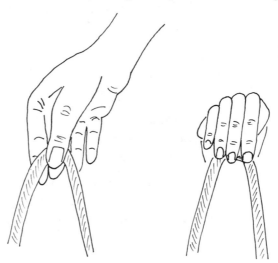

Figure 3-2.

The audience sees all of the rope and gets the impression that both hands are empty and that the rope is unprepared, without calling direct attention to these points.

100

5. Place the center of the rope held by the RH finger tips into the LH. Keep the back of the LH toward the audience. As the center of the rope is placed in the LH, the little finger and ring finger of the LH curl into the palm and hold the center of the rope in the LH. At the same time the right fingers pull the loop of rope into view at the top of the fist formed by the LH. (See Figure 3-3.)

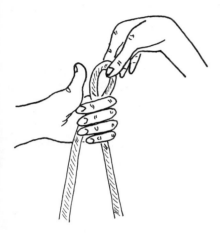

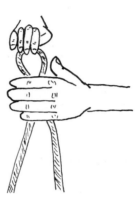

Figure 3-3.

As far as the audience is concerned, you have simply placed the center of the rope into the LH and have pulled it into view. Practice this move until it is smooth and natural.

6. With your scissors, cut the loop of rope. As far as the audience is concerned, you have now cut the rope in the center.

7. In order to dispose of the evidence, you continue to cut small pieces out of the loop and allow them to fall to the floor or onto your table if you are using one.

8. You will finally reach a point at which you will be left with one small piece of the loop. Don't worry about it because it will fall from your hand when the rope is restored and will be taken by the audience as just another piece of the rope.

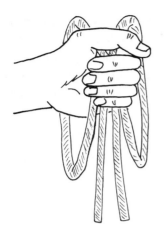

Figure 3-4.

9. In order to restore the rope, thread the ends of the rope that are hanging down from the LH back through the left fist. (See Figure 3-4.)

At this point you can make a magic pass, say a magic word, wave your magic wand or charm over your hand, or any combination of the above.

10. If you pull slowly on the ends of the rope that have been threaded back through the left fist, the true center of the rope will come into view.

11. You have now proved your ability as a magician by restoring the rope and you may even allow the audience to examine it, if you wish, because the rope is "clean."

thinking time Make up some patter to be used with this version of the cut and restored rope.

method B In this method an extra loop of rope is also used, but in a different manner. In this version of the trick, the larger piece of rope is gimmicked. Take the piece of rope that you are going to use, three or four feet in length; cut the ends diagonally; put rubber cement on the cut ends; allow the cement to dry; and then stick the ends together. What you have is a large loop of rope that appears to be one unbroken strand. Take a short piece of rope and tie it around the longer rope, opposite the rubber-cement joint (as indicated in Figure 3-5).

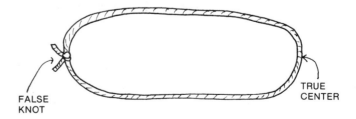

FALSE
KNOT

TRUE
CENTER

Figure 3-5.

The rope appears to be tied at the ends. In reality, you have a rope that is joined at the ends with rubber cement and opposite this you have a false knot. If your hands were clean when you made the joint, you will discover that the joint is invisible except at very close range. In fact, I once used some narrow red rope for this trick and *I* could hardly see the joint.

presentation

1. Display the rope.

2. Cut the rope at the rubber-cemented joint. You now apparently have two pieces of rope. You might also trim off a piece of rope from each end to get rid of the "evidence."

3. Tie the two ends together. Apparently, you have two ropes tied together at the ends. (See Figure 3-6.)

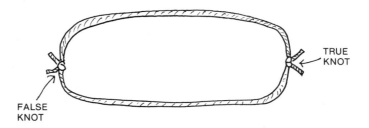

TRUE KNOT

FALSE KNOT

Figure 3-6.

4. Ask a spectator to touch either knot. Here, you are going to use the "magician's choice." No matter which knot the spectator touches you are going to use the knot that you want to use. If he selects the real knot you say, "All right, this is the knot that we will cut away." You do so and let him keep the knot as a souvenir of the show. You then untie the fake knot, holding the rope so that the audience cannot tell that you have a small piece of rope looped around a long piece. If your "assistant" selects the fake knot, you say, "all right, this is the knot that I will untie." You do so, concealing the fact that you have a long and short piece of rope. You should then cut off the real knot and let the spectator keep it.

5. You are now ready to restore the rope. Bring one of the ends of the long rope up with your RH and allow it to overlap one of the ends of the short rope held in the LH. Get a firm grip on the short rope and rapidly slide the LH down the long rope while moving your RH to the right. (See Figure 3-7.)

HAND OMITTED FOR CLARITY

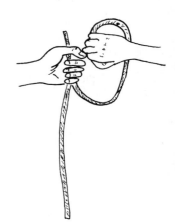

Figure 3-7.

You will now be holding the rope in a horizontal position in front of your body and the short piece of rope will be in your RH. The audience will assume that this is a continuation of the longer piece.

6. You can get rid of the short piece by simply coiling the rope around your RH and placing it in your pocket, table, or case. If you are using a table with a servant, a small bag or shelf concealed from the audience, on the back, you could allow your RH, the hand holding the short piece of rope, to touch the edge of the table, releasing your grip on the short piece of rope and allowing it to fall into the servant. If you wish to use the long piece of rope for another trick, you can get rid of the short piece by coiling the long piece around your LH while, at the same time, folding the short piece so that it can be palmed in the RH. In this case you will dispose of the short piece of rope by putting your RH in your pocket or magic case to get another magic prop.

thinking time   Make up some patter to use with this version of the Cut and Restored Rope. Think of other ways of disposing of, or using, the short piece of rope.

bonus time   This trick can be done with a piece of string as an excellent close-up bit of magic. Make up the string just as you would the rope. The joint in the string is almost impossible to detect, even at close quarters. If you get the right kind of string, you can even eliminate the extra piece. You will need the thick, white string that is often used for wrapping packages. This kind of string is actually composed of a number of smaller, individual fibers. With care you can separate these fibers, and, by twisting them at the point of separation, you apparently have two ends. (See Figure 3-8.)

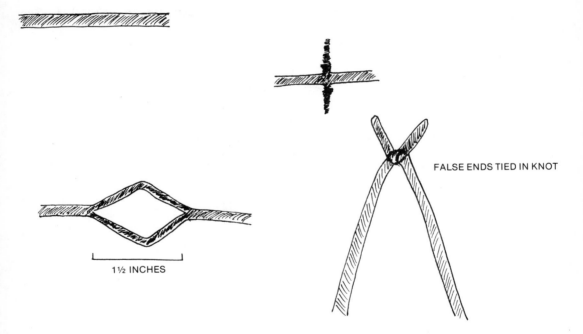

FALSE ENDS TIED IN KNOT

1½ INCHES

Figure 3-8.

You can now tie these two fake ends into a knot. By untying them and pulling on the ends of the string, you can make the string return to its original state. This action apparently makes one string out of what was two strings. In performance this act of restoration should be concealed in your hand; otherwise, the audience will see what happens.

method C   I have used this method in my own shows for years. It can be done without any special preparation of the rope, so you are "clean" at the end of the trick. This method relies on a secret move that is simple and direct. As with all secret moves, no matter how simple, it must be practiced again and again until it is almost a reflex for the performer. In order to learn the move, you should do the following: get a piece of rope six to eight feet long. (Please note that we are using a slightly longer piece of rope with this method than in the other two methods.) Clip one end of the rope (the left end, for example) in the crotch formed by the left thumb and LH and place the other end of the rope between the index and middle fingers of the LH. (See Figure 3-9.)

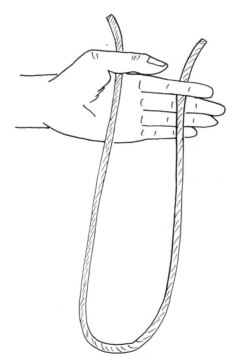

Figure 3-9.

Note that the rope projects a few inches past the points at which it is held. Now take the center of the rope with the index finger and thumb of the RH and lift it up to the LH and clip it

106

with the left thumb against the index finger of the LH. (See Figure 3-10.)

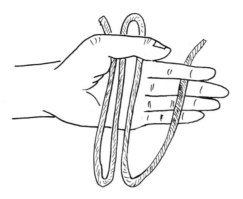

Figure 3-10.

In this sequence of moves, you have simply displayed the rope and have placed the center of the rope between the two ends of the rope in your LH. *Now* for the secret move. Go through the same motions as described above, but this time, as the RH approaches the LH, allow the center of the rope to slide over the right thumb and index finger. (See Figure 3-11.)

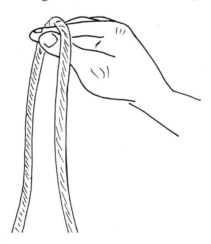

Figure 3-11.

As the RH goes behind the LH, use the index finger and thumb of the RH to pick up the rope just below the point at which the center loop crosses the end of the rope that is clipped between the left thumb and LH. (See Figure 3-12.)

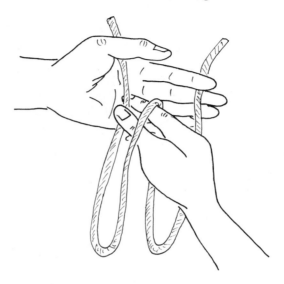

Figure 3-12.

This piece of rope is brought up between the two ends of the rope and is clipped against the index finger of the LH by the left thumb. (See Figure 3-13.)

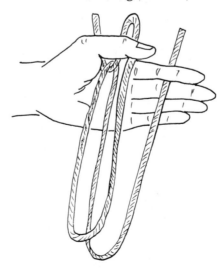

Figure 3-13.

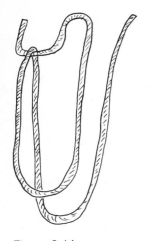

Figure 3-14.

At this point it appears that you have simply displayed the rope and placed the center of the rope in the LH. In reality, you have looped one end of the rope around the remainder of the rope. (See Figure 3-14.)

If you now cut the rope at the point indicated in the illustration, you will apparently cut the rope in the center, but you will have, in fact, a short piece of rope looped around a long piece of rope. If you now tie the ends of the short piece of rope around the long piece of rope, you have apparently tied the ends of two long pieces of rope together. In reality you have one long piece of rope with a short piece tied around it, and the short piece of rope will slide on the long piece.

presentation   Once you have mastered the move, you should practice doing the trick. In this presentation I include some lines of patter that I have used in my own shows. In addition to the six- to eight-foot piece of rope, you will need a pair of scissors and some object that you can use as a magic object, perhaps a silver dollar or another large or unusual coin. Place the magic object in your right pants or jacket pocket. Place the scissors in your inside jacket pocket, or in your magic case or on the table. You are now ready to begin.

1.   Ask a spectator to assist you. I usually pick a young lady for this trick. When she comes on stage or to the front of the room, have her stand to your left. If you are using a table you should both be standing to the left of the table and slightly in front of it.

2.   Display the rope as you ask the spectator, "Do you know much about mathematics?" No matter what the reply, you say, "Today I'm going to teach you a mathematical formula, the formula for finding the center of a piece of rope."

3.   As you say these lines you should be getting the rope into position. That is, you clip the left end of the rope in the crotch formed by the left thumb and LH and the right end of the rope is clipped between the index and middle fingers of the LH. The center of the rope is hanging down.

4. Pick up the center of the rope with the index finger and thumb of the RH and place it in the LH. *Do not do the move at this time.* As you do this you say to the spectator and to the audience in general, "The formula is that the center of a piece of rope is located halfway between the two ends."

5. You then say, "Now we need a pair of scissors." As you reach for your scissors, allow the center of the rope to drop from your LH; retain your grip on the ends of the rope.

6. Hand the scissors to the spectator as you ask, "Do you know how to operate heavy machinery?" (You will get a number of interesting replies to this question and most of them, or the question, will get a laugh from the audience. I once had a young lady about 17 years old assisting me, and she said, "Sure, I drive my father's tractor." In this case, the laugh was on me, but I didn't mind because the audience was being entertained.)

7. The spectator is holding the scissors and you still have the rope. You now say, "It's test time. Do you remember the formula for finding the center of a piece of rope? Let's review it. The center of a piece of rope is located halfway between the two ends." As you say the last line, pick up the center of the rope with the index finger and thumb of the RH. As the RH moves behind the LH, you do the secret move and end up with the end of the rope looped around the remainder of the rope. Remember, as far as the audience is concerned, it should appear that you are doing the same thing that you did a few moments before, displaying the center of the rope between the two ends in the LH.

8. Holding what is apparently the center of the rope toward the spectator, you say, "Please cut the rope in the center."

9. As the spectator starts to comply with your instructions, quickly move your hand back toward your body and add, "Please keep in mind that the very white thing is the rope. The pink things covered with freckles and hair are my fingers. Please don't cut them." (Obviously, if your fingers do not fit this description, alter the line to fit you.)

10. Allow the spectator to cut the rope. She thinks that she is cutting the center of the rope.

11. Holding on to the ends of the short piece of rope, allow the ends of the long piece of rope to drop. You now apparently have two pieces of rope, approximately equal in length, hanging side by side. What you really have is a short piece of rope looped around a long piece of rope. The audience will not know this if you don't separate the fingers of the LH and if you keep the back of your LH to the audience.

12. You now pretend to tie the two ends of the short rope together. In reality, you are tying them *around* the long rope with one knot. This will take some acting ability on your part since it is impossible to tie two separate pieces of rope together with only one knot. I usually tie the short piece of the rope around the long rope with one knot and then I just wrap the ends of the short piece around each other as I mutter something like "Let's see, left over right and right over left, I think that's the way to do it." The illusion is very strong.

13. At this point, the false knot should be slightly off center; you apparently have one piece of rope that is a few inches longer than the other piece. (This is the way that you want it for what follows in the routine.)

14. Holding the rope by the false knot, allow the two ends to hang down. Point out to the spectator that the ropes are uneven and ask her to even up the ropes by cutting off the extra length. At this point you should take the blame for the fact that the ropes are not even. Have the spectator measure the ropes very carefully before she cuts off the extra piece.

15. While the spectator is cutting off the extra length of rope, you should slide the fake knot a few inches in either direction. This should be easy to do since the attention of the audience will be focused on the spectator. Your action will make the ropes uneven again.

16. Tell the spectator to throw the piece that has just been cut off into the audience as a souvenir, and, at the same time, you hold the rope up by the false knot. At this point someone in the audience will notice that the ropes are still uneven. You pretend not to notice for a few seconds, and then, looking at the rope in amazement, you say to the spectator, "I don't think we got that quite right. Let's try again."

17. Repeat steps 14 through 16 one or two more times. Don't repeat them more than two more times because the laugh peak for this bit of business will pass, and the audience might begin watching your actions rather than the actions of the spectator with great care.

18. After you have had the spectator attempt, unsuccessfully, to even up the ropes a few times, stop her and say, "I predict that you have a great future in the Department of the Budget. Why don't you give me the scissors; they seem to be a dangerous weapon in your hands."

19. Take back the scissors as you say, "We'll try something different with these ropes."

20. Put the scissors away and begin wrapping or coiling the rope around your LH. This should be done rather rapidly.

21. The RH, in wrapping the rope around the LH, will eventually reach the false knot. At this point clamp down on the knot with the RH and allow it to slide down the rope as you continue to wrap the rope around the LH. It will be concealed by the RH and the audience will assume that it is coiled around the LH with the rope. The audience cannot see the knot because it is on the side of the hand away from them. As you are coiling the rope around the hand, ask the spectator, "Have you ever done any magic before?" Most of the time, she will say "No." In this case you reply, "Then you are about to give your first magical performance." If she says "Yes," you reply, "It's good to have an experienced magician helping me."

22. Tell the spectator, "I'm going to let you use one of my treasured pieces of magical apparatus." As you say this, put your RH with the palmed false knot in your right pants or jacket pocket. Leave the false knot in the pocket and bring out the coin or other magical thing. A hint: If you judge that the false knot is going to be too large for you to palm with ease, trim off the ends of the knot until you get it to a size that you can palm. Do this *before* you start the business of having the spectator attempt to even up the ends of the rope.

23. Hand the coin to the spectator and instruct her to touch the rope three times with it.

24. After she has done this, take back the coin and say with relief, "I'm glad you didn't touch the rope four times. If you had, you would have turned into a toad."

25. Hand the spectator the end of the rope that is on the outside of the coil.

26. Move to your right, allowing the rope to uncoil. The spectator and the audience will see that the rope has been magically restored.

27. Say to the spectator, "You did a fine job of putting those two ropes back together. I don't understand how you did it."

28. Ask the audience to applaud the spectator for her fine work and allow her to return to her seat in the audience. If you are wealthy, you might allow her to keep the rope as a souvenir. If you are not wealthy, you may keep the rope for other rope tricks.

A VANISHING KNOT

The Vanishing Knot is also a staple of rope magic. This specific version has been used by magicians for many years. It is a fairly simple knot to tie, once you practice it enough to get the knack, and it is very impressive when tied; it looks very realistic. For this trick you will want to use a piece of rope about four feet long. It can be done with a longer rope, but if the rope is shorter than four feet, you may run into some problems. This is a trick that is much easier to teach by drawings than by written descriptions. Get a piece of rope and follow along.

method and presentation

1. Take a close look at Figure 3-15.

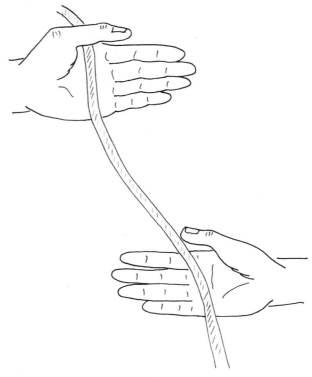

Figure 3-15.

You will note how the rope is displayed. The palms of the hands are facing up; the backs of the hands are roughly parallel to the floor. The rope is clipped between the index finger and thumb of each hand. The hands should be approximately in the center of the rope and there should be about six inches of rope between the two hands.

2. The LH turns until its palm is parallel to the floor, and, at the same time, it moves toward the RH. (See Figure 3-16.)

3. The index and middle fingers of each hand open, somewhat like a pair of scissors. The index and middle fingers of the RH clip the rope that lies over the back of the LH; the index and middle fingers of the LH clip the rope that is hanging from the RH. (See Figure 3-17.)

114

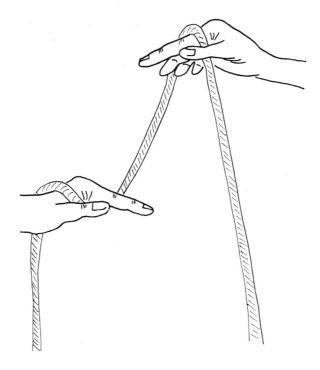

Figure 3-16.

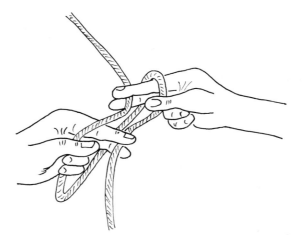

Figure 3-17.

4. The LH and RH separate. The rope remains clipped by the index and middle fingers of each hand, and, at the same time, the thumbs of each hand release their hold on the rope. (See Figure 3-18.)

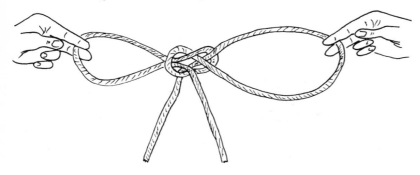

Figure 3-18.

If this is done properly, you will be left with a bow, or shoe-lace, knot.

5. At this point, you will be holding the bow knot by each loop. You must turn the right loop slightly so that the arrangement of the knot looks as it appears in Figure 3-19.

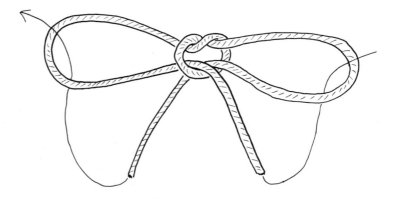

HANDS OMITTED FOR CLARITY.
NOTE THAT RIGHT LOOP HAS BEEN STRAIGHTENED.

Figure 3-19.

This is critical to the success of the trick. This adjustment should be made without releasing your grip on the knot.

6. You should now reach through each loop with the index finger and thumb of each hand and clip each trailing end of the rope with the index finger and thumb.

7. Once the trailing ends of the rope have been clipped, they should be pulled back through the loops. The proper direction in which to pull the ropes is shown in Figure 3-19.

8. Now, if you will pull gently on the ends of the rope, a very realistic knot will be formed; however, if you continue to pull on the ends of the rope, the knot will vanish because it is a false knot. Note: If you have reached this point and have a real knot, you have not followed these instructions correctly. Go back to step 1 and go through the entire process again until you are able to make the Vanishing Knot. Practice the Vanishing Knot until it can be done with ease. Once you have practiced enough you should be able to make the bow in less than a second. Completing the knot should take you only a little longer.

In performing the trick, you would display the rope and then make the knot. In order to cause the knot to vanish, you should place it in your LH; close your LH over it; pull alternately on both ends of the rope until you feel the knot "give" in your hand. You could allow two spectators to pull on the ends of the rope instead of pulling the ends yourself. You would not want to simply pull on the ends of the rope with the knot in full view to make it vanish; this would not be good showmanship. After you feel the knot release in your LH, you can wave your RH over your LH in a magic pass and then open the LH to show that the knot has vanished.

thinking time Make up a story for the Vanishing Knot. You might relate the knot to the problems that children have with tying their shoe laces or you might claim to be the "fastest bow knot tier" in the West (or East, North, or South).

bonus time By using a ring and one more piece of information, you can use the Vanishing Knot above for a very effective ring release or ring-off-the-rope. I have used this release as part of my close-up routine for years and as a part of one of my programs for children's birthday parties. It can also be done as part of a stage or platform act if the ring is large enough. A solid plastic, wooden, or metal ring (or bracelet) about three inches in diameter will work nicely for this trick.

1. Place the ring in the position indicated in Figure 3-20.

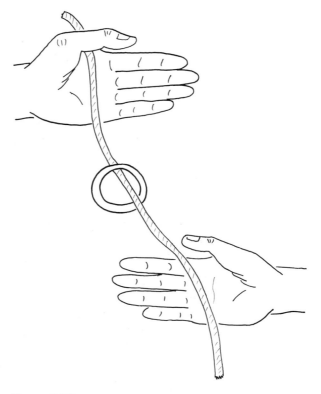

Figure 3-20.

2. Follow the instructions for the Vanishing Knot. This will leave the ring "tied" in the knot. If you were to pull on the ends of the rope at this point, the ring would be released from the knot since the knot would dissolve, but the ring would still be on the rope. (The next step will show you how to get the ring off the rope for maximum magical impact.)

3. In order to get the ring off the rope, you should thread the left end of the rope through the ring as indicated in Figure 3-21.

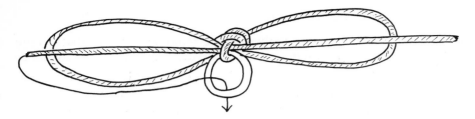

Figure 3-21.

If you pull on the ends of the rope, you will discover that not only does the knot dissolve, but that the ring falls away from the center of the rope. Note: if you have tried this and the rope knots around the ring or the ring remains on the rope, either you have failed to follow the instructions for the bow knot, or you have not followed the illustration for threading the rope back through the ring.

4. In performing the trick, once the ring has been tied into the knot and the end has been pulled back through the ring, you can slowly pull on the ring or the ends of the rope, and the ring will visibly penetrate the rope. This is one way you might end the trick.

5. My ending for the trick is somewhat different. I have one spectator hold one end of the rope and another spectator hold the other end of the rope. I then cover the ring knotted on the rope with one hand. After the knot is covered, I ask the spectators to pull slowly on the ends of the rope. This causes the knot to dissolve and the ring is free of the rope. When I know that the ring is free, I pause for a moment and then I slowly open my hand. The ring drops away from the rope and the spectators are left holding the ends. Because neither the ring nor the rope is gimmicked in any manner, they can be examined by the audience. Children are not the easiest audiences to impress (as you will discover if you do magic for them), but this trick has brought many *oohs* and *aahs* from little ones at more than one birthday party.

extra bonus By using a piece of cord or thick string instead of a rope, a borrowed finger ring, and a specially prepared envelope, you can turn this effect into a first-class close-up trick.

119

You will need a fairly small, rectangular envelope that has the flap on one of the *short* sides. I use a 3⅛" × 5½" coin envelope. These can be obtained at most office-supply stores. Once you have obtained the envelope, you should seal the top flap. Now, very carefully peel back the bottom flap. Coat the inside of the bottom flap and the area indicated in Figure 3-22 with rubber cement.

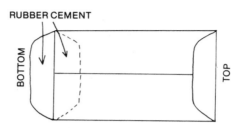

Figure 3-22.

Allow the rubber cement to dry and then cut a piece of cardboard that is a little longer than the envelope plus flap and almost as wide as the envelope. This piece of cardboard will prevent the envelope from closing accidentally. In performance, the piece of cardboard will be replaced by a small magic wand or pencil. The wand or pencil should be a bit longer than the envelope. In performance, this small wand or pencil serves three functions: to keep the envelope from closing before it should, to act as a guide for placing the borrowed ring in the envelope without any fumbling, and to give you a logical reason for reaching into your pocket at the right time.

In performance, the envelope should be in your left inside-jacket pocket with the open end up and the magic wand or pencil in place. (See Figure 3-23.)

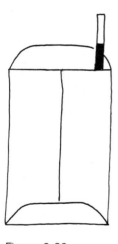

Figure 3-23.

1. Borrow a finger ring from a spectator. A fairly heavy ring works best.

2. Display the cord or thick string and have a spectator thread the ring on the string or cord.

3. Go through all the steps of the trick, up to and including tying the ring on the string.

4. When you reach the point at which the ring is apparently hopelessly knotted on the string, cover the ring with the LH. The closed hand is held palm down about a foot in front of your body.

5. Ask a spectator on your right to hold the right end of the string.

6. Once the spectator has a grip on the right end of the string, you should tug on the right portion of the string nearest your left fist. (See Figure 3-24.)

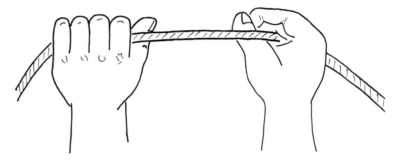

Figure 3-24.

Keep tugging until you feel the knot dissolve and you feel the ring free from the string. At this point, your patter might be, "That's a tight knot." The string is now running through your left fist and the ring is free. Allow the ring to slide down until it is held against the heel of the LH by the pressure of the left finger tips only. (See Figure 3-25.)

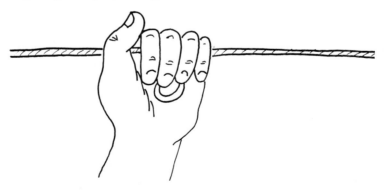

Figure 3-25.

7. Reach *under* the left fist with the RH to tug at the string on the left side of the fist. At this point, you allow the ring to drop from the fingers of the LH into the RH. (See Figure 3-26 A and B.)

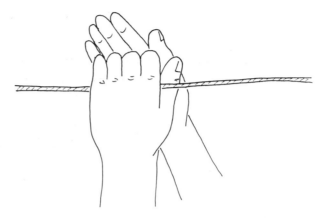

Figure 3-26 A.

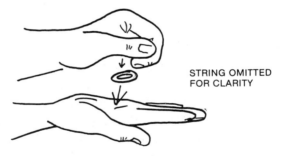

STRING OMITTED
FOR CLARITY

Figure 3-26 B.

This is the key move in this routine. Remember to practice it until it can be done smoothly and quickly. When the ring falls into the RH, it should be concealed by partially closing the index, middle, and ring fingers of the RH.

8. After you tug on the portion of the string on the left side of the left fist, ask a spectator on your left to hold this end. If you have executed the moves correctly, the spectators will believe that the ring is knotted on the string inside your left fist. In reality, the ring is in your RH.

9. Tell the spectators, "I'm now going to cause the ring to free itself from the string, but I will need my magic wand [or pencil, if that's what you're using]."

10. Reach into your left jacket pocket with your RH. As your hand touches the wand (or pencil), allow the ring to drop into the envelope.

11. Bring out the wand and hand it to a spectator.

12. Ask the spectator to wave the wand over your LH. You may even ask him to say a few magic words, either of your choosing or his.

13. Open your LH. The ring has vanished! Act surprised. Accuse the spectator (in a good-natured manner, of course) of having taken the ring. Mutter things like "I don't know what could have gone wrong." Accuse the spectator who waved the wand of having used too much magic power.

14. After playing the apparent mistake for a few moments (don't overdo it), apologize to the spectator who loaned the ring and offer to replace his ring with an object of "great value."

15. Allow the spectators to see that your RH is empty. Do this casually without calling undue attention to it. Then reach into your inside left jacket pocket with your RH. Fold down the flap on the envelope and take it out of the pocket. Because of the rubber cement on the envelope and the flap, it will seal.

16. State that the object of "great value" is contained in the envelope and call attention to the fact that the envelope is sealed. You can let them look at the envelope quite closely.

17. Tear off the top of the envelope and dump the ring into the hands of the spectator who loaned it to you. Ask him to identify it and while he is doing this, crumple the remainder of the envelope into a ball and discard it. This gets rid of the evidence in a casual manner.

I think you will find that this close-up routine has real impact when properly executed. You have caused a knot to dissolve, a ring to vanish from a string and to reappear inside a sealed container. Not bad!

thinking time Can you think of a way to make the ring appear on the center of a small wand or pencil while both ends of the wand or pencil are being held by a spectator? It can be done.

THE CARVER ROPES

In my opinion, this is one of the finest rope tricks ever devised. Since it is relatively angle-proof, it can be done under almost any conditions. Because ropes are not bulky, this trick can be used as part of a close-up routine. And because the ropes have a high degree of visibility, the trick can be used as a stage effect. I was taught this routine by my first instructor in magic, Bob Carver, when I was in my teens, and I have used it frequently since then. It has become very popular in the world of magic because it is such an effective illusion, and it is known, in various forms and under a variety of names, by many magicians. I include it here so that you too may be able to present one of the world's finest rope tricks.

To do this effect you need three pieces of rope. The short rope should measure twelve inches, the medium rope twenty-eight inches, and the long rope forty-two inches in length. These measurements are approximate and can be varied as long as the ratios remain equal: the length of the medium rope should be equal to one-half the length of the short rope plus one-half the length of the long rope. The plot of this trick is that you cause these ropes of different lengths to become ropes of the same length. No other ropes are used. That sounds like magic! It also looks like magic when it is done properly.

method and presentation This trick has three phases, the "equalizing," the "count," and the "unequalizing." All phases must be mastered to do and to "sell" the trick.

1. Show the short rope and place it in the LH. It is placed near the base of the thumb and is held in place by thumb pressure. Several inches of the end of this rope hang over the back of the LH. The back of the LH is toward the audience. (See Figure 3-27.)

2. Show the medium rope and place it in the LH. It goes near the tip of the left thumb and is held in place by thumb pressure. The position of this rope is shown in Figure 3-27.

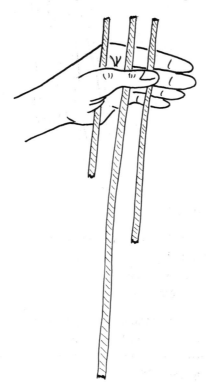

Figure 3-27.

3. Show the long rope and place it in the LH. Note that it goes *between* the short rope and the long rope, as shown in Figure 3-27. You might have to tilt the LH slightly forward so that the medium rope does not slip out when you are positioning the long rope. Once the long rope is in place, you should tilt the hand back so that the back of the LH is facing the audience.

125

4. Bring the dangling end of the medium rope up and place it next to the end of the medium rope already held in the LH. This is shown in Figure 3-28.

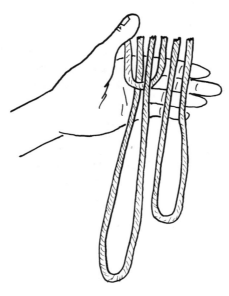

Figure 3-28.

5. Bring the dangling end of the short rope up and place it in the LH *between* the end of the long rope already held in the LH and the two ends of the medium rope. This is shown in Figure 3-28. Note how the short rope now crosses over the long rope.

6. Bring the dangling end of the long rope up and place it on top of the end of the long rope already held in the LH. Note how the long rope crosses over the short rope. This is shown in Figure 3-28.

7. To prepare for the equalizing move you now need to do the following: take one end of the medium rope (the end furthest to your right) and both ends of the long rope in your RH. You will observe that the long rope is now looped through the short rope. The audience cannot see this because the point at which the ropes are looped is concealed in the LH. The spectators believe they see the opposite ends of each rope in each hand. In reality, the LH holds both of the ends of the short rope and one end of the medium rope; the RH holds both ends of the long rope and one end of the medium rope. Separate the hands slightly. (See Figure 3-29.)

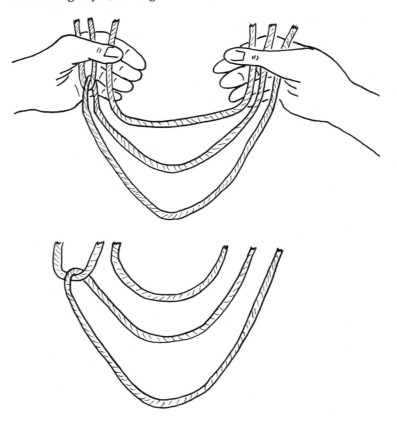

Figure 3-29.

8. The equalizing move is done by slowly pulling the hands apart while moving them away from and toward the body. The movement of the hands helps to conceal that only one rope is moving.

9. In a few seconds, the ropes are apparently equalized. (See Figure 3-30.)

They should now be displayed by releasing the grip on the ends of the ropes held in the RH and allowing the ropes to dangle from the LH.

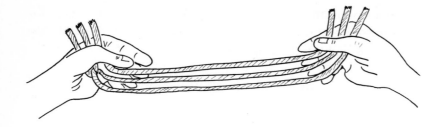

Figure 3-30.

the count phase **1.** The ropes are held in the LH, as shown in Figure 3-31.

2. The RH grasps the end of the medium rope projecting from the top of the LH and pulls it up and away from the LH. This is shown in Figure 3-31.

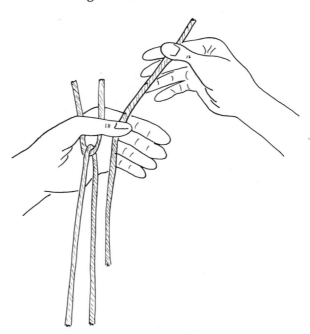

Figure 3-31.

3. The RH again approaches the LH, apparently to pull out the second rope. What actually happens is that the medium rope is switched for the two looped ropes. This is done in the following manner. The end of the medium rope is clipped

128

between the index and middle fingers of the RH as it approaches the LH. As the hands come together, the index and middle fingers of the LH clip the medium rope while the index and middle fingers of the RH release their clip on this rope. At the same time, the index finger and thumb of the RH close on the two ends of the short rope that extend above the LH. (See Figure 3-32.)

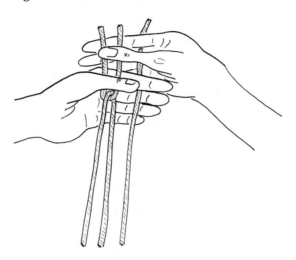

Figure 3-32.

The medium rope is retained in the LH while the two looped ropes are pulled up and away by the RH. (See Figure 3-33.)

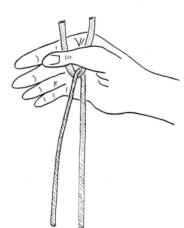

Figure 3-33.

The loop is concealed by the RH. This gives the illusion that you have simply pulled another of the equal ropes from the LH. In reality, you have transferred the looped ropes from the LH to the RH.

4. The RH returns to the LH and again pulls the medium rope up and away from the LH. Now all of the ropes are in the RH and the audience has the impression that they have seen each of the "equal" ropes.

the unequalizing phase   At this point in the routine you cause the "equal" ropes to return to their original state.

1. The ropes will now be in the position in the RH as shown in Figure 3-34.

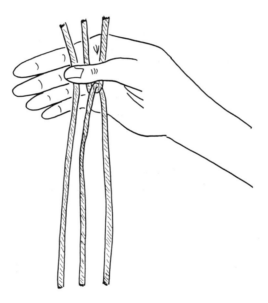

Figure 3-34.

2. Transfer the ropes from the RH to the LH without letting the audience see the looped portion of the long and short ropes. After the transfer the position of the ropes appears as shown in Figure 3-35.

3. Take the ends of the ropes hanging from the LH with the

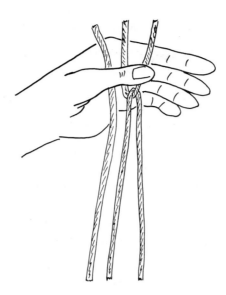

Figure 3-35.

RH and bring them up, one at a time, positioning them beside the ends of the ropes in the LH. (See Figure 3-36.)

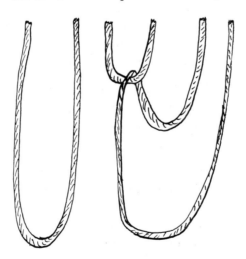

Figure 3-36.

Note that the ends of the medium rope are now side by side.

4. Pull on one of the ends of the short rope until it is free of the LH. Do not allow it to pull the loop into the view of the

131

audience. Display the rope and drop it on your table, or throw it into the audience if you want them to have it as a souvenir.

5. Do the same with the medium rope.

6. Do the same with the long rope.

The routine is now over. You are "clean" and all of the ropes can be examined if you wish. I often use this as a closing effect for banquet and birthday-party shows.

bonus time   Since I often use this as a closing effect, I have developed patter for the trick that relates to audiences.

1. "In my career as a magician, I have performed for many audiences, and I have discovered that there are three types of audiences." (If you are going to have the ropes examined by members of the audience, it should be done before you begin this patter.)

2. "I've discovered that there are little audiences." Display the short rope and position it in the LH. "I don't mean small audiences or audiences of little people. I mean audiences that almost dare you to entertain them."

3. "I've discovered that there are medium audiences." Display the medium rope and position it in the LH. "These audiences seem to be willing to meet you half-way when it comes to being entertained."

4. "And I've discovered that there are big audiences." Display the long rope and position it in the LH. "I don't mean big in numbers, I mean audiences that really get involved in the show. They really want to be entertained and they participate in the entertainment. These are the kind of people that every magician likes to perform for."

5. "I've known for years that these three types of audiences exist—the little, the medium, the big." As you are saying this, you position the ropes for the equalizing move.

6. "There have been times when I have wished that I could make all my audiences equal." Do the equalizing move.

7. "If I could do that, then all my audiences would meet me halfway, and they would get more entertainment out of the show." Do the count to show that all the ropes are equal.

8. "Of course, I know that isn't possible." Place the ropes back in the LH and bring up the dangling ends to get the ropes in position for the unequalizing phase.

9. "I know that I will always have little audiences." Remove the short rope from the LH. "I know that I will always have medium audiences." Remove the medium rope. "And I know that I will sometimes get big audiences." Pull one end of the long rope with the RH while holding the other end of the rope with the LH until the rope is stretched between the two hands. Smile at the audience as you say, "And you've been a big audience. I thank you."

thinking time How many patter stories can you devise that fit this trick? It does have many possible patter applications and, after some time spent thinking, you should be able to develop many interesting stories.

THE ROPES THROUGH THE BODY

This trick is good for the stage or platform because visibility is high and the impact is strong. Two ropes apparently penetrate the body of a spectator! To do this trick you need two pieces of rope, each about eight feet long, and a small piece of white thread. The thread should not be too strong because its purpose is to hold the ropes temporarily in position. The principle employed in this trick is very old and is used in a number of magic tricks.

method Make a small loop out of the white thread. The loop should be large enough to fit over both ropes and it should be fairly snug. It should not be so snug, however, that it will not slide up and down the ropes easily.

The only sleight that you have to do is to reverse the position of the ends of the ropes, so that you apparently have two ropes side by side when, in reality, you have two ends of one rope on one side and the two ends of the other rope on the other side. (See Figure 3-37.)

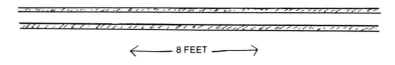

←———— 8 FEET ————→

Figure 3-37.

This can easily be done with one hand if the ropes are held as indicated in Figure 3-38 A and B.

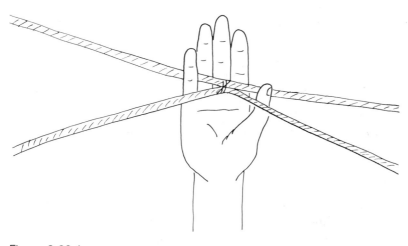

Figure 3-38 A.

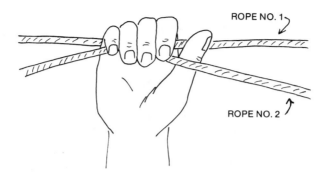

Figure 3-38 B.

By simply moving the right thumb to the left and turning the RH palm down at the same time, you can reverse the ends. (See Figure 3-39.)

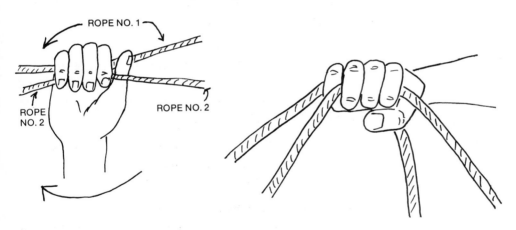

Figure 3-39.

presentation 1. Get two spectators from the audience to assist you. One of them should be a boy or a young man (or even an old man if you can't find a boy or a young man) who is wearing a coat or jacket. (The reason for this will become obvious as we proceed.) Position your "assistants" as indicated in Figure 3-40.

2. Pick up the two eight-foot pieces of rope and display them. The loop of thread should already be on the ropes near the ends that you are going to hold.

135

MAGICIAN

SPECTATOR "B"

SPECTATOR "A"

Figure 3-40.

3. Let spectator "B" hold the other ends of the ropes. Ask him to pull on his ends of the ropes. At the same time, you pull on your ends. This establishes the fact that the ropes are solid. After you have both pulled on the ropes, instruct the spectator to drop his ends of the ropes.

4. With your LH, pull the ropes through your RH until the RH is in the center of the ropes. You are apparently still displaying the ropes. In reality, you are moving the loop of thread to the center of the ropes.

5. Turn to your right so that you are facing the two spectators. This puts your left side to the audience. Allow your RH, holding the ropes at the center, to drop to your side.

6. Ask spectator "A" if he is brave and courageous. You will get a variety of answers, but the audience has now focused attention on the spectator, so there is little attention on you as you reverse the ends of the ropes. Because your body is blocking the audience's view of your RH and because attention is focused on spectator "A," you should have little difficulty executing the move *if* you have practiced it sufficiently.

7. Place your RH behind the back of spectator "A." The hand goes behind his back and beneath his jacket. (The reason for picking a spectator who is wearing a jacket should now be obvious.) The jacket will mask the fact that the ropes are doubled back on themselves. (See Figure 3-41.)

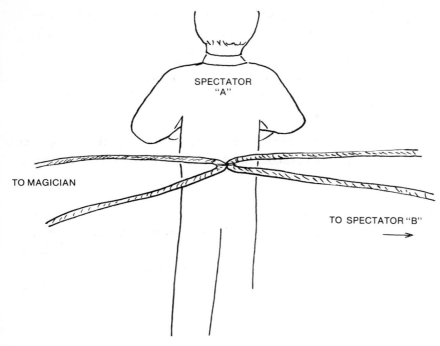

SPECTATOR
"A"

TO MAGICIAN

TO SPECTATOR "B"

Figure 3-41.

8. You now ask spectator "B" to hold one set of the ends of the ropes. He is holding the ends of the same rope but he does not realize this. You will apparently retain the other ends of the ropes. In reality, you are holding both ends of the other rope. The ropes will stay in place because of the loop of thread.

9. You now exchange one of the ends that you are holding for one of the ends that the spectator "B" is holding and proceed to tie a large single knot in the ropes over the chest of spectator "A."

10. Ask spectator "B" to hold tightly to his ends of the ropes and you should hold tightly to your ends of the ropes.

11. At this point you should recap what has taken place: Two ropes have been placed behind the spectator and one of the ropes has been wrapped around the spectator and tied in a knot. Point out that he is imprisoned in the ropes.

12. While you and spectator "B" hold tightly to the ends of the ropes, instruct spectator "A" to count to three, take a deep breath, and move three steps backwards.

13. If spectator "A" does as he has been instructed, the thin white thread will snap and the ropes will apparently pass through his body.

14. Commend spectator "A" for his courage; thank spectator "B" for his assistance and allow them to return to the audience.

thinking time   Develop some patter for this trick. You might consider the idea that this is a form of exotic trial by ordeal, used in some distant land, or you might think about the theme of impossible escapes, mentioning Harry Houdini. As another exercise in magical thinking, try to develop other applications and tricks that use this principle.

CONCLUSION

You now have at your disposal a number of rope tricks. Obviously, there are many more routines that could have been included in these pages, but you have been taught a number of tricks and several basic principles of rope magic. Use your imagination to create new effects and your powers of reasoning to analyze the rope magic that you see others do, in order to add to your repertory.

4

Close-up
Magic

INTRODUCTION

In the 1960s and 1970s, close-up magic came into its own. There are books devoted entirely to the area of close-up magic. Some magicians specialize in this branch of the craft. During most magic conventions some time is given to close-up performers, and, in recent years, entire conventions have featured nothing but close-up performances and lectures.

Close-up magic is not only popular with magicians, but most magicians have more opportunities to perform close-up magic than stage magic. You are much more likely to have the chance to do a few tricks after dinner in your own home or in the home of a friend than you are to perform on the stage of a theatre.

Naturally, the tricks that you learned with cards and coins can be considered close-up magic, and the trick with the borrowed ring (in Chapter 4) could also be considered a close-up trick, but in this chapter I deal with some other props to broaden your repertory and to show you that there are many items that can be used in close-up magic.

A BRIEF TRIBUTE TO A CALLOW YOUTH

I noted in the description of Coins Through the Table that one of the first really good magic tricks I learned used lapping. I also mentioned that I had abandoned the trick for many years because I thought, wrongly, that it was beneath my abilities because it was so simple. Because this is such an effective piece of magic and because it has a number of possible applications, I am going to pass it on to you. I trust that you will be wiser than was I and realize that this trick is worthy of your rehearsal and performance.

The preparation is very simple. You should be seated at a table and should have a paper napkin rolled into a ball in one of your pockets. You should also have a duplicate napkin somewhere on your person. This is an ideal after-dinner trick if you are provided with paper napkins rather than cloth ones. If not, you may have to carry your own. Before you even offer to show the trick, you should secretly place the rolled-up napkin in your lap. You are now ready to do the trick.

method and presentation

1. Display and unfold the duplicate napkin. Allow the spectators to see that both of your hands are empty and that you have only one napkin. You should do this without calling undue attention to either of these facts.

2. Tear the napkin into several strips and then roll the strips into a ball. The ball should look as much as possible like the whole napkin, which is balled up and resting in your lap.

3. Display the ball between the index finger and thumb of your RH. With your left index finger, touch the ball. The hands should be in line with the center of your body and you should be sitting back in your chair so that your hands are directly over your lap. The audience should be able to see that your hands are empty, except for the torn and balled pieces of the napkin in your RH. As you touch the ball, say, "If I touch the pieces of the napkin like this, nothing happens."

4. Lean forward and to your right; hold the ball in front of a spectator as you say, "But if you touch the napkin, this begins a chain reaction." As you lean toward the spectator and extend your right arm to him, your LH should fall naturally into your lap and onto the duplicate napkin that has been placed there. This movement should look and feel natural. When the LH falls into your lap, it should secure the whole napkin in Finger–Palm position.

5. After the spectator has touched the napkin, you lean back in your chair, bringing the RH back toward your body. The RH stops about four inches from the edge of the table and on a line slightly to the right of the center of the body. At the same time that the RH is being drawn back across the table, the LH should casually return to the top of the table. It should rest several inches from the edge of the table and in line, roughly, with the line of the left leg. The back of the fingers should be toward the audience and the whole napkin is held in a loose Finger–Palm position. As soon as the RH reaches its position, it should release the torn napkin, and be lifted several inches above it. Look at the torn napkin and say, "Ah, yes, I can see that the chain reaction is taking place."

6. You now apparently take the napkin from the table and place it in the LH. This is exactly how the move should appear to the spectators. The RH covers the napkin on the table by placing the fingers in front of the napkin, that is, between the spectators and the napkin. (See Figure 4-1.)

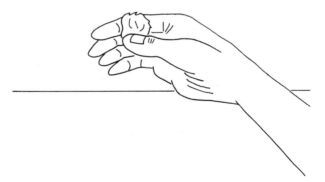

Figure 4-1.

This forms a natural screen and the napkin is temporarily lost from view; the right thumb goes behind the napkin. The RH draws the napkin toward the edge of the table, and, once it reaches the edge of the table, the napkin is allowed to fall into your lap.

7. There must be no pause at this point. The RH moves away from the edge of the table and to the left. The right thumb presses against the fingers as though it were holding the balled-up strips of the torn napkin. As the RH moves away from the edge of the table, the LH moves up and to a position in front of you. The two hands should meet about chest-high, directly in front of your body, well above the top of the table.

8.   As the two hands meet, the RH appears to place the torn and balled-up napkin into the LH. The LH, of course, contains the duplicate napkin, a whole one; and the torn napkin is, by this time, safely in your lap. The LH moves straight away from your body over the center of the table and the RH opens wide so that the audience may see that it is empty.

9.   Open the LH and allow the napkin to fall to the table as you say, "And this completes the chain reaction." The RH will naturally fall to the top of the table.

10.   Sit back and relax as you ask one of the spectators to unroll the torn strips of the napkin. To their surprise they will discover that the "chain reaction" has restored the napkin. Before you leave the table, find an opportunity to dispose of the torn napkin by placing it in your pocket. You need not be in a great hurry to do this, but be sure that you do not leave any evidence behind.

thinking time   As I mentioned earlier, this trick has a number of applications. For example, it can be used impromptu as a vanish or it can be used for transforming one object into another. Spend some time playing with it after you have mastered the basic moves, and see how many different tricks you can invent.

GLASS THROUGH

In this trick, the magician apparently passes a glass through a table. This feat is worthwhile to learn because it is a good table trick and it provides a strong lesson in timing and misdirection. To do this trick you need a drinking glass that has sides that are straight or that slope inward from the mouth of the glass to the base. (See Figure 4-2.)

Figure 4-2.

You also need a sheet of newspaper and a coin, but because the coin is used for misdirection, its denomination does not matter.

method and presentation

1. You are seated at a table with the spectators seated at the other sides of the table or standing opposite you. You have the proper type of glass and a newspaper. On some occasions these items can be borrowed, but if you are planning to perform the trick, it would be wise to have the required props with you.

2. Place the coin several feet from the edge of the table on a line with the center of your body. It should be far enough away from you so that it would be natural for you to lean forward when you are covering the coin with the glass. Ask the spectators, "Would you like to see me make this coin vanish without even touching it?" In all probability, they will say, "Yes."

3. You then state, "That's what I'll do. In fact, I'll cover the coin with this glass so that my hands never come in contact with it." Suit your actions to your words and cover the coin with the glass *mouth down* over the coin.

4. "But I can't allow you to see *how* I make the coin vanish, so I'll have to cover the glass." Remove the glass from the coin and proceed to wrap it in the sheet of newspaper. Some magicians do this by placing the glass on the edge of the

144

newspaper and rolling the paper around the glass, twisting the top of the paper when the wrapping is complete. (See Figure 4-3.)

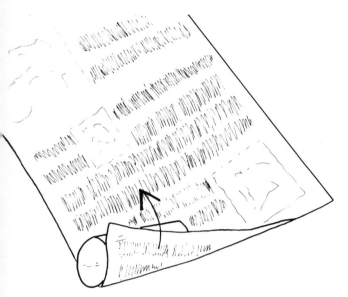

Figure 4-3.

Other magicians prefer to simply place the paper over the glass and crush the paper until it is formed around the glass; the magicians who use this method argue that it appears much more "natural" than carefully wrapping the glass. (See Figure 4-4.)

You should experiment to see which of these methods you prefer. This step is a very important one because later in the routine you will want the audience to assume that the form made by the paper is both the paper and the glass. The form made by the paper should be loose enough to allow the glass to slide out of it at the appropriate time. Make sure that the mouth of the glass is at the bottom of the setup; make sure that the mouth of the glass is not covered by the newspaper.

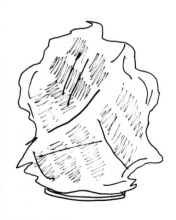

Figure 4-4.

5. Holding the glass through the paper, place it, mouth down, over the coin. You should lean forward while doing this. Then make a magic pass over the glass and say, "Passe, passe, coin under glasse." (I know that this may not be the most impressive magical incantation, *but* it will get a small laugh, or at least a smile or two from the audience.)

6. *Without looking down at the coin,* remove the paper and glass and sit back in your chair. You should be looking at the audience and smiling as you say, "And as you can see, the coin has completely disappeared." The hand holding the glass should be resting on the back edge of the table on a line with the center of your body. (See Figure 4-5 A and B.)

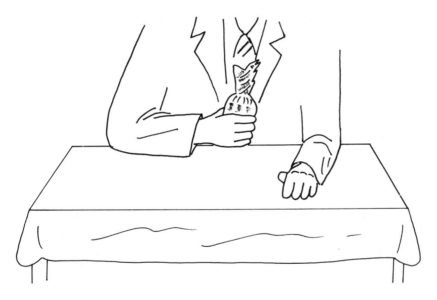

Figure 4-5 A.

It should be in such a position that if you relaxed your grip on the glass it would slide out of the paper form and fall without a sound into your lap.

7. The spectators will quickly point out that the coin has not, in fact, vanished. For the first time, you look down at the spot where the coin is located. Allow a look of surprise or anguish to cross your face as you lean forward from the waist, without moving your hands or arms, and say, "What?!" At this moment, you should allow the glass to slip from its paper shell and fall into your lap.

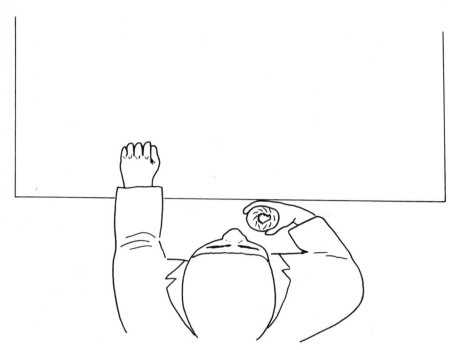

Figure 4-5 B.

8. Slide both of your hands away from the edge of the table toward the center of the table as you continue to look at the coin and say, "I can't believe this. I'll have to try again." Place the paper form over the coin. The audience should believe that the glass is still under the form.

9. Repeat the magic pass and incantation from step 5.

10. When you uncover the coin this time, you should be looking at it, unlike the procedure in step 6. You should also be leaning forward and you should *not* move the paper form anywhere near the edge of the table; it should be moved only a few inches to the side of the coin and should continue to be held in the hand.

11. Once again the coin has not vanished and your attitude should reflect frustration and disgust. Quickly place the paper form back over the coin and say, "I'm going to give up on this."

12. Quickly bring your free hand down sharply on the top of the paper form, while at the same time removing the hand that has been holding the form. This will cause the paper form to collapse. The coin will not have vanished but the glass has.

13. After allowing a few seconds for the vanishing of the glass to sink in, you proceed to reproduce it by reaching beneath the table with your RH and leaning forward at the same time. When your right shoulder comes in contact with the edge of the table, the arm should bend at the elbow so that the RH can pick up the glass from your lap. As you sit back in your chair, the RH emerges from beneath the table with the glass. (This is basically the same move that is used at several points in the Coins Through the Table.)

Some spectators may say that the glass vanished from the top of the table and reappeared beneath the table; others may look upon this as a penetration of the table by the glass. It really does not matter; in either case you have done some fine magic.

bonus time   This bonus might well be entitled "And the Coin, Too" because in this version of the trick, the coin as well as the glass penetrates the table. The only additional prop that you will need is a coin that is a duplicate of the one that is on top of the table. This duplicate coin should be placed on your left thigh before the trick begins.

1. Follow steps 1 through 7 of Glass Through.

2. When you reach step 8, you will need to make a slight change. As you lean forward to place the paper form over the coin, your free hand (the hand not holding the paper form) must move to your lap and turn the glass mouth up and position it between your thighs. This hand should then return to the top of the table to assist in the vanish of the glass.

3. Next follow steps 9 through 12 of Glass Through.

4. A few changes need to be made in step 13. The paper form is crushed on top of the coin. Do not remove the paper from the coin, but, after allowing a few seconds for the vanish of the glass to sink in, move your left leg slightly causing the duplicate coin to slide off the left thigh and into the glass. It will arrive with a satisfying "clink." This may take a bit of practice, but it can be done. Now do the recovery-of-the-glass sequence in step 13 of Glass Through. At the same time that the RH, holding the glass with the coin in it, appears from beneath the table, the LH, which has been resting on the paper on the table, pulls the paper back to the edge of the table. You should apply enough pressure so that the coin that is beneath the paper comes along as well. All of the audience's attention should be focused on the glass and the coin in the RH. When the LH reaches the edge of the table, the coin should be permitted to fall into your lap. The LH crumples the paper into a ball and tosses it to a member of the audience as a memento.

extra bonus   Although "Pass the Salt" is, in many ways, very much like Glass Through I include it because it can be presented under more impromptu conditions than can Glass Through, and I am suggesting an alternate ending that makes the conclusion of the trick far different from Glass Through.

1.   Using a paper napkin and a salt or pepper shaker (instead of a drinking glass and a sheet of newspaper) follow all of the steps in Glass Through.

2.   For the alternate ending, you need to wear a jacket. Leave the jacket unbuttoned so that it can screen the action during a critical part of the trick.

3.   Using a paper napkin and salt shaker, follow steps 1 through 7 of Glass Through. In this version hold the shaker and napkin in your LH.

4.   When you reach step 8, lean forward and, with the back of the little finger of the LH, push the coin toward the edge of the table opposite you, as you say, "Maybe it will help to move the coin." You should lean so far forward that your chest touches or almost touches the edge of the table nearest you. As you are leaning forward the RH drops into the lap, picks up the salt

shaker and shoves it into the left armpit. Your jacket should serve to screen the action of this move. As soon as the shaker is in the left armpit, you say, "No, that's too far." You slide your LH back toward you, pulling the coin back toward you. The pressure of the left arm against your body should hold the shaker in the left armpit.

5. Follow steps 9 through 12 in Glass Through.

6. As soon as you smash the paper form, stand up. Showing your RH obviously empty, reach into the left side of your jacket as though you were going to take something from your inner jacket pocket. Move your left arm slightly away from your body and allow the shaker to fall into your RH. Bring out the shaker and show it to the audience.

It should be noted that the success of Glass Through, The Coin Too, and Pass the Salt all depend upon misdirection and timing. With sufficient practice, you will be able to add these close-up tricks to your repertory.

THE BIONIC VAMPIRE

I had been doing this trick for a number of years but I had never found what I considered to be the ideal theme for it. While working on this chapter, I suddenly had a moment of inspiration and the Bionic Vampire was born. The props that you need for this trick are several envelopes (I use the coin envelopes described for the ring-off-the-string trick), a 1.5-volt size AA battery (the kind used in some games and camera flash attachments), a metal washer (as large a one as you can comfortably hold in the Classic Palm position), and a large nail (the one that I use is very large; in fact, I think it is technically called a "spike"). At the beginning of the trick, the washer and the battery should be in your left jacket pocket; the envelopes and the nail can be in your inside-jacket pocket or in your close-up case.

method and presentation

1. You address your audience: "Have you heard about the latest thing in vampires? You haven't? It seems that vampires, in an attempt to keep up with the changing trends in technology, have started using bionics. We now have bionic vampires. Of course, they feed on electricity rather than blood, so at night they fly to high-tension wires for a little snack. This is really what has been causing the power failures in New York and other parts of the country, but the government doesn't want to admit it. As a good citizen interested in the preservation of energy, I think they should be stamped out, and I am going to show you how they can be destroyed." Pick someone near you on your right to assist with the trick.

2. Remove the envelopes from your pocket and hand one to the spectator. Request that he look inside the envelope, while pointing out that although the envelope appears to be an ordinary envelope, it is, in reality, a vampire trap.

3. "Of course, we will need to bait the trap." At the end of this line, reach into your left jacket pocket with your LH, Classic Palm the washer and pick up the battery with your finger tips.

4. Bring out the battery as you say, "Here's the bait." Drop the battery in the spectator's hand and request that it be placed in the trap and that the trap be sealed. The LH drops naturally to your side while this is being done, and the washer is allowed to slide down into the fingers. You should, of course, make sure that the angle at which you hold your hand does not allow the spectators to get a glimpse of the washer.

5. After the envelope has been sealed, take it by one corner in the RH and transfer it to the LH. The LH and RH should meet in front of your body. The back of the LH will be facing the audience and the envelope should be placed in the LH between the thumb and fingers. The washer will be between the envelope and the fingers of the LH. The left thumb then clamps down the envelope and the LH turns palm up. (See Figure 4-6.)

151

Figure 4-6.

The audience will not be aware of the washer because it is masked by the envelope. As you are carrying out this transfer of the envelope from the RH to the LH, you should remark, "No bionic vampire can resist a nibble at a battery."

6. You now transfer the envelope back to the RH, and take the washer along with it so that the LH can be seen to be empty. This is fairly easy to do. The right thumb clamps down on the upper side of the envelope, the side facing up, and the index finger and the middle finger go beneath the washer, pressing it against the lower side of the envelope. (See Figure 4-7.)

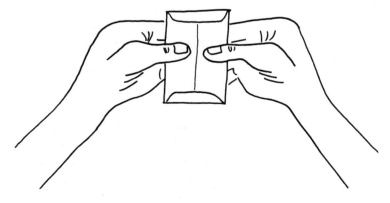

Figure 4-7.

7. The RH gives the envelope a slight shake, "to get the electrons moving," you explain. Do not shake it enough to cause the washer to fall or to expose it in any way.

8. The envelope and washer are now placed back on the open, palm up LH in the same location as they were prior to the transfer. The left thumb clamps down on the envelope again to keep it from shifting and exposing the washer.

9. Point out to the spectators, "I'm sure that a vampire will appear in this trap soon, but, in order to destroy him, we will need a weapon." Bring out the large nail or spike. "I realize that the traditional weapon used against vampires is a wooden stake, but in this case we must use metal since we are not dealing with your common garden-variety vampire."

10. Shake your LH slightly and cry with joy, "Ah! We have one!"

11. Hand the nail to the spectator and allow him to make the "kill." You should guide the point of the nail as it passes through the envelope for two reasons: to make sure that the nail does not pass into your hand or fingers; and to make sure that the nail passes through the hole in the center of the washer. The stabbing should be done from above, that is from the palm up side of the LH. The nail should pass approximately through the center of the envelope, through the center of the washer, beneath the envelope and between the middle finger and ring finger. With a bit of practice, it is not difficult to make sure that the washer is in the correct spot.

12. Ask the spectator to hold firmly to the head of the nail with one hand and to grasp the point of the nail with the other hand. (See Figure 4-8.)

13. Clamp down tightly on the envelope with the left fingers and thumb and pull to your left. The envelope will be ripped open and the washer will fall onto the spectator's hand holding the point of the nail. It will appear that the washer came from the sealed envelope. Not only do you have the production of the washer but it appeared on the nail while the spec-

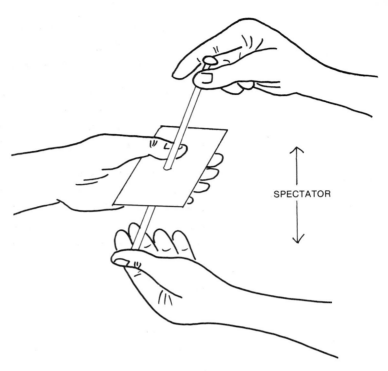

Figure 4-8.

tator was holding both ends! As the washer comes into view, you should say, "I'm sure that this bionic vampire is finished. You got him right through the washer." If you wish and if you can afford it, you might allow the spectator to keep the washer as a trophy of his "bionic vampire hunt."

I think that you will agree that this trick not only has an entertaining theme, but it also gets away from the use of cards and coins, the two items most frequently used in close-up magic.

I GET THE THOUGHT

In recent years, mental magic, magic of the mind, has increased in popularity. There are a number of magicians who specialize in this area, referring to themselves as mentalists or psychic experimenters, who do not wish to be associated with

154

magic and magicians. Because this is a field of magic in which there has been an increase in interest, it seems reasonable to include a few mental effects.

method   In order to perform I Get the Thought, you will need to be able to execute one of the basics of mental magic, the center tear. To perform the center tear, obtain a sheet of paper four inches square. In the center of this piece of paper draw a circle about one-and-one half inches in diameter. Write a number, a word, or a short question inside this circle. Fold the paper once from left to right as shown in Figure 4-9.

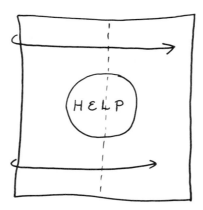

Figure 4-9.

Fold the paper once again from top to bottom as shown in Figure 4-10.

Holding the folded paper with the crease to the right, tear it as shown in Figure 4-11.

Place the pieces from the LH in front (to the audience side) of the pieces held in the RH. Turn the packet of pieces so that the creased edge is up. Now tear the pieces again, as shown in Figure 4-12.

Place the pieces from the LH in front of the pieces in the RH. At this point, all of the pieces are held in the RH between the thumb and the index and middle fingers. The back of the hand

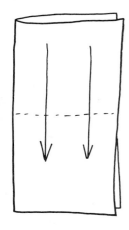

Figure 4-10.

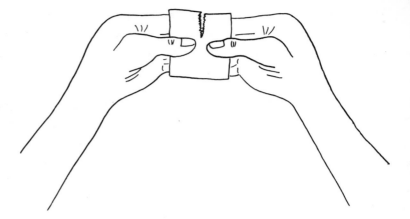

Figure 4-11.

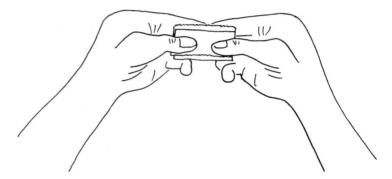

Figure 4-12.

is toward the audience. Turn the RH so that the finger tips point down. Pull up on the piece of paper directly under the right thumb, allowing the other pieces of paper to fall to the table. If you have performed the folds and tears correctly, you should be holding the center of the original sheet of paper beneath your thumb. It is very simple to then shift this piece of paper into the Finger–Palm position. If you were to later open this piece of paper, you would be able to read whatever was written on it. Practice the center tear until you can execute it smoothly. In addition to a sheet of paper four inches square, you need a pen or pencil, a book of matches (in your right-jacket or pants pocket), and an ash tray.

156

1. Make a few opening remarks about recent experiments in the field of extrasensory perception. (If you know nothing about this field, I suggest that you read a book or two on the subject. It is an area with which any contemporary magician should have at least a nodding acquaintance. There are many paperbacks on the market that can supply you with·more than enough information for a few lines of patter.) Offer to perform a simple experiment with the audience. (Notice how this approach can work for you in disarming the audience. You are offering to "experiment," and experiments don't alway succeed, do they?)

2. Select a spectator to aid you in the experiment. Ask for a volunteer who feels that he has psychic power or someone who feels that he has had some sort of psychic experience.

3. Request that the spectator think of a word, a number, or a question. You can be as general or as specific as you wish to be at this point. You might, for example, ask him to think of the name of any city in the world, or you could ask him to think of an active verb because the action is easier to communicate through thought waves. Pretend to attempt to read the spectator's mind. You might even take a guess. (If you do guess correctly, this does not mean that you have psychic power; it means that you are very lucky. If you do hit it with your lucky guess, stop the trick at this point and compliment the spectator for being such a good transmitter.) In most cases, you will miss, giving you a logical reason for going on to the next step.

4. Point out that it is often difficult to transmit thoughts because it is difficult to focus the powers of concentration. Bring out your sheet of paper. If you are performing this trick in an impromptu situation, you can tear the four-inch-square sheet of paper from a larger, borrowed sheet. Draw the circle in the center of the sheet while explaining that the circle aids in concentration.

5. While you turn away from the spectator, have him *print* (to aid in concentration) his thought in the circle. (The printing will make it easier for you to read, but you certainly wouldn't

157

tell the audience that.) Ask him to fold the paper once after he has completed his printing so that you cannot see what he has written.

6. Turn back to the spectator and indicate that he should fold the sheet once more "for good measure." You may decide that you want to make the final fold so that you can make sure that the center of the sheet is going to end up where you want it to be. In this case, you would say that you are going to fold it again "for good measure." It is impossible for the spectator to make the first fold incorrectly since he must either fold from right to left (or left to right) *or* from top to bottom (or bottom to top), and, in either case the fold is basically the same. It is only the second fold that might cause you some difficulty.

7. You now perform the center tear with the folded sheet of paper while saying to the spectator, "You should now have the thought firmly fixed in your mind, and although I can destroy this paper, I cannot destroy your thought."

8. You have reached the point at which the torn pieces are held in your RH between the right thumb and index and middle fingers. Ask someone to pass an ash tray to you.

9. Once you receive the ash tray, execute the pull-away move on the center of the sheet while dropping the other pieces into the ash tray. Let your RH drop to your side or rest naturally on the table as you mutter, "Matches."

10. Before anyone can offer you any matches, thrust your LH into your left pocket. The hand returns without any matches. Now place your RH into your right pocket, leave the center behind, and bring out the matches.

11. Using one of the matches, light the piece of paper in the ash tray. Tell the spectator to imagine his thoughts drifting to you, just as the smoke is drifting away from the burning pieces of paper.

12. In order to aid your concentration, or so you tell the audience, you turn your back and walk away from them. The RH replaces the matches in the right pocket and brings out the center of the paper. You now have ample opportunity to read whatever is written on the center and it is an easy matter to crumple the paper and replace it in your pocket. If you are performing this trick while seated at the table, the center can be dropped in your lap while your RH moves to the pocket for the matches. While the papers in the ash tray are burning, either hand can drop to your lap and unfold the center. You will need to look down in order to read what is written on the center, but this can be covered quite naturally. Close your eyes. Place either elbow on the table and place the corresponding hand over your forehead and lean on it as though in thought. The fingers of the hand will serve to mask your eyes and you can read the center without difficulty.

13. After you have obtained the information you are ready to reveal it to the audience. This should not be done casually. It should be done in the most dramatic manner possible. Pretend to have great difficulty; struggle a bit; you might even spell out the word letter by letter or, in the case of an active verb, you might describe the action. In the case of a city you might describe some of the landmarks and/or the people, if you know anything about the city, that is. Remember, you are performing a mental experiment.

I GET THE VIBES

This is another feat of mental magic. The effect is different from I Get The Thought in that you do not pretend to read minds, but you pretend to get "psychic vibrations" from objects that have been in the possession of the spectators. This trick will involve a number of spectators rather than just one, as is the case in I Get The Thought. To perform this trick you need a small paper bag containing a number of small objects; eight to ten is a sufficient number, and no two of them should be alike. The bag might contain a quarter, a penny, a small piece of color crayon, a button, a book of matches, a bottle cap, and so on. You will also need a packet of small envelopes (I prefer the kind of coin envelopes used in the Bionic Vampire). I do wish to state at this point that I do not own any stock in any stationery-supply store or company!

method Four of these envelopes should be marked by making an impression on them with your thumb nail on the flap side of the envelope. Figure 4-13 will give you two suggestions where to mark the envelopes.

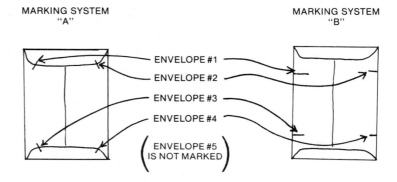

Figure 4-13.

Use any system that you choose, but you must be able to remember the system because this is going to be your key as to which spectator held which object. Once you have marked four envelopes, make a stack of about one dozen envelopes. Place envelope 1 on top, followed by envelopes 2, 3, and 4. Envelope 5 can be identified by its lack of a thumb nick. Place a rubber band around this stack so that the order of the first four envelopes will not be disturbed.

presentation **1.** Make a few opening remarks about how everyone has different psychic vibrations just as everyone has different finger prints. Offer to demonstrate how this works.

2. Show the various items in the paper bag, pointing out that they will be the objects used in the experiment. Replace the objects in the bag.

3. Request five volunteers to help you in the experiment. When five people raise their hands, pass the bag to one of them and ask him to put his hand in the bag, grab one of the objects tightly and bring it out and hold it in his hand so that neither you nor anyone else can see it. After he has done this, ask him to pass the bag on to the next volunteer.

4. Continue this procedure until five people are holding some object from the bag. Have the last volunteer pass the bag to a sixth spectator to hold until the experiment is over.

5. Point out that while the spectators are holding the objects the objects are absorbing psychic vibrations from the spectators.

6. Bring out the stack of envelopes as you state that you do not want any vibrations to become mixed, thus rendering the experiment difficult or impossible. In order to prevent this, you explain, each object is going to be sealed in an envelope.

7. Pass through the audience, giving out the first five envelopes in the stack. This will distribute the four marked envelopes and one unmarked envelope. It is probably best to move from your left to your right since this will make it easier for you to keep up with the numbers. As you become more proficient with this trick you could be more random in the distribution of the envelopes—but I am not at all sure that this adds to the effectiveness of the trick. The audience should not be suspicious of the envelopes if they are given out in a direct and casual manner. As you move from your left to your right, the first spectator on your left will get envelope #1, the next spectator will get #2, etc., and the fifth spectator will get the unmarked envelope. You should think of these spectators in terms of envelopes #1, #2, #3, #4, and #5.

8. While your back is turned, ask the spectators to place their objects in their envelopes and seal them. Ask another spectator to collect and mix the five envelopes. Be sure to tell the spectators not to let anyone see the objects that they are putting in the envelopes.

9. Turn back to the audience and request that the spectator who did the mixing hand you one of the envelopes.

10. In the process of tearing open the envelopes to get the object, casually glance at your secret mark. This will tell you which spectator held the object in the envelope. Crumple the envelope and toss it in the nearest waste basket, or, if there is no convenient waste basket, place it in your pocket. (We don't want people to get the impression that magicians are litter-bugs, do we? This also gets rid of the evidence.) Holding the object tightly in your hand, give a brief description of the person who last held it. This can be as brief or as detailed as you wish to make it, but don't go on too long. Finally point to the spectator and ask, "Am I correct?"

11. Repeat this process with two more of the remaining four envelopes. In each case get the spectator to admit that he did hold the object.

12. When you get to the last two envelopes, take one in each hand, casually look at them for the secret marks, and tell the audience, "Now I will attempt an even more difficult feat. I will attempt to get the vibrations from the last two objects at the same time and without touching them." Crumple the envelopes around the objects, concentrate for a few moments and then hand them to the proper spectators to be opened and identified.

13. Collect the bag and all of the objects. Thank the spectators for taking part in this experiment.

Given the proper presentation and handling, this can be a most impressive feat of mental magic. I have been doing a similar routine for college students for several years, and it often gets more response than much of my more "magical" magic. You should also note that you can, to a great extent, control the running time of the trick by doing as much or as little with the descriptions of the spectators as you wish. There is also an opportunity to inject some humor in the routine, either related to the object or the person selecting it. And, if you are performing for strangers and have been able to find out a few simple facts about one or more of your assistants, you can really bend their minds by casually tossing in a few facts that they have no reason to suspect that you know.

THREE OBJECTS —PLUS ONE

I call this trick Three Objects because I have seen it performed with crumpled dollar bills, with balls of paper made from a napkin, with marbles, with the heads of paper matches, and an assortment of other items. Because of its adaptability, it can be done almost anywhere and is almost impromptu in nature. There is only one small preparation that you must make and that is to have a fourth object that matches the other three; hence the "Plus One" part of the title. The audience should not be aware of this extra object.

In order to learn the trick, use pieces of newspaper. Cut out four pieces of newspaper; each piece should be about four inches square. Crumple each piece of paper until it forms a small ball. Before you begin the trick, one of these balls should be placed in the Finger–Palm position in the RH. In performance, this ball could be in the right-jacket pocket, it being a simple matter to place your hand casually in your pocket and bring out the ball in the Finger–Palm position.

method and presentation

1. With one ball in the Finger–Palm position in the RH, place the other three balls on the table in a row in front of you. Extend your right index finger and touch each ball as you count, "One, two, three."

2. Pick up one of the balls with the index finger and thumb of the RH and toss it into the LH as you say, "One." Quickly close the LH on the ball.

3. You now apparently repeat the same process with the second ball. You pick it up and toss it as you say, "Two." The difference is that you open the fingers of the RH and allow the ball in the Finger–Palm to also be tossed into the LH. The

RH comes very close to the LH, and the right fingers mask the toss. The LH should close very quickly to conceal the fact that you have three balls rather than two in the LH.

4. Pick up the last ball on the table as you say, "And the third ball goes in my pocket." You apparently place the third ball in your pocket, but you place the ball in the Finger–Palm position as your RH goes into your pocket.

5. The RH emerges from the pocket with the extra ball in the Finger–Palm position. The right index finger should be extended, and you use it to tap the back of the LH as you say, "But if I tap my hand like this . . ."

6. Open the LH to show that it now contains three balls and dump these balls on the table.

7. Repeat steps 1 through 6. You have again, apparently, caused the ball to leave your pocket and return to your LH.

8. You are going to produce the same effect for the third time, but this time you change the method. When you toss the first ball and say, "One," you also release the hidden ball and allow it to fly into the LH. Again the RH comes close to the LH, and the fingers of the RH mask the toss. Be sure to close the LH quickly.

9. The RH can now be shown to be empty as you pick up the second ball. This time, instead of tossing the ball into the LH, the ball in placed on the top of the left fist, as shown in Figure 4-14.

The right index finger then pushes the ball into the left fist through the opening provided by the index finger and thumb of the LH.

10. The RH picks up the remaining ball from the table and places it in the right pocket. *This time the ball is really left in the pocket,* and the RH emerges empty. Open the LH and allow the three balls to fall to the table.

11. At this point you say, "To speed things up, I'll do two at a

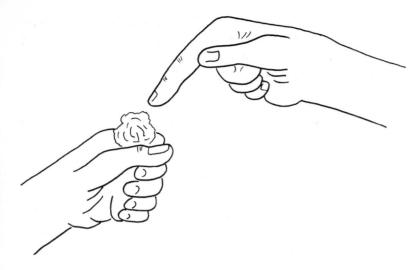

Figure 4-14.

time." Fitting your actions to your words, place two of the balls in the RH in position for the Finger–Palm Vanish.

12. Execute the Finger–Palm Vanish as you apparently place the balls in the LH.

13. Pick up the remaining ball with the index finger and thumb of the RH as you say, "And again the third ball goes in my pocket." Place the ball in your pocket and release the two balls that are in the Finger–Palm position, thus leaving all three balls in your pocket. The empty RH returns to the table.

14. Look at your closed LH and then at the audience and say, "At this point I sometimes ask the audience to guess how many balls are in my left hand. They often guess 'one,' or 'two,' or 'three,' but the real answer is 'none'!" Open your LH to show that all of the balls have vanished.

bonus time   After you have mastered the basic moves, you might want to work on a different ending to the trick. You will need some object that you can comfortably Classic Palm. This object, for example, a rubber ball, should be in your right jacket pocket at the beginning of the trick. When you reach step 10, you should

165

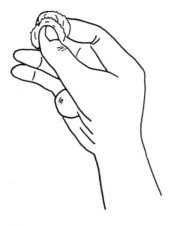

Figure 4-15.

Classic Palm the ball in the RH. Two of the balls on the table are then placed between the right index and middle fingers and the right thumb and are held in position as you say, "I'll do two at a time." (See Figure 4-15.)

The LH approaches the RH as if to receive the balls. The RH revolves palm down over the LH and releases the rubber ball that has been held in Classic Palm, and, at the same time, pulls the two balls down toward the Finger–Palm position. The fingers of the LH and the RH should mask this move. From this point on the ending is as in the original effect except that you ask the spectators how many balls are in the LH. No matter what they say, you say, "The correct answer is one." You open your LH and roll the rubber ball across the table.

Now that you know how to work the trick, I think you can see why I say that it is almost impromptu in nature. It would be fairly simple, for example, for you to tear a piece from a paper napkin and make a small ball out of it during a meal. You could then allow the spectators to make the other three balls. Or, you could have a crumpled one-dollar bill in your pocket and borrow the other three one-dollar bills from the spectators in order to make balls for the trick. (In this case you should have three more one-dollar bills in your wallet to return to the spectators at the end of the trick after all the balls have vanished. You should not reach into your pocket and bring out three crumpled bills. You might even get a laugh as you return three bills that were obviously not used in the trick and say, "The only thing I don't like about this trick is that it costs me three dollars each time I do it.")

THE SHELL GAME

The shell game is an ancient gambling game that has been transformed over the years into an entertaining classic of close-up magic. The game is played with three walnut shell halves and a small pea, actually a small rubber ball or, more recently, a small ball made of foam rubber. The object of the original game is for the spectator to keep up with the pea and to correctly guess which shell the pea is under after the performer has stopped moving the shells. In the hands of a clever operator, it is impossible for the spectator to keep track of the pea.

To perform this feat, you will need three walnut-shell halves. These can be obtained by carefully cracking a number of walnuts and selecting the three best halves in the lot. Once you have selected the three halves, you should smooth out the inside of the shells so that there are no projections left inside to snag the pea. It is not a bad idea to place a light coat of plastic wood inside the rear end of the shell. (See Figure 4-16.)

WOOD PUTTY

Figure 4-16.

This plastic wood can be sanded until it is smooth after it has dried.

You will also need a pea. This is best made from a piece of foam rubber, the kind frequently used in mattress pads or for packing delicate objects. The foam rubber should be cut into small balls, approximately one-quarter of an inch in diameter. You should make several of these small balls at the same time. You will find that a piece of foam rubber of reasonable size will provide you an ample supply of peas.

Although some magicians can perform the shell game on almost any surface, you will discover, at least while you are learning the trick, that it is much easier to perform on a surface that will provide some friction for the pea. A table cloth, close-up pad, or carpet (with a short nap) should be about right.

the basic move

There is one basic move that you must master in order to secretly remove the pea from one shell and place it under another. Although it is fairly simple to master, it should be practiced until it can be done smoothly. The basic grip for this move is shown in Figure 4-17 A and B.

Grip a shell in the basic grip and place it over the pea, using the proper working surface. Now slowly move your hand for-

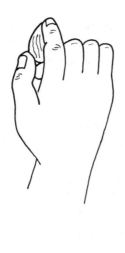

Figure 4-17 A and B.

ward. You will discover that the pea, because of the friction caused by its rubbing against the working surface, rides out of the shell and arrives at the point at which your thumb and middle finger touch. You can now clip the pea between the thumb and middle finger with very little pressure. Remove your hand from the shell without changing the position of the fingers. The pea is now concealed between the tip of your middle finger and the thumb. Without changing the positions of your fingers, move your hand to another shell and grip it with the basic grip. Move your hand and the shell backward. Release your grip on the pea and it will ride unseen under the rear of the shell and inside it. You should practice this move with each hand.

the getaway move

There may be times in a shell-game routine when the spectator, by luck, will guess the correct shell. Over the years magicians have evolved a number of methods to use to show that the shell does not contain the pea when, in fact, it does. The simplest method is to use the basic move to get the pea into the position between the tip of the middle finger and thumb and then lift the hand and the shell a few inches above the working surface. This shows that there is nothing beneath the shell. The shell can be replaced on the working surface and the pea can be reloaded in the shell or it can be moved to another shell.

adding a pea

While the spectators should be only aware of one pea being used in the shell game, you can create a very strong effect by secretly introducing a second pea to the trick. You could, of course, have a number of peas in one of your pockets and bring one of them out at the proper time, but this would mean that you would need some logical reason for going to your pocket at this point in the routine. A cleaner method of obtaining the pea can be employed. Place a straight pin through the material inside your jacket near the bottom edge of the jacket with the point of the pin pointing down. Impale a pea on the point of the pin. (See Figure 4-18.)

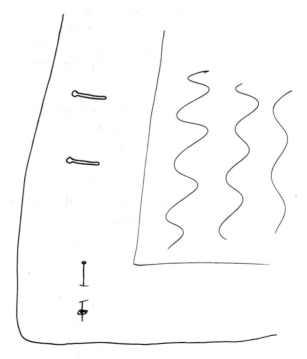

Figure 4-18.

It is now a simple matter to reach beneath the edge of the jacket and to pull off the pea, getting it between the middle finger tip and thumb in position for the basic move. With the pea in such a position, it can now be added secretly to one of the shells by simply moving the shell backward as though adjusting its position.

a suggested routine

Although there are a number of routines that you can perform with the shell game, the one offered here makes use of the material that has already been covered. It is short and to the point. For the purpose of instruction, we label the shells A, B, and C. The routine begins with shell A on your left, shell B in the center, and shell C on your right. In the illustrations, the position of the pea is indicated by an asterisk. In addition to the three shells and the pea, you should have another pea impaled on a pin under the right side of your jacket.

1. Show the three shells and the pea as you talk about the shell game as a gambling game in which millions of dollars have changed hands. Point out that you are going to show the audience how even alert observers can be deceived by the game.

2. Cover the pea with shell C. Place your RH on shell C and your LH on shell B. Grip both shells in the basic-move position. At any point in the routine when you grip a shell, unless otherwise indicated, do so in the basic-move position. This accustoms the audience to this grip. Move shells B and C forward; the pea will ride from beneath shell C into the concealed position in the RH. (See Figure 4-19.)

Figure 4-19.

3. Now shift your hands; your LH grips shell A and your RH grips shell B. Move these two shells backward several inches, and load the pea under shell B. (See Figure 4-20.)

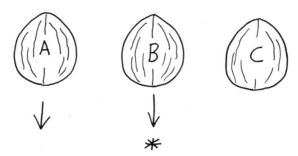

Figure 4-20.

4. Place your RH on shell C and keep your LH on shell A. Reverse the positions of shells A and C. (See Figure 4-21.)

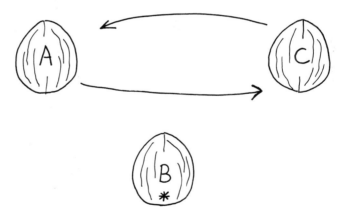

Figure 4-21.

Remove your hands from the shells and ask the spectators which shell the pea is under. If they have been following the moves, they will indicate shell C. You should then say, "That's what I'd say, but . . ." Lift the center shell (shell B) to show that the pea is beneath this shell.

5. Arrange the shells in a row again. Place the pea under shell C. Grip shell B with the LH, shell C with the RH. Move these shells forward, stealing the pea from shell C into the RH. (See Figure 4-22.)

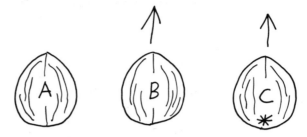

Figure 4-22.

6. Grip shell A with the LH and shell B with the RH. Move the shells back a few inches but *do not* load the pea under shell B; retain the pea in position in the RH. (See Figure 4-23.)

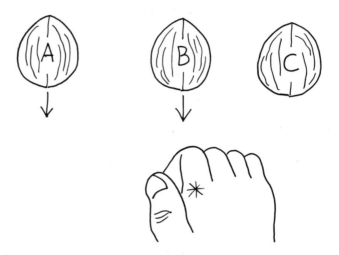

Figure 4-23.

7. Grip shell A with your LH and shell C with your RH. Reverse the position of the two shells; you still do not load the pea. (See Figure 4-24.)

8. Grip shell B with the LH and shell A with the RH and move them backward toward you. At this point the pea is loaded under shell A. (See Figure 4-25.)

Figure 4-24.

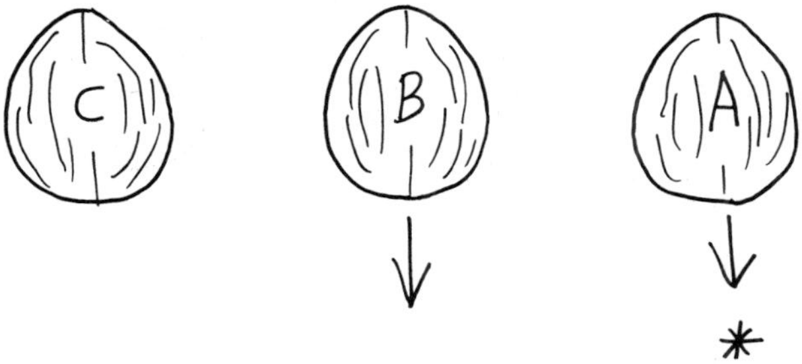

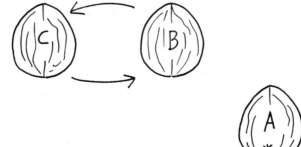

Figure 4-25.

9. Now reverse the positions of the shells B and C and ask the spectators to locate the pea. (See Figure 4-26.)

Figure 4-26.

They should indicate shell C. You say, "That's what I'd say but . . ."

10. With the LH lift shell A to show that the pea is under that shell, and at the same time, steal the duplicate pea from the pin beneath your jacket with the RH. Get the pea in position for the basic move.

11. Tell the audience that you are going to make the game easier to follow by using only two shells. As you say this, use your LH to put the shells in a row.

12. Say, "I'll eliminate this shell," as you move shell C back with the RH. As you move the shell, load the duplicate pea under it. (See Figure 4-27.)

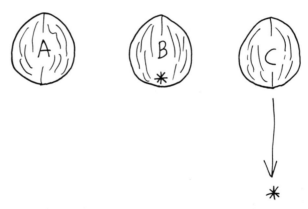

Figure 4-27.

13. Cover the pea that the audience can see with shell B, using your RH. Ask a spectator to place a finger on top of the shell. Move the shell forward and steal the pea. (See Figure 4-28.)

You will discover that the pea can be stolen in the usual manner although the spectator has his finger on the shell.

14. Move shell A toward another spectator and request that she place her finger on top of the shell. As you are moving shell A forward with your LH, allow your RH to come to the back edge of the table and let the pea concealed in the RH fall behind the table. (See Figure 4-29.)

Figure 4-28.

Figure 4-29.

15. Allow the audience to see that your hands are empty and then use your RH to show that there is nothing beneath shell C as you say, "Remember, we aren't going to use this shell." You, of course, use the Getaway Move to show that there is no pea under this shell when there really is a pea under the shell. As you replace shell C on the table, reload the pea under it.

16. Ask the spectators to turn over the shells that they are holding. The pea has vanished. Ask another spectator to turn over shell C. As he does so, the audience will see the pea. You might say to them, "You were watching me so closely that I had to use this shell."

Note: If at any point in the routine the spectators happen to select the shell that does contain the pea, you can either show them that they are correct *or* you can use the Getaway Move to show that the pea is not under the shell. In either case you should then proceed with the rest of the routine.

thinking time   Using your knowledge of the shell game, try to evolve some other routines with it.

THE CUPS AND BALLS

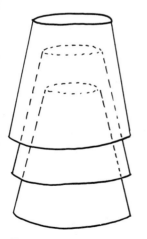

Figure 4-30.

One of the classics of magic, and a trick that has a history several thousand years old, is the Cups and Balls. For this reason, I feel it should be included in a discussion of close-up magic.

The cups may be made from almost any opaque substance. I have seen silver cups, chrome-plated cups, plastic cups, and even styrofoam drinking cups used for this trick. The cups must not have handles and must taper from the mouth to the base so that the cups can be nested. (See Figure 4-30.)

There should be enough space between the bottom of one cup and the next cup so that a ball can be concealed between them. You also need four similar balls. These balls should be approximately one-half-inch in diameter and can be made from a number of substances such as rubber, foam rubber, cork, or paper. You also need a large ball that fits snugly into the cups; a large rubber ball works well. It is useful to have a small cloth bag to hold all of your props.

method and presentation

1. Before your begin the trick, one of the four balls should be placed in one of the cups. This cup should be placed mouth down on top of the other two cups so that the ball is trapped between the top cup and the next cup. (See Figure 4-31.)

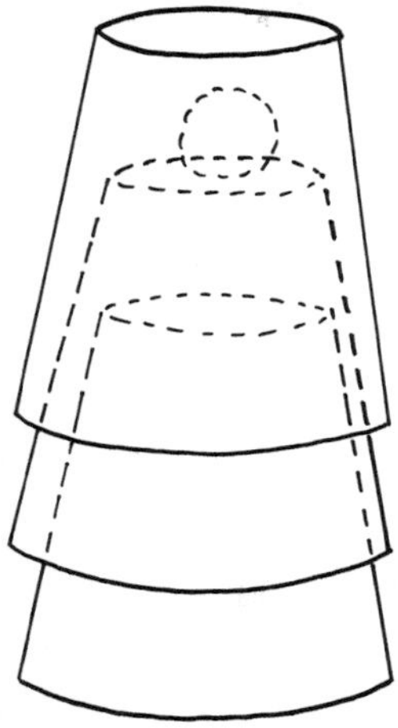

The large ball should be in your left jacket pocket. When you are ready to begin the routine, bring out the stack of cups in the LH. Briefly, let the audience look into the mouth of the bottom cup. Then turn the cups slightly in the LH so that the mouth of the cups point to the left. Peel off the top cup with the RH, and, with a sweeping motion, place it mouth down on the table to your right. (See Figure 4-32.)

Figure 4-31.

Figure 4-32.

The centrifugal force of this move will cause the ball to stay in the cup while it is moving through the air. When the cup comes to rest on the table, the ball (unknown to the audience) is trapped beneath it. Go through the same motion with the next cup in the stack. You may move a bit more slowly with this cup because it does not contain a ball, but you do not want to move too slowly. The rhythm should be about the same for both cups. The third cup should then be placed mouth down on the table in a line with the other two cups. For the purpose of teaching this trick we will number each cup: to your left is cup 1; in the center is cup 2; and on your right is cup 3. The ball is under cup 3.

2. Now show the three balls; during the routine the audience should only be aware of three balls. Place a ball on the bottom of each cup. (See Figure 4-33.)

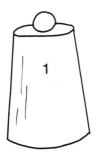  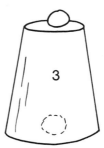

Figure 4-33.

3. Pick up the ball that is resting on the upturned bottom of cup 3 with the RH. Perform either the Finger–Palm Vanish or the Pull-Down Vanish as you pretend to place the ball in the LH. Pretend to toss the ball in the LH into the air and watch it vanish.

4. Pick up cup 2 with the RH. The cup should be picked up with the index and middle finger and thumb of the RH. This action should place the mouth of the cup directly above the ball that is in the Finger–Palm position in the RH. (See Figure 4-34.)

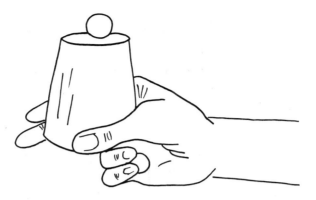

Figure 4-34.

Tip the cup so that the ball resting on the upturned bottom of the cup falls into the LH. As the cup is being tipped, the ball that is in the Finger–Palm position in the RH should be allowed to fall into the cup. (See Figure 4-35.)

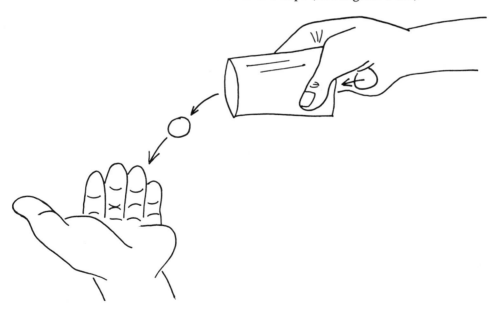

Figure 4-35.

Cup 2 is then quickly replaced, mouth down, on the table. This action will trap the ball under the cup and will leave the RH empty.

179

5. Dump the ball in the LH back into the RH, and, using the Finger–Palm Vanish or the Pull-Down Vanish, pretend to place the ball in the LH while retaining it in the RH. Pretend to place this ball in the LH in your left ear for the vanish.

6. With cup 1, repeat step 4. This time pretend to place the ball in your mouth and mime swallowing it. At the end of this step you should have a ball under each cup (unknown to the audience), and you should have a ball in the Finger–Palm position in the RH.

7. You are now ready to enter the next phase of the trick. With the LH, pick up cup 1 and show the ball under it. Tilt the cup until the bottom of the cup touches the ball, and, with the cup in this position, use it to push the ball a few inches toward the center of the table. Place cup 1 mouth down in its original position and repeat the same process, using your LH again, with cup 2 and the ball that is beneath it. With the RH pick up cup 3, showing that there is also a ball beneath it. Use the same tilting and pushing move to push this ball across the table. This position should cause the mouth of the cup to be in position to receive the ball that is in the Finger–Palm position in the RH. (See Figure 4-36.)

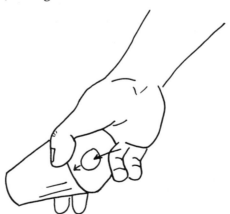

Figure 4-36.

At the moment the cup pushes the ball forward, the ball in the Finger–Palm position should be released into the cup. Cup 3 should then be placed quickly mouth down on the table. You have now trapped a ball under it, once again, unknown to the audience.

8. Take the ball that came from cup 3. Do one of the vanishes that allows the ball to be retained in the RH, while you pretend to place it in the LH. Vanish the ball by tossing it into the air with the LH.

9. Take cup 3 in the RH and lift it to reveal the ball under the cup. Once again tilt the cup and use the bottom of it to push the ball toward the spectators. As this is being done, load the ball from the RH into the cup. This time, however, instead of placing the cup quickly mouth down on the table, tilt the cup until the mouth faces you (taking care not to let the spectators see into the cup) and openly pick up that ball that was just shown to be beneath cup 3 and drop it into cup 3. Quickly place cup 3 on the table, mouth down, thus trapping two balls beneath it. (The spectators should believe that there is only one ball beneath the cup, the ball that they saw you drop into the cup.)

10. Pick up one of the two remaining balls on the table and once again pretend to place it in the LH, while retaining it in the RH. Pretend to vanish the ball from the LH by any means you choose.

11. Repeat step 9, but this time reveal two balls under cup 3 and place these two balls openly in the cup. (The second ball is apparently the ball that you just vanished.) At the end of this step, three balls will be under cup 3; however, the audience should think that only two balls are beneath the cup. There is one more ball remaining on the table.

12. Pick up the remaining ball with the LH and say, "Instead of causing this ball to vanish, I'll just place it in my pocket." Place the LH in the left jacket pocket. Leave the small ball in the pocket and Classic Palm the large rubber ball in the LH. You will find that you are using a modification of the Classic Palm because you will really curl your fingers around the ball in order to hide it. But, since the misdirection is strong at this point, this should not be a problem. As you are doing this, you should say, "But even if I place the ball in my pocket, it has a desire to return to its friends." As you finish this statement, lift cup 3 with your RH by grasping the cup by the bottom with the hand, as shown in Figure 4-37, and lifting straight up.

Figure 4-37.

As the RH is lifting cup 3, the LH should be emerging from the left pocket with the large ball. Your eyes and the eyes of the audience should be on the three balls on the table. The cup in the RH, cup 3, is carried to the LH and placed over the ball in the LH. This should be done casually and smoothly. All attention should be focused on the three balls on the table. If the large rubber ball is the proper size, it will wedge itself into cup 3.

13. As soon as the rubber ball has been loaded into the cup, place cup 3 on the table and stack the other two cups on top of it. If the ball is large enough to wedge into the cup, it is rather easy to place it on the table. But if the ball is not large enough to wedge into the cup, you will need to place the cup down by sliding it off the left fingers onto the table. You should give the appearance that the trick is over. Almost as an afterthought, you say to the audience, "Some people accuse me of using a fourth ball. I must confess that I do, and I'm going to show it to you." As you finish this statement, lift the stack of cups to reveal the large ball, a fitting climax to this routine.

The Cups and Balls trick is a classic of magic that requires a number of hours of practice before you can present it smoothly.

CONCLUSION

I have offered only a few of the close-up tricks that belong to the world of magic, but you should have enough magic to keep you busy for weeks and months to come. I think that you will find your efforts rewarded.

5

Stage
and Platform
Magic

INTRODUCTION

Since the middle of the nineteenth century, magicians have devised many tricks that are more suitable for the platform or stage than for close-up performance. Indeed, many of the larger illusions can be done only on a stage with all the facilities of a theatre. If you have witnessed any of the television specials featuring such performers as Mark Wilson or Doug Henning, you have seen many of these large illusions presented in a most effective manner. I have no intention of telling you how to saw a woman in half or how to float a lady in the air. It would be pointless to describe tricks that would require thousands of dollars of equipment to perform. But I do offer a number of tricks that can be performed on the stage with simple props that you can either buy or construct, although many of the principles that you will learn are used in larger illusions. Remember also that a few of the card tricks and a number of the rope tricks discussed in earlier chapters are suitable for use on platform and stage.

THE PRODUCTION TUBES

Someday you will discover, if you have not done so already, magic dealers and their fascinating catalogues. In these catalogues there are a number of devices designed so that the magician may produce a number of silk handkerchiefs (called "silks" by magicians), livestock, or other items from apparently empty boxes or tubes. You will also discover that these items are rather expensive. However, there are ways to make and use an inexpensive production device.

In order to make the production tubes, you will need two tubes of about the same length, one slighly smaller in diameter than the other; some contact paper or spray paint; the objects to be produced; a small cloth bag; and a hook.

For one of the tubes I use a forty-six-ounce juice can. After you remove the juice, the bottom and the top of the can should be carefully cut away (an electric can opener is good for this), leaving a cylinder, open at both ends. Any paper covering the can should be removed and the can either sprayed (on the outside) with a bright paint or covered with contact paper.

For the other tube I use a round forty-two-ounce cardboard oatmeal container. After emptying the container, the bottom and all of the paper covering the cardboard tube should be carefully removed. The outside of the tube can then be covered with contact paper or spray painted.

These are the containers that I use. If you cannot find these exact containers, any two tubes will do, provided that they are about the same height and that one container is slightly smaller in diameter than the other.

Figure 5-1.

The hook can be made from a bent paper clip or a short piece of very stiff wire. (See Figure 5-1.)

Once the hook has been bent into the proper shape, it should be painted black.

The objects to be produced (silks, candy, small toys, or whatever you like) should be placed in the small cloth bag, and the bag attached to one end of the hook by using a rubber band. (See Figure 5-2.)

This bag of production items is called your "load."

Figure 5-2.

method The load will move from one of the tubes to the other while both tubes appear empty. Place the load in the smaller tube and hook the free end of the hook over the rim of the tube. (See Figure 5-3.)

Figure 5-3.

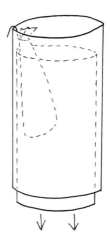

Figure 5-4.

Hold the larger tube in your LH and look through it toward an imaginary audience. Now turn the larger tube to a vertical position and drop the smaller tube through it from the top. (See Figure 5-4.)

The hook should catch the rim of the larger tube, allowing the smaller tube to fall through the larger tube, leaving the load behind in the larger tube. Pick up the smaller tube and show that it is empty.

presentation   **1.**   At the beginning of the trick, the larger tube should be on your table to your left; the smaller tube should be on your right with the load in place.

2.   Pick up the larger tube with the LH and show that it is empty by looking through it at the audience.

3.   Say to the audience, "As you can see, this tube is empty. In fact, it is so empty that I can drop this other tube through it." Pick up the smaller tube on your right with your RH and drop it through the larger tube, allowing the hook to engage the rim of the larger tube, thus leaving the load behind in the larger tube.

188

4. Place the larger tube on the table. Pick up the smaller tube and look through it toward the audience.

5. Place the smaller tube on the table and then lift the larger tube and place it over the smaller tube so that the two tubes nest. You must take some care at this point to make sure that the load slides into the smaller tube without "riding up" and being exposed to the audience.

6. After making a magic pass, reach into the nested tubes and disengage the bag from the hook. Start bringing out the production items. If you have at least one large silk in the bottom of the bag, you can get rid of the bag and the hook by bringing them out under cover of this silk. In this case you can pick up both tubes and show them empty at the end of the trick. This is not really necessary unless you wish to do it. You can just leave the tubes sitting on the table and go on to your next trick.

thinking time   Develop a story about the two tubes. Make a list of the items that you could produce from the tubes. Experiment with some of these items.

bonus time   By making a slight modification in the cloth bag, you can have a very effective candy production. Cut open the bottom of the bag and sew in a number of snap fasteners or use strips of Velcro to hold the bottom together. Fill the bag with candy and proceed with the trick. Have a large bowl or plate on your table. After nesting the tubes, place them on the plate or in the bowl. Reach in the tubes and open the bottom of the bag and the candy will fall into the plate or bowl. The tubes can be lifted away together and the candy distributed to the audience.

THE PRODUCTION BOX

For this production trick, you need a cardboard box with a lid. Although a variety of box sizes might be used, you may discover that the best results can be obtained with a box that is about eighteen inches by eighteen inches and twelve to eighteen inches deep. A hat box works rather nicely for this trick. The load should be attached to the rear of the underside of the lid by a strong piece of string; fishing line or a strong thread can be used for this purpose. To reduce visibility, you might paint the underside of the lid black and use black thread. The length of the string is important. It should be short enough so that when the top of the lid is tilted forward the load rides up out of the box and is concealed behind the lid. You may use a cloth bag to contain the load as in the production tubes. However, other containers for the load can be used. For example, I was doing a Halloween show several years ago and I wanted to tell a story about The Great Pumpkin from the *Peanuts* comic strip. I obtained a large, hollow, plastic pumpkin with a jack-o-lantern face and used it to hold all of the items that I was going to produce. After I had produced these items, I produced the pumpkin, after first disengaging the thread, and told the audience that this was The Great Pumpkin.

method and
presentation

1. The box, with the load in place, is sitting on your table. Turn the box to show all four sides, but make sure that the final turn places the box so that the point at which the string is attached to the underside of the lid is nearest your side of the table.

2. Lift the lid of the box up from the front so that the audience can see the underside of the lid. (See Figure 5-5.)

3. Tilt the lid forward, apparently to show the top of the lid. This motion allows the load to ride up out of the box and hang behind the lid. (See Figure 5-6.)

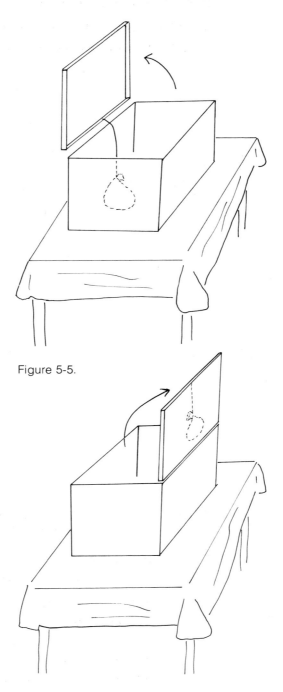

Figure 5-5.

Figure 5-6.

4. With either hand, lift the lid, still held in the vertical position, a few feet above the box. (See Figure 5-7.)

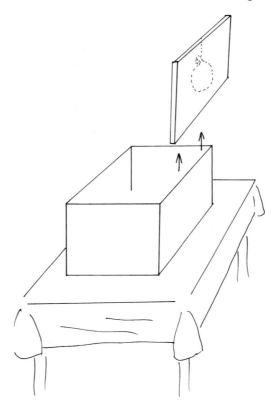

Figure 5-7.

5. With your free hand, tilt the box on its side so that the opening of the box faces the audience. (See Figure 5-8.)

You have now demonstrated that the box is empty. You may even lift the box and turn it upside down.

6. Place the box on its bottom and lower the lid to replace it on the box. This must be done with care so that the load returns to the box without being exposed to the audience. The best way to do this is to lower the lid slowly with the front rim of the lid going in front of the box. (See Figure 5-9.)

Figure 5-8.

Figure 5-9.

As soon as the load is safely in the box, the rear of the lid can be placed on the box. (See Figure 5-10.)

193

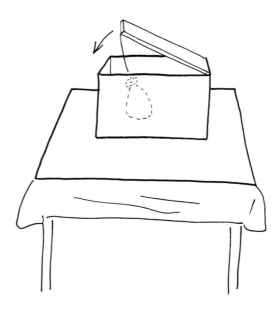

Figure 5-10.

7. After making a magic pass or saying a magic word, lift the lid *from the front to the back* and begin your production.

These moves are not difficult, but you must be able to execute them smoothly. All you are apparently doing is showing the lid and the box, proving that the box is empty.

The production box will hold more items than the tubes, but the tubes are more angleproof than the box. You should use the production device that best fits your performing needs.

THE BURNED BILL

A familiar theme in magic for more than two centuries has been the apparent destruction and restoration of a spectator's item of property. Watches, snuff boxes, handkerchiefs, and gloves have been used in this trick. In this version, you use something that has great sentimental value for most people: money.

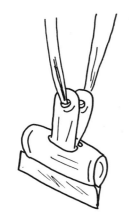

Figure 5-11.

You will need several props to do this trick. First, prepare a coin envelope like the one used in the ring-off-the-string trick. Place this envelope in your inside right-jacket pocket with the small magic wand or pencil in it, just as in the ring trick. You need a few feet of ribbon, strung through the handles of a fairly large Bulldog paper clip. (Figure 5-11.)

This prop should also be in your inside right-jacket pocket. Next, prepare an ordinary envelope (3⅝″ × 6½″) by cutting a slit, no longer than one inch, in the face of the envelope. (Figure 5-12.)

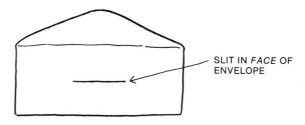

SLIT IN *FACE* OF ENVELOPE

Figure 5-12.

Place it either on your table or in your left outside-jacket pocket with a book of matches. In addition to these props, you also need a fairly large ash tray.

method and presentation

1. Begin by asking for a "small loan." Attempt to borrow a one-hundred dollar bill from a member of the audience. (You are not likely to get one!) Work your way down. You will usually find someone who will loan you at least a ten or a twenty. Ask this spectator to come forward with his money to "keep an eye on it."

2. Place the spectator to your right; your table should be to your left. Take the bill from the spectator, examine it, and then tear off one corner and give it to the spectator as a "receipt."

3. Fold this bill, from side to side, in half, in quarters, and in eighths, and then fold the bill once from top to bottom. Hold

the folded bill by the tips of the thumb, index, and middle fingers of the RH. (See Figure 5-13.)

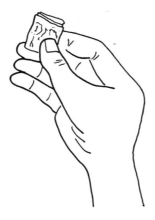

Figure 5-13.

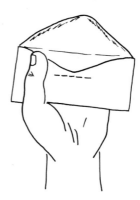

Figure 5-14.

4. Now offer to show the spectator the latest in flameproof paper. Pick up the letter envelope from your table or take it from your pocket. Hold the envelope with the face side down across the fingers of the LH so that you conceal the slit. (See Figure 5-14.)

5. Slowly and carefully place the bill into the envelope. It should appear that the bill is being put cleanly into the envelope. If you have cut the slit at the proper point, however, the bill should go onto the fingers of the LH and into the Finger–Palm position.

6. Take the envelope in the RH and lift it to your mouth in order to lick the flap. Make sure that the fingers of the RH cover the slit. Allow your LH, holding the bill in the Finger–Palm position to drop naturally to your side. Lick and seal the envelope.

7. As you say "We'll need some safe way to hold this envelope," reach into your inside right-jacket pocket with your LH. Drop the bill into the gimmicked coin envelope and bring out the bulldog clip on the ribbon. Clip the bulldog clip to one end of the envelope, keeping the envelope face down.

8. Place the ribbon over the spectator's head and allow the envelope on the bulldog clip to swing back against his body. He will not be able to see the slit because the rear of the envelope is facing outward; the slit side (face) of the envelope is against his body.

9. Bring out the book of matches, again pointing out that the envelope is made of the latest in flameproof paper. Give the spectator the matches and ask him to tear out a match and prepare to strike it.

10. Hold the envelope away from the spectator's body by grasping it at the end near the bulldog clip and holding it in a horizontal position. Use your RH for this. Ask the spectator to strike the match and hold it under the end of the envelope that is away from his body. As he does this, you should look at the audience and patter about the remarkable flameproof quality of the envelope. The envelope will soon begin to burn. At first you do not notice this. When you do notice it, appear to be surprised and mutter something about things not working properly or flaws in the paper.

11. By this point the envelope should be burning merrily away. Allow it to burn for a few more seconds and then quickly get the ash tray with your LH and place it beneath the flaming envelope. Open the clip with the RH and allow the burning envelope to fall into the ash tray. Continue to watch it burn with increasing alarm and distress. You should take great care in this step of the trick. You do not want to burn yourself or the spectator, nor do you want a burning envelope on the floor.

12. After the envelope and its contents (the spectator and audience should believe that his money is in there) have been consumed, thank the spectator for his contribution to science and then ask the audience for the loan of another bill. The spectator will, of course, still be on stage. At this point you notice his presence and tell him that he can return to his seat. It is not likely that he will be willing to do this. He wants his money back.

13. Almost as an afterthought, you remember that after all, you are a magician and that you can bring his bill back. Take the wand or pencil from your inside right-jacket pocket and hand it to the spectator. Tell him that if he taps the clip with it that his bill will appear in the clip. He taps the clip but the bill does not appear. Say something about this being one of those days and offer to give him something that is of equal value to his bill.

14. Before he can refuse, reach into your inside right jacket pocket with your LH, seal the gimmicked envelope and bring it out. Point out that this envelope contains an item as valuable as his bill. Let him see that the envelope is thoroughly sealed. Tear off the gimmicked end of the envelope and allow him to reach into the envelope to get the "valuable object." He will find a bill. Have him unfold it and match the corner, that he has been holding all the while, to show that it is his original bill.

15. Retrieve the bulldog clip and ribbon. Allow the spectator to retain the envelope, minus the gimmicked end, and his bill. Thank him for his cooperation and encourage the audience to applaud him as he returns to his seat.

In addition to the mystery involved in this trick, I hope that you can see the possibilities for comedy. I have suggested a line of comic patter for the trick, and, with a little imagination, you should be able to build on this.

IDENTIFIED FLOATING OBJECTS

One of man's oldest dreams has been to defy the laws of gravity. Many popular magic tricks give the impression that gravity can be defied, as objects rise and float. Here we consider a method of making a number of objects float. What we employ is a black thread, one of the magician's best friends.

The magic wand is a fairly common object for most magicians and it can be made to float with some simple preparations and a bit of practice. For this trick you might want to make your own wand. To do this, get a section of dowel 14 inches long and ½ inch in diameter. Measure off 2 inches from each end and cut a small groove into the dowel at these points. (See Figure 5-15.)

Figure 5-15.

Paint the two tips of the wand white and paint the center portion black. You also need a fairly strong black thread. You will need to experiment to find the right thickness of thread. It should be thick enough to support the weight of the wand, but it should be as thin as possible, so that the audience does not see it. The thread should be attached to the wand at the grooves. There are two possible lengths that you might use. A length of thread about two feet long can be used for many floating motions. (See Figure 5-16 A and B.)

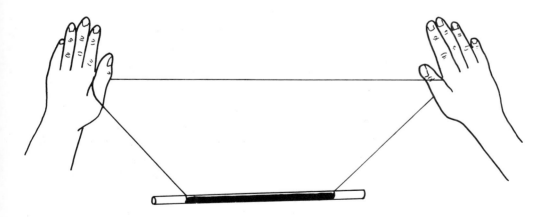

Figure 5-16 A.

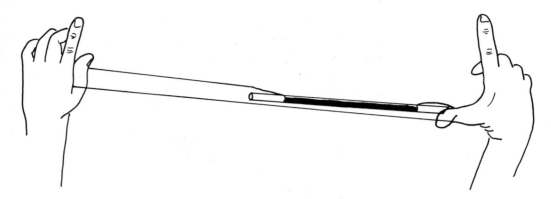

Figure 5-16 B.

For more variety in the floating wand, you might want to use a thread that is long enough to pass around your body. Once you have made your wand, you should experiment with both lengths of thread to see how many different rising and floating motions you can discover. In either case, you will need to break the thread from the wand if you are planning to use it later in the show, especially if you plan to allow some member of the audience to use it. The same technique can produce a floating broom. This has good patter possibilities for Halloween (a witch's broom).

You can also float a ball of paper by using a black thread. For this trick you need a piece of thread about two-and-one-half feet long and a small piece of double-stick transparent tape. One end of the thread should be tied around a button in the center of your shirt or attached to your belt buckle. The other end of the thread should have a piece of double-stick transparent tape wrapped around it. The taped end of the thread can then be stuck to a button on your jacket or even to the cloth inside your jacket. When you are ready to perform, take a sheet of tissue paper (about one-and-one-half square feet should work nicely), show it on both sides, and crumple it into a ball. In the process of crumpling it into a ball, with either thumb, disengage the end of the thread that has been wrapped in tape and stick the taped end to the center of the sheet of paper. The double-stick tape should adhere to the paper, and once the sheet of paper has been formed into a ball the thread will be caught in it. The ball can now be made to float. (See Figure 5-17.)

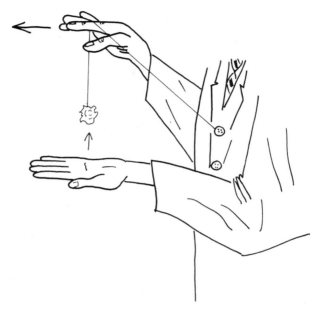

Figure 5-17.

Obviously, the thread will need to be broken at the end of the trick, and it is best to break the end that is tied around the button so that you do not go through the remainder of your program trailing a piece of thread.

You can have an even more ambitious floating object routine with the use of two off-stage assistants. These people should be trusted friends who will keep the secret of the trick. You *must* rehearse with them. Put in a good deal of rehearsal time before you attempt to put this trick in your program.

The floating or dancing handkerchief can be done with your two assistants, a piece of black thread that is long enough to extend across the stage, and a handkerchief, even a borrowed one. Before the show begins, you must run the thread from one wing of the stage to the other. Position an assistant on each side of the stage and have them hold the ends of the thread firmly so that it does not get kicked away. At this time, the thread should be on the floor.

When you are ready to perform, either bring out the handkerchief that you plan to use or borrow a handkerchief from some member of the audience and return to the stage. Hold the handkerchief up by one corner, and, at this point, the assistants should raise the thread until it is level with one corner of the handerkerchief. You then proceed to tie a knot in one corner of the handkerchief. The knot should be tied around the thread.

You now make some magic passes and the handkerchief magically comes to life. It jumps, it moves, it dances. All of this action is due to the movement of the thread by the assistants in the wings. Only practice will show you how many different movements are possible. Your assistants can gain a good deal of height by standing on chairs. When you are ready for the routine to conclude, one assistant can release or cut his end of the thread and the other can reel in the remaining thread. The handkerchief can then be returned to the owner.

By using a black thread, a styrofoam ball about four inches in diameter, and your two assistants, you can have a very effective floating-ball routine. If you are using the ball, it must be threaded before the show begins. It is wise to have the ball on a table upstage from your working area, so that you don't trip over the thread while doing the rest of the show. The thread should pass through the center of the ball. If you wish to show that the ball is free of any outside influences (such as thread) at the end of the trick, one of your assistants must cut or release his end of the thread while the other reels in the thread as you walk toward the audience with the ball. A subtle way to show that nothing is attached to the ball might be to use its "magic power" in a trick that follows the Floating Ball, handling the ball freely.

For years countless magicians have apparently torn asunder such items as playing cards, paper napkins, and newspapers and have then restored them to their original states.

To perform this trick, you need two similar napkins. One of these should be formed into a small ball. The best way to do this is to unfold the napkin, and, beginning at one of the corners and working diagonally, roll or form the napkin into a ball. (See Figure 5-18.)

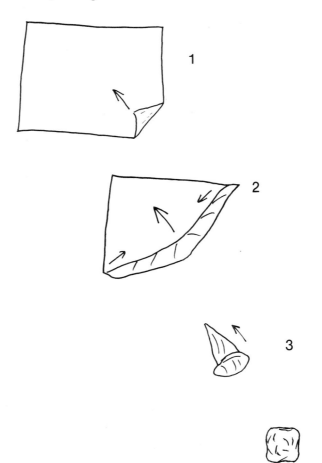

Figure 5-18.

Note that one corner of the napkin should project a bit. This makes it easier for you to unroll the napkin at the proper time. The other napkin should be left in its normal folded state. You will also need a "magic thing" in your right jacket or right pants pocket.

method and presentation

1. At the beginning of the trick, the rolled napkin and the folded napkin should be in such a position that you can pick them up, holding the rolled napkin behind the folded napkin. The best place to have them might be on your magic table.

2. Pick up the folded napkin and the rolled napkin as one with the RH, holding the rolled napkin in place behind the corners of the folded napkin with the right thumb. (See Figure 5-19.)

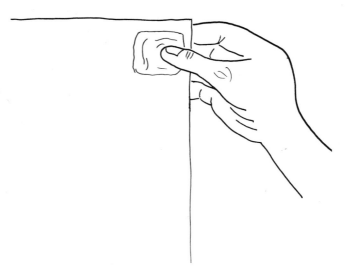

Figure 5-19.

3. Unfold the folded napkin with the assistance of the LH, keeping the rolled napkin behind one corner of the now un-folded napkin.

4. Using the LH, tear the napkin into several pieces. Always place the pieces, as they are torn away, in front of the piece that conceals the rolled napkin. (See Figure 5-20.)

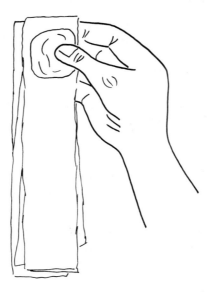

Figure 5-20.

5. After you have torn the napkin into several pieces, using the index and middle fingers and thumbs of both hands, begin to mold the torn pieces into a ball. This ball should resemble the rolled, but still whole, napkin.

6. In the process of molding the torn pieces of the napkin into a ball, reverse the position of the torn napkin and the whole napkin so that the whole napkin comes to the tips of the index and middle fingers of the RH and the whole napkin is moved to the Finger–Palm position in the RH.

7. Openly and obviously, place the whole napkin (its rolled shape will cause it to look like the balled-up pieces of the torn napkin) in the LH, continuing to conceal the torn napkin in Finger–Palm position in the RH.

8. While holding the whole napkin at the finger tips of the LH, reach into your right-jacket pocket or pants pocket with your RH and remove the "magic thing." At the same time, you leave behind the torn napkin.

205

9. Make a magic pass over the napkin held at the finger tips of the LH, and then return the "magic thing" to the pocket from which it came.

10. While making it obvious that your hands are empty, slowly and dramatically unroll the rolled napkin and show that you have restored the napkin to its original state.

patter suggestions

1. "As a magician, people often ask me to define the word 'illusion.' A dictionary definition of illusion might be that it is a mistaken perception of reality. In other words, we think that we see something when, in reality, we do not. Let me show you what I mean by using this napkin." Display and unfold the folded napkin.

2. "You, of course, can see that this is a napkin, but now I am going to create the illusion that I am destroying this napkin." Begin to tear the napkin into pieces.

3. "Doesn't that look real? Aren't the sound effects fantastic?"

4. "I haven't really torn the napkin, of course, but I am going to roll it into a small ball." Roll the napkin into a ball and don't forget to make the switch.

5. "Now if I were presenting this as a feat of magic rather than the demonstration of an illusion, I'd say, 'I now need my magic coin to restore this napkin.' I think I'll say that: 'I now need my magic coin to restore this napkin.'" Get the coin (or other "magic thing") from your pocket and leave the torn pieces of the napkin behind.

6. "Of course, then I'd wave the magic coin over the napkin and pretend that it had been restored." Fit your actions to your words and show them the "restored" napkin.

7. If you wish to stop the trick at this point, you should say, "I was kidding you about what I was doing. I really did tear the napkin into several pieces, but I *didn't* restore it. I just got the

pieces so close together that it appears to be restored." At this point you can toss the napkin into the audience if you wish.

bonus time   After having performed the trick as given, you can do it again and apparently show the audience how it is done; however, they will still be deceived. For this extension of the trick, you need another rolled and folded napkin setup and an extra rolled napkin.

1. If you wish to extend the trick, after you have given the final line in the suggested patter, say, "I'm sure that you all realize that this was a magic trick, and since you have been such a nice audience, I'm going to teach you how to do it. You see, I use an *extra* napkin."

2. Hold up the extra rolled napkin. "It's placed in my left hand." Place the extra napkin in the LH and hold it there rather awkwardly. Do not attempt to do a good palm; after all, you don't want the audience to realize that an object can be concealed in either hand.

3. Now follow steps 1 through 5 of the original trick.

4. At this point you have two whole napkins in your LH (the audience should think that one of the balls is the torn pieces of the original napkin) and you have a balled-up, torn napkin concealed in Finger–Palm position in the RH. Say to the audience, "The only reason that I reach into my pocket for a magic coin is to give me a chance to switch the whole napkin in my left hand for the torn napkin in my left hand. You don't really believe in magic coins, do you?"

5. As you reach into your pocket with your RH to get the coin (and to leave the torn napkin behind), you slowly and deliberately, in full view of the audience, reverse the position of the two napkins in your LH, pointing out to them that this is what they didn't notice before.

6. Touch the visible napkin in the LH with the magic coin and replace the coin in your pocket.

7. Your next step is to unroll one of the napkins to show that it has been restored. Point out to the audience that it is very important to keep the ball of torn pieces concealed.

8. Discard the restored napkin and hold the other napkin (the one that the audience believes to be the torn pieces) at the tips of the left fingers. Say to the audience, "Now just suppose that I was doing this trick and someone caught a glimpse of these torn pieces and wanted to know what I had in my hand? What could I do? Well, because I am a real magician, I would simply take my magic coin, because it really is a magic coin, touch the pieces, and restore the napkin." Suit your actions to your words and "restore" the napkin.

A TRIPLE PREDICTION

Because mental effects are very popular with audiences, I have decided to include a simple, but effective, prediction.

There are some advanced preparations that need to be made in order to perform this feat. From a deck, select three cards, such as the Jack of Spades, the Six of Clubs, and the Three of Hearts. Place these cards aside and return the remainder of the cards to the card case. You need three large ten-inch by thirteen-inch manila mailing envelopes. On a piece of cardboard slightly smaller than the envelopes, print the following: "I predict that, during my performance today, three spectators will select from a freely shuffled deck the following cards: the Jack of Spades, the Six of Clubs, and the Three of Hearts." Seal this prediction in one of the envelopes and place it aside. This is the prediction envelope.

The second envelope is gimmicked. Drop the three predicted cards, Jack of Spades, Six of Clubs, and Three of Hearts, into the bottom of one of the remaining envelopes. Cut off the bottom third of the last envelope and, using double-stick transparent tape, affix this third of the envelope inside the top of the envelope containing the three predicted cards. (See Figure 5-21.)

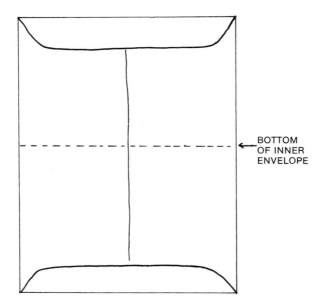

BOTTOM
OF INNER
ENVELOPE

Figure 5-21.

You now have a gimmicked envelope that contains the three cards predicted. The top third of the envelope will trap anything that is dropped into it. Do not seal this envelope at this time.

In addition to the deck of cards (minus the three predicted cards), the prediction envelope, and the gimmicked envelope, you also need a felt-tip marking pen and a tray; a TV serving tray will do nicely.

method and presentation

1. On your magic table, you should have all of the props used in the trick. At the beginning of the trick make some remarks about the powers of the mind, psychic phenomena, predictions, and so on, and ask for three spectators to assist you in an experiment.

2. When the three spectators come forward, greet them, and place them to your right. You should position yourself between the table and the three spectators. (See Figure 5-22.)

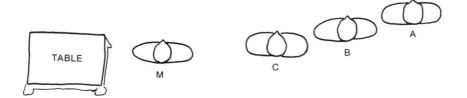

Figure 5-22.

3. Hold up the prediction envelope and point out that you have attempted to predict something that is going to happen during the show and that you have sealed your prediction in this envelope. Take the envelope to spectator A; have him initial it with the felt-tip marker and allow him to retain the envelope. Return to your position between the three spectators and the table.

4. Ask spectator C to come to you. Give him the deck of cards and ask him to shuffle it as much as he likes. Pick up the tray and ask him to spread the deck *face down* across the tray. You should hold the tray while he is doing this. After he has spread the deck, ask him to carefully push one card, *face down*, out of the spread.

5. Next, ask him to take the tray to the other two spectators and request each of them to carefully push a card face down out of the spread. There are now three cards that have been pushed from the spread by the spectators.

6. Spectator C should then return to you with the tray. At this point, pick up the gimmicked envelope, hold it with the address side to the audience, and open it slightly. Taking care that none of the spectators, including spectator C, can see the faces of the cards, pick up, one at a time, the three cards selected by the three spectators and drop them deliberately into the gimmicked envelope.

7. Seal the flap of the envelope while pointing out to the audience that nothing now can get out and nothing more can get in. Because of the construction of the gimmicked envelope, the three cards selected by the spectators will now be trapped in the upper half of the envelope.

210

8. Ask spectator B to come to you so that he can become custodian of the envelope holding the three cards. Place him to your left. (See Figure 5-23.)

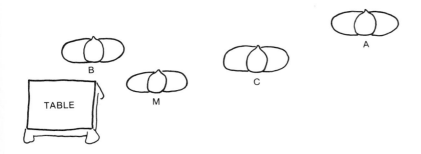

Figure 5-23.

Have him face the audience and hold the envelope up so that everyone can see it. Take the tray and extra cards from spectator C and return them to your table.

9. Now you should recap what has happened, pointing out that your prediction was made before the trick started, that the prediction envelope has been in the hands of a spectator throughout the experiment, that the deck was freely shuffled, and so on.

10. Ask spectator A to open the prediction envelope and read the prediction.

11. After he has read the prediction, take the gimmicked envelope from spectator C and turn it in your hands, showing and pointing out its sealed state.

12. You now open the envelope by *tearing it in half.* (See Figure 5-24.)

The top half, containing the gimmick, should be in your LH, and the bottom half, containing the three cards that match the prediction, should be in your RH. Hand the bottom half to spectator B so that he can "verify the prediction," and while he is taking out the three cards, you should casually crumple the top half of the envelope and drop it into your magic case.

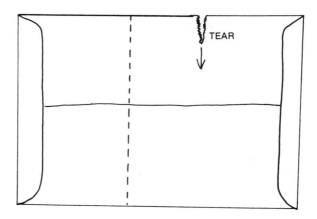

Figure 5-24.

13. The experiment has now successfully concluded. Make some final remarks about the powers of the mind. Thank the spectators for their help and allow them to return to their seats.

IT'S A GAMBLE

Tricks with gambling themes, especially those in which the magician may lose his bet, are popular with most audiences. This trick combines the supense of the gambling theme with an opportunity for comedy and audience participation.

In order to perform this trick, you need one piece of special equipment, although it should not appear to be special, in the form of a simple tray. The tray can be made from plastic, metal, or wood, although it is probably easiest to make it from cardboard. The overall dimensions of the tray are 8½ inches by 14 inches. The cardboard should be fairly thick. The sheet of cardboard used as backing on legal pads serves nicely, although any thick, uncorrugated cardboard should work. You need three 8½-by-14-inch sheets. They should be cut and assembled, as shown in the illustration, in order to build in the secret compartment necessary for the trick. (See Figure 5-25 A and B.)

212

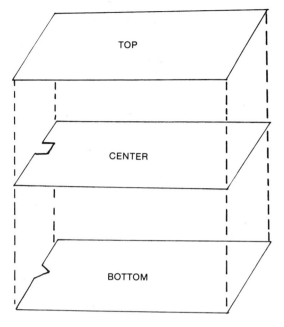

Figure 5-25 A.

ASSEMBLED TOP

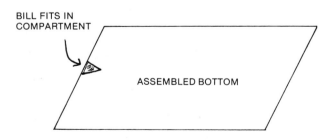

BILL FITS IN
COMPARTMENT

ASSEMBLED BOTTOM

Figure 5-25 B.

Use a good quality white glue to attach the three sheets together, and then cover the top and bottom of the tray with contact paper. Do not forget to cut the contact paper on the bottom of the tray so that the "V" notch is open.

In addition to the gimmicked tray, you need five coin envelopes, five pieces of play money, one real bill of any denomination that you choose to use, and a felt-tip marker.

Before the show, fold the bill into halves, quarters, eighths and, then, fold it once from top to bottom and insert it in the secret compartment in the bottom of the tray. Fold each of the play-money bills in the same manner and place one in each of the five coin envelopes. You might write little messages on each of these bills such as "Too Bad," "Better Luck Next Time," "I Get To Keep My Money," or whatever. Bend back and then restraighten one of the corners on one of the envelopes. This is a distraction for sharp-eyed spectators. They will think that you have "marked" the lucky envelope for yourself, and they will make every effort to keep this envelope in their possession. Be sure to seal the envelopes.

method and
presentation

1. Tell the audience that since they have been so delightful you are going to give a few of them a chance to make some money. Ask for four spectators, who would like a chance to win ten dollars (or whatever amount you are using) without any risk or investment, to raise their hands. (The larger the bill that you use, the greater the audience interest.) Pick four volunteers and ask them to come to the stage. Place two to your right and two to your left.

2. Pick up the tray, which should have the five sealed coin envelopes on it, and point out that one of these envelopes contains the ten-dollar bill. You should grip the tray as is shown in Figure 5-26.

Ask one of the spectators nearest you to take the felt-tip marker and number the envelopes one through five.

3. After he has done this, extend the tray to your right and ask each of the spectators to take one of the envelopes. Do the

Figure 5-26.

same for the spectators on your left. The envelope remaining on the tray is "your" envelope, but you do not touch it.

4. Allow the four spectators to exchange envelopes with each other. This will give you some comic possibilities because some of them may want to keep the one that they are holding. Point out that they must not refuse to exchange them. Let this go on from one to two minutes and then call "Time."

5. Starting with the spectator on your extreme right and moving to your extreme left, allow each spectator the opportunity to exchange his envelope that he now holds for the envelope resting on the tray.

6. After you have done this, ask the spectator on your extreme left and the spectator on your extreme right to open their envelopes. They will, of course, find play money. Allow them to return to their seats and say to the remaining spectators, "It's down to the three of us."

7. Tell the two remaining spectators to exchange envelopes and then allow each of them, starting with the spectator on your right, to exchange their envelopes for the one on the tray.

8. Ask the spectator on your left to open his envelope. He will find play money. Allow him to return to his seat.

9. Look at the spectator on your right as you say, "It's just between you and me, one-on-one." Allow the spectator to exchange envelopes with the one that you are holding on the tray. Ask him if he is sure about his choice. Play this up a bit and then tell him that it is his last chance to make a change.

10. You both open your envelopes at the same time. This is the one critical point in the routine for you. You should tip the tray to the left so that the envelope slides down the tray into your left hand. The fingers beneath the tray grip the bill in the compartment in the bottom of the tray. The left thumb presses down on the envelope from the top while the fingers press the bill against the envelope from the bottom. With your RH, put the tray aside.

11. To open your envelope, you transfer it from the LH to the RH. You do this by placing your right fingers on top of the envelope, and your right thumb goes beneath the envelope and presses the bill against it. The RH then lifts and turns the envelope so that the side opposite the bill is facing the audience. Tear off the uppermost end of the envelope with your LH and, showing the LH obviously empty, pretend to reach into the envelope with the left index finger and thumb. In reality, your left thumb and index finger go behind the envelope to grasp the bill and pull it up. (See Figure 5-27.)

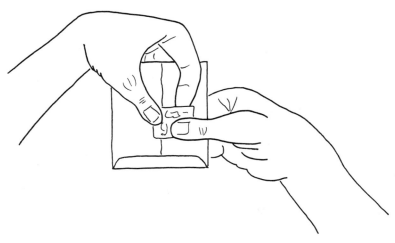

Figure 5-27.

The other three fingers of the LH serve to mask this action. It will appear that the bill has come from the envelope.

12. Crumple the envelope and place it in your pocket. Unfold the bill to show that "luck was with you." Thank the last spectator for his participation and allow him to return to his seat.

THE WORLD'S FASTEST WIZARD

The trick of the little figure that vanishes, the Bonus Genius, as it was called, can be traced back to the seventeenth century, when this trick was recorded in one of the earliest magic books, *Hocus Pocus Junior*. Here, I offer a modern version of this effect.

You need to make a special figure to use in this trick. This can be done by combining a small styrofoam ball, a short piece of dowel, some cloth for the body of the figure, and some foam rubber to stuff the body of the figure. Part of the short piece of dowel is attached to the figure at the point where the neck of the figure would be. The projecting end of this small piece of dowel then fits into a hole made in the base of the styrofoam ball. The fit should be snug, but not so tight that it is difficult to remove the head from the figure. Follow Figure 5-28 A and B with care in making the figure.

You will note that, once the figure is completed, you can easily slip the head off the piece of dowel, thus separating it from the body of the figure. By using false hair (like the kind of hair sold by theatrical suppliers for use in stage makeup), you can make a beard for your wizard.

In addition to the figure of the wizard, you also need a simple cloak for it. It should be made as shown in Figure 5-29.

You can use braid and other materials to make the outside of the cloak as fancy as you wish, but it is important that the cloak be somewhat longer than the figure. Strips of Velcro can be used to keep the front of the cloak closed.

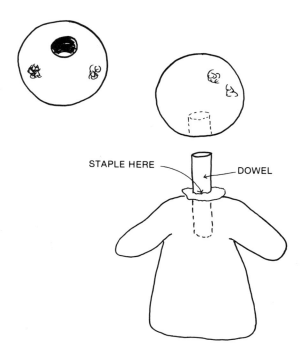

STAPLE HERE

DOWEL

Figure 5-28 A.

CREPE HAIR

Figure 5-28 B.

CLOAK

Figure 5-29.

1. Show the figure of the wizard and point out that not only is he your friend, but that he is also the fastest wizard in the world. Offer to send him on a journey.

2. Display the cloak, showing it inside and out and wrap it around the wizard. (See Figure 5-30.)

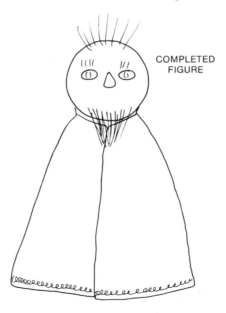

COMPLETED FIGURE

Figure 5-30.

3. In wrapping the cloak around the wizard, keep your RH inside the cloak. As soon as the wizard is covered by the cloak,

219

and while you are making the final adjustments with your LH, pull the body of the wizard away from his head and fold it into as small a ball as possible in the RH. Because the body is stuffed with foam rubber, you should be able to make a very small ball of the body.

4. Point out that the wizard must have his magic wand in order to make the trip. After saying this, place your RH into your right-jacket or pants pocket. Leave the body behind and bring out an imaginary magic wand. You should claim that it is so small that the audience probably will not be able to see it. Because the audience can still see the head of the wizard above the cloak, they assume that the body is still there. Pretend to place the small wand beneath the cloak.

5. Transfer the wizard's head and the cloak to your RH. You should hold these so that the spectators will continue to believe that the body is beneath the cloak.

6. Tell the audience that the wizard must be completely covered by his cloak in order to begin his trip. As you say this, push the wizard's head into the cloak with your LH. Your RH grips the cloak so that it does not fall.

7. As you push, or pretend to push, the wizard's head into the cloak, palm it in your LH. Withdraw your hand, being sure not to let the audience get a glimpse of the head.

8. Using both hands, open the cloak quickly to show that the wizard has already begun his journey. Show both sides of the cloak, keeping the head concealed in your LH.

bonus time   Would you like the wizard to reappear? This can be done if you make two wizard figures. The second figure could be loaded in one of the production devices, the production tubes or the production box. After making the first wizard vanish, you can proceed to reproduce him (actually the duplicate figure) from the production device.

INSTANT COW

The final trick I am including in this section comes from my lecture for magicians. I am including it because it fulfills what I consider to be a very important function of magic: entertainment. As you read the instructions for this trick, you will discover that the emphasis is on the entertainment rather than the trickery. The magician produces an "instant" (and invisible) cow and it is "milked" by a spectator.

You need a number of props for this trick: a thin rubber glove, a cowbell (the kind that cows wore about their necks when I was a lad; perhaps they still do), four to six feet of fairly thick rope (one end of the rope should be frayed to make it look somewhat like a cow's tail; if the rope is light brown or yellow, this adds to the effect), two identical brown paper bags (the twenty-five-pound grocery bag is about right) about 2 cups of finely chopped styrofoam (real powdered milk can be used but it is rather messy), a chair or stool for the spectator to sit on, a container to pour the "milk" into after the "cow" has been "milked," and a blindfold for the spectator.

Place the styrofoam in one of the paper bags; fold the bag as flat as it will go and place it in your magic case or in a box on your table. Place the rubber glove, cowbell, and rope in the other bag and place this bag in your magic case or in the box on your table. The blindfold is in the case or box but *not* in either bag.

method and presentation

1. Obtain a spectator from the audience to assist you. (If you are working for a group in which all or most of the people in the audience know each other, it is helpful to pick an assistant who has "importance" for the group. This best way to do this is to ask, in advance, the program chairman for the names of a few people who are popular with the group and who are also good sports.)

2. Say to your assistant, "I'm so glad that you agreed to help me today because I understand that you are the blindfold milking champion of this area. We're going to give you a

221

chance to demonstrate your ability." Play up his reaction. If he denies the title say, "Oh come now, don't be so modest." If he agrees say, "I'm sure the audience would like to see you in action."

3. Have the spectator sit on the stool or chair facing the audience.

4. Point out, "Since it's very difficult to carry a cow around for demonstration purposes, we have the next best thing, an instant cow. That's not really unusual for our age since almost everything else is instant: instant coffee, instant tea, instant grits."

5. Bring out the bag containing the props. "And I have everything in this bag that we'll need for the instant cow."

6. Take out the glove, inflate it, twist it so that the air cannot escape, and place it firmly in one of the spectator's hands as you say, "I'm sure that a champion milker knows what this is."

7. Have him, with his free hand, give you the rest of the props and then ask him if that is everything. He will say "yes" because the bag is empty; this establishes the fact that the bag is empty.

8. Fold up the bag to match the duplicate bag in your case or in the box as you look puzzled and say, "I thought I had a blindfold in there."

9. Look into your magic case or into the box, as you note, "Ah, here it is." Reach into the box or case *with the hand that is holding the bag* in order to get the blindfold. As you get the blindfold, switch the two bags. As long as you do this in a natural manner, you will have no problems. You now have the blindfold and the bag containing the "instant" milk.

10. Place the bag on the table and then proceed to blindfold the spectator.

11. Say, "We'll just let you milk this bag," as you place the bag, now opened, under the inflated glove held by the blind-folded spectator.

12. Tell him, "When I say 'Go,' you can start milking."

13. Stand a few feet to one side of the spectator. Hold the cow bell and the unfrayed end of the rope in the hand furthest from the spectator. Use your other hand to get a grip on the rope about two feet from the frayed end of the rope; this will give you control over this end of the rope.

14. Say, "Go." As the spectator "milks" the glove, you ring the bell and flick the frayed end of the rope (gently) in the spectator's face. At the same time give the best "moos" that you can manage. Continue this action for about 45 seconds. There should be considerable laughter.

15. Stop the action and place the bell and rope on your table and then say, "That's a fine job; I've never seen better milking."

16. Ask the spectator to remove his blindfold. As he is doing this, pick up the paper bag and say, "Let's show the audience how much you got."

17. Pour the "milk" from the bag into another container as you remark to the audience, "What did you expect? An instant cow gives instant milk."

18. Congratulate the spectator on his skill, thank him for coming forward, and send him back into the audience.

CONCLUSION

You have now learned a number of tricks than can be used when you have the opportunity to perform on stage or platform. Just because you are using apparatus and, in many instances, basically simple methods, do not be tempted to present them without proper rehearsal. When a magician is on a stage, it is very important that he be at ease and in command of the situation. With these tricks and with the proper amount of practice, you can achieve these two goals.

6

The
Real
Secrets

INTRODUCTION

By this time, you may have gathered that I consider the presentation of the trick as important as the method. I think it worthwhile to explore even more deeply the areas that lie at the very heart of successful magic, misdirection, practice, dealing with anxiety, and so on—the *real* secrets of magic. If you read, absorb, and apply the material with care, your study will be more than amply rewarded and your magic will show a marked improvement.

PRACTICE AND REHEARSAL

Throughout this book I have stressed the need for practice. It is now time to consider some of the specifics concerning practice and rehearsal. Practice is necessary because magic *is* a craft, and in order to pursue and master a craft you must first master the basic skills. In learning to play the piano, you spend hours practicing the scales and simple pieces of music before you are ready to attempt more complex works. You would spend many hours in practice before being ready to play in public. If you were learning to play football, you would spend hours on the basics before learning the plays and executing them in game situations. In either music or athletics, once you master (or at least become familiar with) the basic skills, you move on to use these basics in situations that simulate performing or playing conditions, all of which might be called rehearsal.

As you will discover, there are many people in the world who call themselves magicians because they have bought some tricks. In general, these performers do rather poor magic,

226

usually because they ignore practice and rehearsal. It is certainly true that you can learn the secret of most magic tricks in a few moments from a book, from the instructions that come with a trick, or from another magician. *But*—and this is an important but,—the degree of success that you are likely to have in performing a trick, and your feeling of reward in having learned to perform it properly, is likely to be in direct proportion to the amount of time you have spent in perfecting it through practice and rehearsal. And it is important to develop a sensible system of practice and rehearsal.

The first thing that you should do is to select a single effect that you wish to master. It is not only impractical to attempt to learn an entire magic program at one time, it is impossible. Once you have mastered this trick, you can then go on to others, eventually building up an extensive repertory of magic.

After having selected the trick, you need to read the directions several times in order to get an overview of the trick. At this point you might want to ask yourself what impact the trick should have on the audience. It is a production? a vanish? a destruction and restoration? You might also note the props that you need. You will want to consider the conditions under which the tricks can be performed. Is it basically a closeup or a stage trick? Can it be done surrounded by spectators, or are there problems with angles? In general, you want to make sure that you understand what is happening in the trick, how it is happening, and what impression the trick is supposed to have on the audience. If the trick is complex, you might, at this point, wish to gather the props and go through the routine. It is not likely that you will be able to do the sleights at this time, but you will be able to get the feel of the entire routine.

The next step in practicing the trick is to break it down into its basic parts or units. Sound educational theory says that a complex activity is most easily mastered by first mastering the parts or basic units that make up the complex activity. This is what you are going to be doing. Ask yourself what kind of setup or pre-performance preparation is needed. How many sleights or secret moves are there? What comes first? The directions for the tricks in this book are written in terms of such learning units. You will, however, not find this true with all magic books or directions, and you may need to work out some details for yourself.

After you have broken the trick down into its basic units, it is then time to begin practicing the units. There are two ways that you might do this. You might begin with the first unit in the trick and go over it again and again until you feel fairly confident with it, and then go on to the next unit in the trick. Or you could begin with the most difficult unit first and practice it until you feel comfortable with it. For example, let's say that you are doing a coin trick that requires two sleights and that you consider one of them to be more difficult than the other. Using the second method, you would begin by attempting to master the more difficult sleight. Either of these methods will work. The one you use will, at times, depend upon the complexity of the trick that you are trying to master and your own preference. I suggest that you try both methods a few times to discover which works best for you.

Once you have practiced the basic units of the trick, it is time to move on to the next step: putting all the units together in proper sequence and going through the entire trick in order to get the flow of the trick. You should begin to think of the trick in terms of its total impact rather than in terms of the individual units.

When you move to the stage of doing the trick as a total unit, you add the patter that you are going to use. You should coordinate the patter with the flow of the trick. Practice saying the patter aloud rather than simply running the words through your mind. If you only say the words to yourself in practice, you may discover, in performance, that the patter is not coordinated with the movements of the trick.

After you reach the point at which you have the patter integrated with the trick, you are then ready to begin to practice with a mirror. For stage or platform tricks, or even close-up tricks that you will stand to present, you will find that a full-length, or at least a dresser-top mirror, will be best. For practicing close-up tricks for which you are seated at a table, a simple set of practice mirrors can be made for a reasonable price. (See Figure 6-1.)

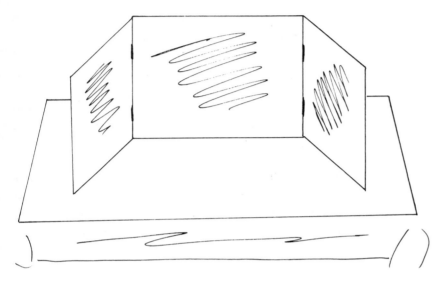

Figure 6-1.

The mirrors allow you to view the trick *as the audience will see it.* This is important because you may discover that you will need to make slight adjustments in your body position, the position of your hands, and so on.

You are now ready to rehearse. I think it is possible to distinguish practice from rehearsal in that in rehearsal you attempt to simulate the conditions that you will find in the actual performance situation. You use all of the props and accessories that you will use in the actual performance. You wear the clothing or costume that you plan to wear during the performance. You go through the trick from beginning to end as though you were doing it for an audience. If you make a mistake, you should not stop to correct it, but attempt to work yourself out of the difficulty just as you would do in performance. In so doing, you gain useful experience in confronting those situations in which things do go wrong, and you gain experience in learning how to deal with such situations. During this rehearsal period, you may want to make extensive use of your practice mirror.

The use of a "sample" audience can be even more helpful than the mirror at this point of your rehearsal, supplementing your mirror practice. Get a member (or members) of your family or a friend (or several friends) to watch you closely while you do the trick. You should, of course, get them to promise to keep your secrets *and* you should stress that you want *honest* and *objective* criticism from them. This can certainly be, at times, a blow to the ego of the budding magician if your mother, wife, brother, or friend says, "I saw you holding the coin in your right hand," or "It looked like you did something funny with that rope." If you want to be a magician, however, you must learn to accept constructive criticism. It is much better to have your ego bruised in rehearsal than to have it shattered in performance.

You have probably realized that the procedure for learning even one magic trick is somewhat lengthy, and you are probably asking yourself, "How can I do all of that at one time?" The answer is that you can't. You will find that it is best to set up a time for practice that allows you to practice for a short period each day, or perhaps every other day, on a regular basis. If you can set a practice schedule of thirty minutes to an hour on a regular basis and stick to it, you will be amazed at how much you can accomplish. You will also find that there are moments in your daily schedule during which you can work on mastering a sleight or a move. Because watching television does not usually require a great deal of concentration, I often find that I can get in some useful practice time while watching the tube.

Before leaving this section on practice, there is one more technique that I want to suggest to you. This technique is practice by visualization. Without using any props or sleights you attempt to see yourself doing the trick. You visualize or imagine that you are performing the effect. Attempt to see yourself going through the routine, to hear yourself saying the patter. You will find that, once you have the routine firmly in mind, this is not difficult to do, and it will reinforce what you have already learned in your earlier practice sessions. Experiments have demonstrated that this technique can be used to improve athletic skills, and it can also improve your magic. The advantage of this method is that you can use it almost anywhere at any time, riding on buses, sitting in dentists' waiting rooms, or waiting to fall asleep at night.

BUILDING CONFIDENCE

Before you have been in magic for very long, you will make an interesting discovery. You will observe that the magicians who are good magicians are good, at least in part, because they know that they are good. They possess the kind of self-confidence (not conceit or arrogance) that enables them to do their magic under a variety of conditions. This self-assurance communicates itself to the audience, and, in turn, the audience becomes more receptive to the magic. The reverse is also true. The magician who lacks self-confidence often finds himself with a bad case of dry-mouth and wet arm pits. Nothing seems to work for him, and performing becomes a frustrating chore rather than a pleasant experience.

How, then, can you build confidence? What can you do to avoid or minimize frustration? By following three simple and sensible principles, you can improve your magic and your confidence.

The first step in increasing your confidence is to improve your ability. It should be obvious that you are not going to be confident about doing something unless you know how to do it. I say this *should* be obvious, but I hate to think of the number of times that I have seen so-called magicians attempt to do a trick that they had obviously just bought or read about and had tried only a few times. It was apparent from the mumbling and fumbling that they really didn't know what they were doing. If you will follow the program of practice and rehearsal offered above, you will be able to improve your ability. You can also improve your ability at magic by continuing a serious study of the craft. Read other books on the subject. Watch other magicians. Talk to other magicians. If you can find a good instructor in magic, take lessons. If you ever get the chance to take courses in theatre or stagecraft, take them. All of these activities help deepen your knowledge of magic and should also improve your skill. Above all, continue to practice, and never be tempted to do a trick unless you feel that you have practiced it enough to be confident of success.

Set reasonable goals for yourself. Let's say, for example, that you want to put together a close-up magic show that runs for about twenty minutes, one that you can do when you have some friends in for dinner. It would be ridiculous to think that you could work out such a show in a week, or even several weeks. Such a program would take you several months of study and practice. You could buy a number of so-called self-working tricks from a magic dealer, but the audience would likely get the impression that you were doing some "almost" self-working tricks that you bought from a dealer. You could find twenty minutes worth of good close-up magic in this book, and you could "learn" it in the broadest sense of the word, but your presentation would not likely be very effective. The temptation is very great when one is getting started in magic to want to do everything in magic right away. I know this is true because I was this way when I started out in magic and I have observed other magicians who have fallen prey to the same temptation. Fortunately, most of us grow out of this phase, but I know magicians who have been in magic for years who still think that they can master every magic trick that has ever been invented or that will ever be invented. They usually end up playing with a lot of magic, never learning to do any of it effectively. Some of them become frustrated and eventually get out of magic. Others continue to deceive themselves more than they ever deceive their audiences, and they continue to accumulate tricks. What, then, are reasonable goals? They are goals that you can, with justification, hope to reach. Instead, for example, of setting out to master a twenty-minute program of close-up magic, start with one trick. Once you have mastered that trick, you can move on to another trick. You will discover in a relatively short time (but not in a few weeks) that you do have a twenty-minute program. By following the same procedure over the years, you will be able to add many tricks to your repertory. The same principle can be applied to learning a single routine of magic. Some magic tricks are more complex than others. For example, a billiard-ball routine or a linking-ring routine are both classics of magic, but they are somewhat lengthy and complicated. You could find yourself frustrated if you attempted to master the entire routine at one time. But, by breaking the routine down into its separate parts, as suggested in the section on practice and rehearsal, and by mastering one part at a time, a reasonable goal, you can learn the routine. Several years ago, I saw Tony Slydini perform at an International Brotherhood of Magicians convention. I was very impressed with his work and even took a private lesson from him. His various coins-through-the-table routines are classics of magic. I returned home determined to learn to perform at least some of his routines. I broke them down into their basic elements and practiced each element until I felt that I could do it effectively. It took me several months, but when I had finished, I had a routine that I could perform and one of which I was proud.

The third step in building confidence is to set a proper value on the goals that you are trying to reach. Your goal should be high enough so that you feel rewarded when you have reached it, but it should not be so high that it is impossible to attain. In other words, put your goal in perspective. Every magician will sooner or later make a mistake—a coin will drop, a thread will break—not only in rehearsal, but in performance. Be assured that you will not die even if you feel awful. You are not performing brain surgery, so no one in your audience will die either. The earth will continue to rotate. Be assured that your audience will not remember your mistake as long as you will, and one day you will either have forgotten it or will look back on it with amusement. On the other hand, if your magic is successful, you are likely to feel elated. Performing a magic trick well can be a real ego trip, but this should not give you a feeling of overconfidence. Success in performance should reinforce your faith in yourself as a magician.

By improving your ability, setting reasonable goals for yourself, and putting your goals in perspective, you should find that your confidence in your ability to master the craft of magic grows with your experience.

MISDIRECTION

Perhaps the most powerful weapon that the magician has in his arsenal is that of misdirection. Misdirection might better be defined as controlled direction because what is actually happening is that the magician is controlling, or directing, the attention of the audience. He is guiding them or even forcing them to focus on what he wants them to see, believe, or think. Misdirection may be considered physical or psychological, although, in most cases, it is usually a combination of both.

Physical misdirection is present in any sleight that a magician performs. For example, when performing the coin vanishes described in this book, you are carrying out physical misdirection. You are pretending to place the coin from one hand into the other hand, yet you are retaining it in the hand in which it was orginally held. The hand that is to receive the coin closes and pretends to hold the coin while the hand retaining the coin is held in a natural manner. (You will note that when performing the Finger–Palm Vanish, for example, that you are instructed to point with the index finger of the hand retaining the coin and to curl the other fingers in toward the palm of the hand. This is a natural way of holding the hand if you are going to point at something.) This implies that the coin has been transferred from one hand to another.

Physical misdirection depends on four basic techniques: use of the eye, body language, natural actions, and repetition.

By the use of the eye, I mean looking where you want the spectators to look. The importance of such a technique in theatre and in magic has been recognized for centuries. Contemporaries of the great eighteenth-century English actor David Garrick often commented on his use of his eyes in his performances. Similar comments were made by contemporaries of Alexander Herrmann, the great nineteeth-century magician. In many of the tricks in this book, you have been told to *look* at a specific hand, or you have been told to *look* at the spectator at a critical point in the trick. The reason for this is that the spectator's eyes will follow the direction that your eyes take. If you pretend to place a coin in your left hand and *look* at your left hand, the spectator will also look at your left hand, while your right hand drops to your side. If you look at the spectator, and, perhaps, address a remark to him while you are executing a sleight, the tendency of the spectator will be to look at you rather than at your hands. By the same principle, if you cast a guilty glance at the hand that is really holding the coin or ball, be assured that the spectator will realize that something is wrong and he will also look in that direction.

The concept of body language has received a good deal of attention in recent years in the field of communication, and some of the implications of these studies are being applied to magic. Since there are a number of books available on this topic, some sound and some not so sound, it would be impossible to summarize all of the material on this topic in this book, *but* a basic concept of body language, and one that is useful to the magician, is that our actions do often speak louder than our words. We frequently convey our true attitudes and meanings in our physical actions, our body positions and tension, rather than in what we say. I think that this tells the magician that he must be able to pretend that what he is doing is real until he reaches the point at which he can "believe," at least on one level, that what he is doing is "real." I am not suggesting a form of self-hypnosis, but the kind of pretense that the actor carries out in doing a role in a play. Most actors are certainly aware, even in the midst of a performance, of who they are and where they are, *but* they are able to pretend that they are the character whom they are playing at least to the extent that the audience believes them. The magician has the same task in pretending that his magic and actions are real. If, for example, you really placed a coin in your left hand, and closed the hand around the coin, there would be a certain degree of tension in the mucles of the left hand. You would not hold the hand too loosely because the coin might fall out. At the same time, you would not need a "death grip" on the coin, either. The converse is also true. If a hand is supposed to be empty, it should be treated as if it were empty. Let's say that a coin has apparently been placed in the left hand, while being retained in the right hand. You allow the right hand to drop to your side, while you focus attention on the left hand. The force of gravity should do the work. You do not fling your right hand to your side nor do you allow it to s–l–o–w–l–y move down as if an invisible wire were attached to it. The muscles of the right arm should be relaxed and the right hand should have only enough muscular tension to retain the coin in palm position. Your whole body should say, without a single word on your part, "The coin is in my left hand." In summarizing this point, your motto for magic might well be, "Let your body do the talking."

Natural actions are a technique of misdirection. If what you do looks unnatural or strange, the audience will notice and become suspicious. In general, I agree with this idea, but I think it can be modified somewhat. For example, in each of the three coin vanishes (see Chapter 2), the coin is first displayed in the right hand and transferred to the left. You know, of course, that this is necessary in order to make the vanish work, but, if the magic were real, there would be no reason to first display the coin in one hand and then transfer it to another. The magician could simply close his hand around the coin and it would vanish. What I am suggesting is that a great many of the movements used in magic are not natural in the final analysis (I would be willing to bet that I get some cards and letters from other magicians on that point), but that the audience is never troubled by this if the magician performs these moves in a natural manner and "believes" in the move. The audience is led to accept what the magician is doing as a natural, acceptable, minor idiosyncrasy. After all, we don't all shake hands, wave goodby, or even scratch our chins in the same way. I think that one excellent way of achieving naturalness in your sleights and moves is to do the move or sleight as though it were real. That is, practice putting the coin in the left hand and really leave it there—in the early stage of practice, of course. This will show you how your hands would move if you were really doing what you are going to be pretending to do in performance. You will also be able to observe some of your own body language in your practice mirrors.

In some instances, however, the action is natural because the action is what you would do even if you were not doing a magic trick. In A Tribute to A Callow Youth, for example, the act of picking up the paper napkin from the table (see Chapter 4) is very natural because you draw the napkin to the edge of the table in order to pick it up rather than drop your hand from above like a crane scooping up earth or a bird of prey diving on a rabbit. In It's A Gamble (see Chapter 5), it is also natural to slide the envelope from the tray into your left hand since both hands are holding the tray. Therefore, a magician's actions and movements must either be natural or give the appearance of being natural.

Repetition can also be used as a device of misdirection. If the audience sees the magician repeat the same action several times, their attention lags and the magician can carry out the sleight with a very low chance of detection. There are two good examples of this technique in The Maximum Misdirection Card to Pocket. Notice how many times the right hand goes into the pocket *before* the card is palmed from the deck and placed there. In the same trick, notice how the bottom card of the first two piles is shown and then dealt face down on the table before the glide is used on the third pile to keep the bottom card in place.

There is one more technique of physical misdirection that I want to cover, although it is not used as frequently as the others. In the Click Pass used in the Coins Across and in the counting of the coins in Reflex Test, sound is used to misdirect the spectators.

Certain elements of physical misdirection can also be seen in magic props as well as in sleights. Many of the larger stage illusions depend on the clever use of design, painting, and optics to make a piece of apparatus appear smaller than it is, or to hide secret compartments necessary to the trick. The special tray used in It's A Gamble might be considered an example of this. The element of the natural is often used in a magic prop, in that the prop appears to be an ordinary object while, in reality, it has been modified or changed. The envelope in A Triple Prediction that allows the magician to switch the selected cards for the cards that the magician has predicted falls into this category.

In the area of psychological misdirection, I think there are three significant techniques: justification, implication, and multiple focus.

Justification is having a reason for doing what you are doing so that the audience does not become suspicious of your actions. In many tricks, it is necessary for you to put your hand in your pocket in order to secretly leave something behind, make an exchange, or secure some object. If you were to simply put your hand in your pocket, the spectators might wonder, with cause, "Why is he putting his hand in his pocket?" and they might conclude, with cause, that you were doing something "funny." But if you are putting your hand in your pocket to get a "magic thing," or a book of matches, you have a justification for what you are doing and this answers any question before it is asked. In A Triple Prediction, the three cards selected by the spectators *could* be left on the tray, but you would have to make a difficult switch if they were, so you justify sealing them in the envelope (thus making the switch) by claiming to do this for the reason of security. In the tricks in this book, I have offered points of justification when needed, but as you start to invent your own magic or learn more magic, be aware of this important consideration.

Psychological misdirection by implication is the implication that one state exists when, in fact, the opposite state exists. By giving the spectator the deck and allowing him to shuffle it in A Triple Prediction, you imply that the deck is an ordinary one, containing 52 cards, but you do not say this. (No magician, unless he is doing a spoof of magic for other magicians, should ever say, "This is an ordinary deck of playing cards, an ordinary piece of rope, an ordinary coin, and so on." Any magician guilty of violating this law should have his wand broken and all his gimmicks trampled on.) The envelope used in The Burned Bill is gimmicked, but as long as you do not call attention to it, the spectator will take it for what it appears to be, an ordinary envelope. Implication is involved in the performance of sleights. When you apparently place a coin from your right hand into your left hand, while retaining it in your right hand, you are implying that the coin is now in the left hand. At times the magician may use the false statement for misdirection, as in It's A Gamble when the audience is told that one of the envelopes contains a real bill. However, most of the time you will discover that magic operates more by implication than by direct false statement.

Multiple focus is the dividing of the spectator's attention so that his full attention cannot be focused on any one point. You give your audience more than one thing to think about. This idea is unconsciously parodied in a line of stock patter used by many magicians: "Keep one eye on my right hand, one eye on my left hand, and another eye on me." The Maximum Misdirection Card to Pocket contains an excellent example of multiple focus. At one point in the routine, the spectator is attempting to watch the card under the coin that he believes to be the selected card, and, at the same time, he is attempting to watch the card that the magician has *said* is the selected card. There is very little attention left to watch the magician put his hand in his pocket, especially because he has justified his action and is repeating an action that he has performed several times already.

It may have occurred to you that it is very difficult to isolate physical misdirection from psychological misdirection. I agree. Most of the time I think that you will find that the physical and the psychological work together to create the illusion. You may have also noticed that several techniques of misdirection may be operating at the same time: you may be employing the eyes, the body, implication, and justification in the same sleight. You are right again. The reason that I have attempted to discuss the basic kinds of misdirection and the techniques in their "pure" form is twofold: I wanted you to focus on some specifics of misdirection, and I wanted you to begin doing some probing thinking about the concept of misdirection. As you think, go back over the tricks and note the points at which misdirection operates and *how* and *why* it works. You should also study the work of other magicians to learn more about this fascinating area of magic.

MAGIC AS ENTERTAINMENT

A real and serious problem faced by many beginning magicians (and also by far too many long-time magicians) is that they forget about working for the audience and work primarily for themselves. I call this "audience-bypass" magic. They are more concerned with performing some complicated sleight that they have learned or displaying some new piece of equipment that they have purchased than with entertaining the audience.

A magician should never lose sight of the fact that he is first and foremost an entertainer. The nineteenth century's great French magician Robert-Houdin is credited with saying that a magician is an actor playing the part of a magician. I think it should be added that the basic goal of the actor is to entertain. There are three basic ways in which a magician can entertain his audience: He can mystify them; he can impress them; and/or he can amuse them.

If you are planning to entertain your audience by mystifying them, I think it is very important that you adopt the proper attitude. If you use the approach that says to the audience,

"See how much smarter I am than you," you are asking for trouble. You should know, having read all or most of the chapters on tricks, that many of the secrets of magic are rather simple. If you present your magic as a mental challenge to the spectators with a "see if you can figure this out" attitude, that may be just what happens. The audience may take up your challenge and devote their efforts to figuring out how you did what you did. You should also be aware that there are a number of books on magic available in bookstores and on library shelves that tell how to do magic, and some members of the audience may have read some of these books.

Am I saying that mystery does not have a place in modern magic? Not at all. However, in the twentieth century, magicians who wish to pose as masters of mystery do not have it as easy as did their counterparts in the eighteenth or nineteenth centuries. In our time there has been a great deal of interest in pyschic phenomena and the occult, so you may discover that mentalism is your cup of tea. Many books have been written about flying saucers and ancient civilizations. If you read some of these books, I think that you will be able to develop patter and ideas for tricks that relate to these unusual fields, fields that, for many people, border on the scientific. You might, then, present your magic as "experiments" rather than as tricks, creating an aura of mystery around your work.

Another way to entertain your audience is to impress them with your skill at performing. In some cases some members of your audience may know (or think they know) how you are doing a trick, but, if you perform smoothly and efficiently, they will be impressed. This is especially true for any magicians who happen to be in your audience. At times, watching magic can be like watching an athletic event. Spectators appreciate a well-thrown pass, a well-hit ball, or a well-executed gymnastic feat. They can also appreciate a magician who makes his magic look easy and flawless.

A third way of entertaining your audience is to amuse them. Humor can be an important device in magic in more than one way. It can serve as an important means of misdirection because if people are in a good mood, if they are laughing, they are less likely to worry about *how* you did a trick. Humor can also keep the audience interested in what you are doing. You may have noticed that many of the bits of patter and patter suggestions that I have given you are of a humorous nature. I do feel that the humor used in magic should be done in the spirit of having fun *with* the audience (or an assistant from the audience) rather than *making* fun of them. You will notice that in no trick that I give you is the assistant made to appear stupid, and any trick using an assistant has a "happy ending," in that nothing "bad" happens (in reality), to the assistant or his property. In additon to having fun with the audience, I do not think that it is beneath the dignity of the magician (unless you are posing as a "serious man of mystery") to have a few laughs at his own expense, provided the trick ends successfully and the magician proves to be the master of the situation.

The ideal situation would be to combine mystery, skill, and humor. This can be done by many performers and in many tricks. Whether you attempt to use one, or any combination of these approaches, either in a routine or in a single trick, always remember that the greatest crime that any magician (entertainer) can commit is to bore his audience. Bend all of your resources of mind, talent, and will to entertaining your audience.

FINDING YOUR STYLE

Closely related to the idea of magic as entertainment is the task of finding your own style as a magician. Why is finding your style important? It is important because it will determine out of the thousands of possible tricks which ones you can do best. Once you find your style, the magic that you do will be comfortable to you because it is natural. Once you find your style, you will discover that your magic is more readily accepted by your audiences because what you are doing, the personality that you are projecting, rings true.

In attempting to develop your own style, you should be prepared to experiment with all of the various branches of magic in order to find the one that best fits you. When I was a teenager I wanted to be a stage magician doing large stage illusions; a skilled exponent of manipulative magic, using billiard balls, coins, and cigarettes; and an escape artist, like Houdini, performing death-defying feats. None of these types of magic was really right for me, but I continued the struggle into my early twenties, getting little positive reinforcement from the magic I was doing. When I started to work on my master's degree, I discovered that I had neither the time nor the money to keep up my interest in magic so I "dropped out" of magic for several years. My break was total; I packed away all of my apparatus and tricks; I let my membership in the International Brotherhood of Magicians lapse. It was not until I had finished my degree, started teaching in college, and married that my interest in magic was rekindled. This period of abstinence from magic was probably the best thing that could have happened to me, because, during this time, I learned a great deal about *myself*. Therefore, when I was ready to "wield the wand" again, I had a much better idea of the kind of magic that I was able to do most effectively. Another change took place several years later when one of my teachers and closest friends in magic, J. C. Doty, convinced me that I could be an effective close-up magician. Prior to that time, I had done little close-up magic and I had not really been pleased with the results. Now, close-up magic is one of my favorite fields. I am not suggesting that you will have to drop out of magic in order to find your style, but I do think that finding your style is a gradual process for most magicians and that it is necessary to experiment with magic and to get to know yourself in order to accomplish this goal.

You should also be prepared to spend time and money to find your style and the tricks that best suit you. A successful professional magician once told me that he went through about $5000 worth of magic tricks before he found the $500 worth of magic that he used in his one-hour show. You will discover that you will purchase, while in the process of developing your style, tricks that you will not use. Almost every magician has a drawer, closet, or, in some cases, a room, filled with magic that he does not use. This should not be depressing because you may be able to trade or sell equipment to other magicians, or you may discover that you can use much of this magic after you have developed your style and learned to alter the trick to fit your style. In 1968 I bought a trick for the princely sum of one dollar. I tried it a few times but discovered that the patter, as supplied by the dealer, did not fit my style. Three years later, the "right" patter idea came to me, and now, that dollar purchase is one of my favorite close-up tricks. You will also discover that your magic bookshelf grows as you attempt to learn more about magic and to find your style. This is a very healthy sign because, in comparing books with tricks, books can be a far better investment. From books, you will learn the secrets of many tricks, you will encounter ideas for patter, and you will get tips on presentation. All of this knowledge can be valuable in developing your unique style of presenting magic.

Many beginning magicians are tempted to develop their style in magic by imitating other magicians. This is entirely natural because much of our personalities are built upon the models of people whom we admire. There have been a number of successful magicians who began their careers in this fashion. One of the outstanding magicians in the nineteenth century, Robert Heller, began his career by doing the tricks of and attempting to duplicate the personality of Robert-Houdin. Although Heller was English, he wore a dark wig and spoke English with a French accent, imitating the great French magician. Later in his career, Heller became very successful in his own right, but, by this time, his presentation of magic was all Robert Heller. The danger of imitation is that you can find yourself becoming merely a carbon copy of another magician, and this situation will not really permit you to express your own personality in magic. I suggest that, if you are tempted to imitate another magician, you first ask yourself, "Is that really me? Am I exactly like that?" It is possible to be stimulated by another magician without becoming an inferior copy of him.

After you find your style as a magician, you will notice many changes. You will discover that you enjoy performing magic more and more because your magic has become an extension of your personality. You will discover that your magic is more warmly received by your audiences because they sense that what you are doing is right for you. You will discover that you are buying fewer tricks because the tricks that you buy you use. You will also discover that you can adapt tricks to fit your style. Finding your own style is indeed one of the real secrets of magic.

ROUTINING YOUR ACT

Routining the magic act may be defined as the process of putting several tricks together to form a pleasing and unified performance. Routining is very important in almost any situation, whether it be a close-up, platform, or stage performance. Although there are a number of different ways to approach routining, I think it is helpful to regard the magic routine as one might regard the structure of an effective speech. That is, the routine should have an introduction, a body, and a conclusion, or a beginning, a middle, and an end. (I am sure that I have been conditioned to this approach by years of teaching speech, but it *does* work.)

Your opening trick, or introduction, is important because its basic function is to get the favorable attention of the audience, to establish a rapport between you and them. When I started in magic years ago, the thinking was that the opening trick should be quick and flashy, perhaps a quick production or vanish. While there is much merit in this approach, especially for the magician who does a silent stage act, I am not sure that it is good for all magicians or all situations. If, for example, you do a talking act, a silent, quick production may be out of place because it may not lead logically into the rest of the magic. It is also possible that a quick opening trick may be so quick that the audience is not aware that anything has happened until the trick is over. To me, it is important that the opening trick serve to establish the fact that you are a magician and to establish your performing style. This may mean that you use a quick, flashy trick, but it might also involve a trick that takes several minutes and good deal of patter. For example, since I am a comedy-patter magician, I do a humorous patter presentation for my opening trick.

The body, or middle, of your routine may involve one or several tricks, depending on the length of the routine. In the body of the act, if you are doing several tricks, I think that variety is important. You do not want the tricks to be repetitious. For example, you would not want to use, in the same routine, a cut and restored rope and a cut and restored ribbon. Nor would it be wise to use both the production tubes and the production box in the same program. There are, of course, a limited number of basic magic effects, such as productions, vanishes, destructions and restorations and so on, but different variations of a basic effect will be viewed as "different" tricks by the audience if there are sufficient changes in the details. For example, the basic effect of the Cut and Restored Rope and the Burned Bill are the same: An object is either mutilated or destroyed and then restored. But, because the objects are different and because they are destroyed in a different manner, you could use both tricks in the same program.

Variety is also important in terms of tricks that require audience participation and those that do not. I think it is wise to break up your program by alternating tricks that require audience participation with those that do not. In one of my most successful programs, a platform show, I use eight tricks. The opening trick requires no audience participation; the second and third tricks use members of the audience; the fourth trick requires no audience participation; while the fifth, sixth, and seventh tricks make use of members of the audience; and the eighth does not. Many magicians feel that each trick should be stronger than the previous trick in the program, but this is frequently difficult, if not impossible, to judge. As long as each trick is a self-contained unit with a definite climax, I think you should have a satisfying program.

Your closing effect is important because it says, or should say, to the audience, "This is it. My act is over." Many magicians feel that the closing trick should be the most impressive trick. There is a good deal of validity to this approach *if* you can determine what is your most impressive trick. I do think that your final trick should be a strong one, but more importantly, it should be a trick that tells the audience that your show is over and one that focuses attention on *you*.

Another area that must be considered in routining a magic show is the conditions under which you are going to perform. By the conditions, I mean the proximity of the audience to the performer (close-up, platform, or stage) and the time limits of the performance (impromptu or scheduled in advance). You would, for example, not be able to do certain tricks in a close-up performance that you could do on a stage or platform. On the other hand, there are many fine close-up tricks that simply could not be seen if performed on a stage or platform. You would also make different choices of tricks if you knew that the spectators were expecting you to perform rather than apparently giving an impromptu performance.

Timing is important in routining a magic performance because many beginning magicians (and far too many "experienced" magicians) are tempted to go on far too long. In performing impromptu, that is, when someone asks you to do a few tricks without any prior warning, I think the rule of three is a good one to keep in mind. By doing three tricks, you have what amounts to an introduction, a body, and a conclusion. It is permissible, under these conditions to do only one trick if you wish. Under more formal conditions, that is, when you have been asked in advance to perform, you should plan on a longer program. For example, you might select five tricks for a close-up act, an act that might run from fifteen to twenty minutes, depending on the selection of tricks. In doing a program of magic for the stage or platform, you are usually expected to perform twenty to thirty minutes or longer, depending on the circumstances. For example, as part of a longer program with other magic acts, or even other variety acts, thirty minutes would probably be too long. If you were the only performer and were expected to do a thirty-minute program, you would want to select six to ten tricks—depending on the length of the tricks—to fill out your program.

Drawing upon the tricks in this book, I have devised some sample routines that you might want to use for your magic shows.

sample routine #1   This routine is for an impromptu, close-up situation. The assumption is that you have the necessary props on your person or that you can borrow them. I always carry several coins for coin tricks. You could probably borrow a deck of cards, pencil, paper, and so on in most homes.

1. Coins Across. This is a good opening effect because it is visual, fast, involves money, and, if you have practiced, it should establish you as a magician.

2. I Get The Thought. This is good for a change of pace because it is a mental effect and it takes somewhat longer than Coins Across.

3. Maximum Misdirection Card to Pocket. This is a good closing effect because a card apparently vanishes from the deck and appears in an impossible location, your pocket. For maximum effectiveness, you might have the card signed at the beginning of the trick.

sample routine #2   This routine is for an impromptu, close-up situation when you are seated at the table.

1. A Brief Tribute To A Callow Youth. Using an item found at the table, a paper napkin, you can tear and restore it, cause it to vanish, or change it to another object, things that only a magician could do.

2. Reflex Test. This trick happens in the spectator's hand, and you should be able to borrow enough coins for this trick even if you don't have any on your person.

3. Glass Through, or Pass the Salt. You use items, once again, that can be found at the table for a penetration, an impressive closing effect.

sample routine #3   This routine is for an impromptu, close-up situation in which you have been caught with only your coins, and it is impossible to borrow the props for Sample Routine #1.

1. Ambitious Coin. This trick involves a number of vanishes and reappearances with a single coin.

2. Coins Across. In this trick you move from using one coin to several.

3. Reflex Test. For this item in your program it might be wise to borrow the coins, even if you have enough on your person, because this seems to make a stronger impression. It has enough impact for a closing trick because it happens in the hands of the spectator.

sample routine #4   This routine is for a planned, close-up situation. That is, you are expecting, or expected, to perform. Note that it involves some tricks that require a prior setup or special props. Also note that it is longer than the impromptu routines.

1. Mongolian Clock. This is a visual, off-beat card trick, and is, therefore, a good opening effect.

2. Coins Across. In this trick you move from cards to another traditional prop for close-up magic, coins.

3. Bionic Vampire. The basic effect in this trick is that of a production, and the patter theme is unusual.

4. I Get The Vibes. With this trick, you once again change the pace of the routine by presenting a mental effect that calls for audience participation by several members of the audience.

5. Ring In the Envelope. This is a good closing trick because an object borrowed from a spectator vanishes and then reappears in an "impossible" location, a sealed envelope.

The conditions for this routine are the same as for Sample Routine #4.

1. Ring Off The Rope. This is quick, visual penetration.

2. Two-Card Reverse. This is an offbeat card trick that has good visual impact.

3. Three Objects—Plus One. You may use any objects of your choice and either ending for this trick. Although one may argue that this trick is a transposition, just as in the Two-Card Reverse, because you use different props and the transposition apparently takes place in a different manner, the effect is another trick in the minds of the audience.

4. I Get The Thought or I Get The Vibes. Either of these mental tricks provides a change of pace with strong audience participation.

5. The Coin In The Bag, In The Box, In The Sock. The impact of this trick is very much like that of trick 5 in Sample Routine #4; this is why the trick was chosen as the closing trick for this routine.

This routine is designed for a performance on a stage or platform. I am suggesting only six tricks because this routine should take from twenty to thirty minutes, depending on how fast you work and how the audience responds. This is long enough to be on stage for any beginning magician and for many advanced magicians, as well.

1. Production Box or Tubes. This opens your show with an impressive production number. You might consider producing some of the items that you are going to use in the show such as ropes, scissors, and so on. You could then refer to the tubes or the box as your magic traveling case.

2. Cut and Restored Rope (any version). This is a strong effect and allows you to make use of audience participation.

3. Triple Prediction. This trick adds variety to your routine

250

because it is a mental effect and uses three assistants from the audience.

4. The Burned Bill. This trick, although in a way like the Cut and Restored Rope, is different because it involves an object borrowed from a spectator and introduces the concept of magician failure, because it appears, at one point in the routine, that you have failed in the trick. As you can see, it affords many possibilities for comedy and byplay with the spectator. You might substitute It's A Gamble for this trick if you wish.

5. Instant Cow. This is a production trick, and it uses a spectator from the audience in a comedy situation. You might substitute the Ropes Through The Body for this trick.

6. The Carver Ropes. I have found, over the years, that this is a very good closing trick. It uses no assistants and no apparatus other than the three ropes. It focuses attention on you as the magician.

You may have noticed that I have suggested many more close-up routines than stage routines. There is good reason for this. You will have many more opportunities to perform close-up magic than to perform stage magic. As you learn more about magic, by reading other books on the subject, buying tricks, and coming in contact with other magicians, you will not only add to your repertory of individual tricks but you can add variety to your routines as well.

DOING THE MAGIC SHOW

In actually doing the magic show, there are several steps or phases that you should go through in order to be successful. The same basic rules apply to the close-up, stage, or platform situation.

The first phase is learning the tricks and selecting the routine. You can begin from either side. You might, for example, already know a number of individual tricks, and, from them, you might select the proper tricks to make up a pleasing routine. Or you might begin by first selecting the routine and then learning the individual tricks. In either case, your first and most basic task is to practice the tricks until you can do them effectively. Remember that a "rehearsal" should simulate performance conditions, so you should enlist observers when you have built up your confidence through careful practice.

The second phase is to develop a checklist for all of the props used in the tricks in the routine. Make sure that nothing has been left behind or put in an incorrect place. This is very important. It is far from reassuring to discover, after you are ready to perform or after you are into the trick, that you have left an important gimmick at home or to discover that a prop that should be in your right jacket pocket is in your left jacket pocket. Indicate on your checklist what the props are and where they are going to be at the beginning of your show, then use the checklist to make sure that they are there. If you are performing close-up magic, most of your props will probably be on your person; some may be in your magic case. If you are doing a stage or platform show, most of your props will probably be in your magic case or on your magic table, but in most cases you will have a few props on your person.

This seems to be a logical point to say a few words about magic cases and tables. For close-up work, it would be wise to purchase an attaché case in which to store and carry your magic props. You will discover that a great deal of close-up magic can be contained in such a case. In order to keep the inside of the case neat, so that you can find the props that you want when you want them, it is wise to make a series of dividers. These can be constructed by making the partitions out of balsa wood and gluing them to a thin plywood base. (See Figure 6-2.)

For a magic table, you can use a TV tray (the kind often used for serving snacks or meals in front of a TV set). (See Figure 6-3.)

To make this a bit more elegant, you can add a top made of a

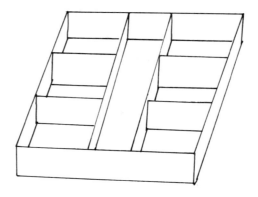

Figure 6-2.

Figure 6-3.

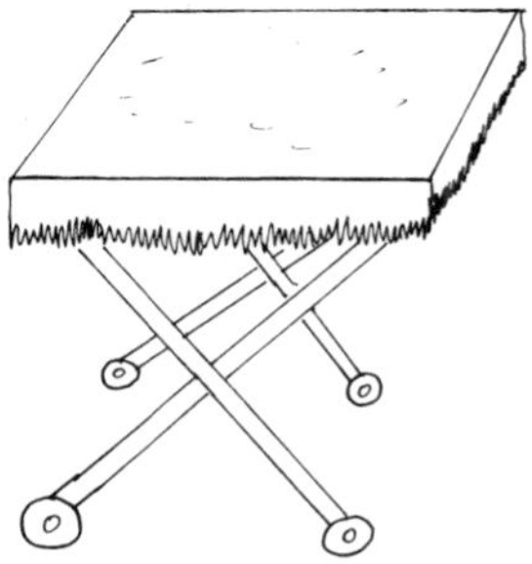

Figure 6-4.

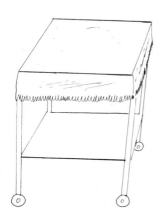

Figure 6-5.

thin sheet of plywood, covered with cloth and a fringed border. (See Figure 6-4.)

A serving cart, covered with a plywood top and with a drape attached can make a nice roll-on table. (See Figure 6-5.)

You will note that the drape does not extend to the back of the cart and that the two shelves of the serving cart provide ample space for a number of props. A card table, covered with a simple table cloth, can also serve as a magic table for stage and platform performances. For carrying your props to and from a stage or platform performance, a small suitcase is usually sufficient. By having a cover made that can slip over the open lid of such a suitcase and by placing this case on a card table

253

with a cover, you can have a very effective setup for perform-ing magic. (See Figure 6-6 A and B.)

Figure 6-6 A.   Figure 6-6 B.

I have used this combination of card table and suitcase for a number of years in doing birthday-party shows, and it works effectively.

The third phase in doing the show is to use your checklist to set up your props in their appropriate places, whether on your person or in your magic case. Many times many of your props can be set up before you actually get to the place where you are going to perform. Once you arrive, it is not a bad idea to go over your checklist once again.

The fourth phase is to get to the location where you are going to perform early, and prepare to do the show. It is always wise to double-check with your host or prospective employer about where you are supposed to be and when you are supposed to be there. Then you need to make sure that you start in plenty of time to get there without feeling rushed. Once you arrive, you should find out exactly where you are performing and get your equipment set up. Obviously, if you are doing an im-promptu performance or performing in your own home, this phase is minimal.

In phase five you actually do the show. I think it is important that you start on time and that you end on time. Move the show along so that the audience does not get distracted or bored. In doing any show, is important to keep your props out of sight until they are needed, and to put them away after you have finished with them.

Phase six could be called the "cleanup." In this phase, you pack your props away, fold up your table, and so on. This should be done as soon as possible after the performance. If you are working close-up, the chances are that all of your props will be back in your case or pockets at the conclusion of the performance; however, if you are working on a stage or platform, you may have a few props that are still on your table. You want to get these away from prying eyes. You will often discover that people will want to talk to you after the show to tell you how good you were or, sometimes, to ask you how you did a certain trick. It is perfectly all right to talk to them, but don't be tempted to give away any of your secrets.

A good name for the seventh phase might be the "debriefing" phase. This occurs after you return home. You should carefully put away your props, after first examining them for any damage or wear. Any needed repairs should be done as soon as possible. It is then advisable to sit down and review the performance you have given. You might even make notes and ask yourself such questions as "What trick seemed most effective as far as the audience was concerned?" "Did anything go wrong? If so, how could I have prevented it?" Questions like these, if you ask and answer them honestly, can help you improve your magic and give you a great deal more satisfaction from performing.

DEALING WITH ANXIETY

One of the greatest problems that you may face as a beginning magician, or even as an experienced magician, is the anxiety that comes in the performing situation. This reaction can be called anxiety, tension, or stage fright. No matter what it is called, it can work a great hardship on your ability to do magic unless it is properly understood and controlled. Trembling hands, shaking knees, a dry mouth, and a quivering voice are not strong assets for your magic.

This anxiety can occur when anyone is placed in a situtaion in which what he is doing is important to him and in which the outcome is unknown or uncertain. Studies of professional actors, teachers, athletes, and speakers have shown that all of these people experience some degree of this emotion. Bear in mind that these people are professionals, not beginners. Remember that the reaction is perfectly normal and that you are not alone.

The key to dealing with this anxiety is to control it. Please note that I did not say "eliminate it." Some tension before performing is actually good for you. Studies have shown that the professionals mentioned above look forward to the feeling of tension in the performing situation, whether in sports or acting, as an indication that they are "up" for the game or performance. This tension, properly channeled and controlled, gives them that extra bit of energy or "fire" needed to put forth their best effort. You should take the same attitude as a magician and welcome the tension because of the energy that it can give you in performance.

At this point, you may logically say, "This sounds good, but how can I control the anxiety rather than let it control me?" There are a number of things that you can do to control the tension or anxiety in the performing situation.

First, you need to develop your confidence by practice and rehearsal so that *you* know that you know what you are doing. (You might want to reread the sections dealing with building confidence and practice.) If you do not really feel prepared for performing your feeling of tension is going to *increase*. But, if you have confidence in your ability to perform a trick or routine, your self-confidence will increase in the performing situation.

You also need to get as much experience as possible. People tend to feel more tense in situations in which they have little or no experience and more at ease in situations in which repetition has built up confidence. This applies to starting in a football game, driving a car, or performing magic. For example, I know a number of very fine close-up magicians who can perform for hours surrounded by an audience, yet they become very tense when they have to get on the stage, simply because they have more experience in close-up magic than stage magic. Although I do not advise that you push your magic on others, I do think that you should take any and every opportunity to perform, provided that you have practiced, of course.

In addition, there is the matter of perspective. You simply cannot allow the performance of a single magic trick or even a single show to become more important to you than it should be. Remind yourself that, even if something should go wrong with the trick, the sun will still rise tomorrow, and that you are not likely to be shot for having made a mistake. I don't say this in order to encourage sloppy magic. I do think that you should care about what you are doing and do your best at it, but if you can place the magic in its proper place in your life, I think you will be much more relaxed while performing.

You should remind yourself that audiences are basically friendly and that they do want you to succeed. Although you may encounter a hostile audience at some point in your magic career, most audiences are on your side. The majority of audiences view magic as it should be viewed, as a form of entertainment, and they *want* to be entertained. They are willing to extend a great deal of support to the performer because they have made an investment of their money (perhaps) and certainly their time in the show, and they don't want it to be wasted.

You can also take comfort in the fact that you usually appear to be more confident than you feel. In some cases, such as trembling hands or a shaky voice, you might indicate tension to an audience; however, *most* of the time, a great deal of the tension is internal. Others, therefore, cannot see it. Only you know for sure how you feel, and if you appear to be confident and avoid saying things like "I'm so scared," others will assume that you are confident. Realizing that no one can tell how you feel should, in turn, make you feel more confident.

"Doing" various physical activities can "drain off" excess energy that leads to shaking hands and quivering voices. Deep breathing, knee bends, running in place, and isometric exercises can help bring your symptoms under control before performing.

Although you may look upon the tension or anxiety of the performing situation as your enemy, keep in mind that it can be your potential friend, provided that you control it rather than let it control you.

FACING DIFFICULTIES

If I were not realistic about magic as a hobby or even a career, and if I were not concerned with being honest about the craft, I would leave you with the impression that the road to success in magic is smooth and downhill all the way. I cannot do this because I have known so many magicians who have had to struggle hard for success and recognition and because I have had so many ups and downs in my own experiences with magic. Because difficulties and discouragement can arise, I think it is fitting to look at some of the situations that can bring this about, and, suggest some possible remedies.

One difficulty that any magician can encounter is making a mistake in performance. I have seen this happen to beginning magicians (many times) and to seasoned, professional magicians (sometimes) as well. It has happened to me. It will happen to you. This can be depressing, but there are several things that you can do about it. You can practice the trick *more*. I know that you must be getting tired of seeing "practice the trick" so frequently on these pages, but I'm not sure that I can stress the need for practice enough. An effective way to relieve your depression is to put your failure in proper perspective. You must ask yourself, "How important is this one trick in the total scheme of my life?" Another factor that you should keep in mind is that many times the audience will not realize that you have made a mistake unless you tell them! This is not true with every trick, nor is it true for every point in any trick; you do reach a "point of no return" in almost every magic trick, a point at which gracefully getting out of the mistake is impossible. But with almost every trick in magic, you do have options, until you reach the "point of no return," for changing or abandoning the trick. It is wise for you to decide, in practice, where this point is and what you will do if something goes wrong. It is not a bad idea to occasionally practice these "outs," as they are called in magic. If the worst happens, you can always pretend that this was the way that the trick was supposed to work (or not work) and attempt to turn the trick into a spoof. Once you learn to bluff your way through, you will be amazed how many people will believe you have achieved the intended outcome of the trick.

Another difficulty that you may face in performance is not getting positive reinforcement for your magic. You have practiced your tricks thoroughly and you do them well, but you don't get much positive response from your audience. The problem may be a lack of experience on your part, or it may be that you have not yet found your proper performing style. The only solution to this problem is to keep working at your magic; keep experimenting with your style. When you do get a good response from an audience, you should then attempt to analyze why.

Yet another difficulty you may encounter in doing magic is dealing with people. Unless you are doing a stage act that requires no assistants from the audience, you will be forced to deal with people. What I am about to tell you may come as a great shock. Not everyone enjoys magic, just as there are people who do not enjoy baseball, or classical music, or coconut cake. Many people who do not enjoy magic will simply ignore it, but there are others who become aggressive toward the magic and the magician. They will grab your hand during a sleight; they will pick up your equipment and in general, attempt to foil or explain your tricks. I have given a good deal of thought to this kind of personality over the years and I have decided that these people are basically insecure. They have such a limited understanding of who they are or see themselves in such a bad light that they cannot stand to be fooled, or to admit that they have been fooled. Magic, for them, is a threat to their egos. My best advice to you in dealing with these people is to avoid doing magic for them. If you are performing for free, you may simply stop your performance. If you are being paid for your work, however, it is difficult to stop, so it is best to ignore these people and attempt to work with other people in the audience. As you gain more experience in performing magic, you will learn how to quickly spot the receptive and the nonreceptive people in your audience and how to deal with both types.

The difficulties that I have discussed may not be the only problems that you may face in doing magic, but I think they are the major ones. You can learn to overcome them if you are dedicated to the craft of magic and to your own improvement as a magician.

WHERE DO I GO FROM HERE?

I have attempted to give you an introduction to the basics of the craft of magic. The logical question that you might ask now is "Where do I go from here?"

My first suggestion is that you attempt to master the basics of magic in this book. This will give you a firm foundation for future work in the field. This does not mean that you must be able to do every trick in the book, but it would be wise to be able to do several from each chapter, and I think you should become as familiar as possible with the Real Secrets.

The next thing that you should do is to get as much experience as possible in performing magic. You should actively look for opportunities to perform. This suggestion assumes, of course, that you have put in the necessary time practicing and rehearsing to do the trick or tricks well. There are many opportunities for beginning magicians to perform. You might start by doing magic for your family and friends. You should next look for opportunities to perform at school or church talent shows or parties. You will discover that there are many worthy organizations that cannot afford to hire a professional magician that will be delighted to have a performance by an *accomplished* nonprofessional. (By professional, I mean a magician who performs for pay either part-time or full-time.) What you *should not* do is to have business cards printed up and attempt to sell your magic act, not until you have had several years of experience. I shudder to think of the number of people I have seen who have been in magic for a few years, or less, who have decided that they are qualified to do magic for money. Some of them do actually manage to get a few paid shows by undercutting the price of a competent magician, but they only manage to put a blemish on our fine craft and to leave a bad taste for magic in the mouths of their customers. These beginners manage to alienate any professional magicians who live near them, making it harder for them ever to be accepted into the magic fraternity.

You should also extend your knowledge of the craft of magic by reading everything that you can locate on the subject of magic. It is truly amazing how many good books have been written on the subject of magic. Keep in mind that the suggested-reading list below is a selected list. It does not attempt to include all of the good books on magic, nor does it attempt to list all of the books that I have read and found useful, but it is a beginning. The abbreviation "n.d." indicates that no date was given.

Bobo, J. B., *Modern Coin Magic* (revised edition). Chicago: Magic, Inc., 1966.
This is the classic work on coin magic. If you decide that you want to do magic with coins, you cannot afford to be without this book.

Christopher, Milbourne, *The Illustrated History of Magic.* New York: Thomas Y. Crowell Co., 1973.

———, *Panorama of Magic.* New York: Dover Publications, Inc., 1962.
Christopher's two books not only give good information on the history of magic, but they also contain numerous beautiful reproductions of magic posters from Christopher's private collection.

Corinda, *Thirteen Steps to Mentalism.* New York: Louis Tannen, Inc., 1968.

Because of its scope and depth, if you read no other book on mental magic, you should read this one.

Ganson, Lewis (ed.), *The Art of Close-Up Magic* Vol. I. London: Unique Studio, 1961; Vol. II, Bideford, Devon., England: Supreme, 1973.

————, *The Dai Vernon Book of Magic.* London: Unique Studio, n.d.

————, *The Magic of Slydini.* Bideford, Devon., England: Supreme Magic Company, n.d.

————, *Routined Manipulation, Part I.* New York: Louis Tannen, Inc., n.d.

————, *Routined Manipulation, Part II.* New York: Louis Tannen, Inc., n.d.

————, *Routined Manipulation, Finale.* New York: Louis Tannen, Inc., n.d.

The books edited by Lewis Ganson provide a very wide range of excellent close-up magic.

Ginn, David, *Professional Magic for Children.* Norcross, Georgia: Scarlet Green, 1976

I have known Dave since he was in his teens. He is now a professional magician who does a great deal of magic for children. He shares some of his favorite routines and techniques in this book.

Kaplan, George G., *The Fine Art of Magic.* York, Pennsylvania: Fleming Book Company, 1948.

This book contains not only some very fine magic tricks but some excellent material on the theory of magic as well.

Lorayne, Harry, and Tarbell, Harlan (Eds.), *Tarbell Course in Magic* (7 vols.). New York: Louis Tannen, Inc., 1941–72.

Tarbell edited Vols. I–VI; Lorayne edited Vol. VII. These books deal with close-up, platform, and stage magic, and, page for page, the Tarbell course is one of the best investments that you can make in the area of literature on magic.

Lorayne, Harry, *Close-Up Card Magic.* New York: Louis Tannen, Inc., 1962.

———, *Deck-sterity.* New York: Louis Tannen, Inc., 1967.

———, *My Favorite Card Tricks.* New York: Louis Tannen, Inc., 1967.

———, *Personal Secrets.* New York: Louis Tannen, Inc., 1964.

All of the books by Lorayne are on card magic and they contain well-written and usable material.

Marshall, Frances Ireland, *Kid Stuff* (6 vols.). Chicago: Magic, Inc., 1954–74.

A number of talented magicians have contributed their favorite routines for children's shows to these books. If you are interested in this type of magic, these books are excellent buys.

Mentzer, Jerry, *Close-Up Cavalcade.* Greenville, S.C.: published by the author, 1973.

This book contains a number of effective close-up tricks that I use, including an effect by one of my favorite close-up workers, Rick Johnsson.

Nelms, Henning, *Magic and Showmanship: A Handbook for Conjurers.* New York: Dover Publications, Inc., 1969.

Not only does this book contain some very clever magic, but it also contains a great many perceptive ideas about the theory of magic.

Pecor, Charles Joseph, *The Magician on the American Stage, 1752–1874.* Washington, D.C.: Emerson and West, 1977.

Well, I did have to get in a plug for my own book, didn't I? This is the only in-depth study of magic and its relationship to theatre in early America. I am rather fond of it.

Poland, Ellison, *Wonderful Routines of Magic.* North Billerica, Mass.: published by the author, 1969.

This is a collection of very fine close-up and platform magic. It contains a number of clever routines and ideas by Bill Spooner, one of the South's leading close-up workers.

You should also make contact with a number of magic dealers. You could do so by visiting any magic shops in your area or by attending a magic convention, a place where many dealers usually assemble. There may be, however, no magic shops near you, and it may not be convenient for you to attend a convention in the near future. The next best solution is for you to get a catalogue from a dealer and to get on the dealer's mailing list. You will find the names and addresses of a number of dealers listed below. This does not represent, by any means, all of the magic dealers, but I have personally dealt with all of these and have been pleased. Some of these dealers have catalogues that they will mail you free; others will sell you a catalogue for a few dollars.

Abbott's Magic Manufacturing Company
Colon, Michigan 49040

Al's Magic Shop
1205 Pennsylvania Avenue, N.W.
Washington, D.C. 20004

Magic, Inc.
5082 North Lincoln Avenue
Chicago, Illinois 60625

Paul's Magic and Fun Shop
903 N. Federal Highway
Fort Lauderdale, Florida 33304

Louis Tannen, Inc.
1540 Broadway
New York, New York 10036

M & M Magic Emporium
4861 Jonesboro Road
Forest Park, Georgia 30050

Magic Methods
Post Office Box 4105
Greenville, South Carolina 29608

It would also help your magic career to join a magic club. Membership in a magic society can be of great value to any magician, and of special value to a beginning magician. At magic club meetings, you get to see new tricks, to share magic and ideas about magic, and to meet and be taught and stimulated by other magicians. It is in the magic club that you are most likely to find a magician or magicians willing to teach you magic and to evaluate your work. If there are any magic clubs in your area, you can usually locate a member who will be willing to invite you to a club meeting. You should not expect to be accepted immediately into the club. Regulations vary from club to club, but most magic societies insist, and rightly so, on a period of apprenticeship so the sincerity of the prospective member can be judged. If you are invited to attend a meeting of a magic club, you should take with you a few of the tricks that you perform best. At the club meeting, be on your best behavior and remember the "rules" of magic. Do not be a smart mouth. Nothing alienates experienced magicians more than a beginner who acts as if he knows everything. If there are no magic clubs near you, you might attempt to become affiliated with one of the national or international magic organizations. For more information on these organizations and for details on how to become a member, you should write to the following addresses:

Mrs. Mary T. Dowd
Executive Secretary
International Brotherhood of Magicians
I.B.M. Headquarters
Post Office Box 227
Kenton, Ohio 43326

Mr. Frank F. Buslovich
Membership Development Chairman
Society of American Magicians
5 Stanley Terrace
Lynn, Massachusetts 01905

Magical Youths International
61551 Bremen Highway
Mishawaka, Indiana 46544

If you follow these suggestions, you will discover that magic is an ever-expanding universe; there is always something new to be learned or something old to be used in a new and different way.

Conclusion
The Art of Magic

I began this book by calling magic a craft and I end it by calling magic an art. How is this possible? It is possible because I feel that there are skills that you can acquire in magic, if magic is right for you, that go far beyond accomplishments and skills of a craft.

Magic begins to be an art when you start inventing your own tricks. This is one reason that I have attempted to teach you principles of magic in this book, so that you might have a foundation to build on. This is also the reason that I have include a thinking-time section after many of the tricks. I want to stimulate the creative forces that are often buried deep inside a potential magician.

Magic begins to be an art when you start figuring out how tricks are done without having to be told the secret. For some magicians, this ability seems to come rather quickly; for others it takes more time. But once you have acquired this magic "mind set," you will be amazed at your ability to analyze what you have seen.

Magic begins to be an art when you find the performing style that is right for you and when you develop the ability to pick or adapt tricks to fit this style. As I have mentioned, this may take time and you may need to invest in a good deal of magic before it happens, but when it does happen, all of the hours that you have spent in magic will be worth it. When you can meld your magic with your personality, you are well on your way to becoming a magical artist.

Magic begins to be an art when you reach the point at which, if something goes wrong in a trick, you can work your way out of it. This will take a good deal of thought on your part and it will come as you acqure experience, but you will gain a great deal of self-confidence in knowing that you can command the situation.

Magic becomes an art when you can relax and enjoy the performance of magic while you are doing it. This is a sure sign that you have arrived. You will and should still feel tension or anxiety before you begin your performance; most magicians do. But, once you are "on," the tension is replaced by a feeling of confidence and well-being. You experience a real and natural emotional "high." You will become involved in what you are doing, but, at the same time, you will be aware of the audience and its reactions to your performance. You will discover that you become sensitive to the attention and interest of the audience and that you can skillfully control spectators.

Magic becomes an art when you are able, in close-up, platform, or stage magic, to establish a rapport with your audience and bring them into your magic world no matter if it be humorous, serious, or frightening. The ultimate goal of magical entertainment is to allow the audience to escape, even briefly, from the real world with its cares and worries to the imaginary world of magic, in which the unusual becomes the ordinary and the impossible is made possible.

With the proper amount of work and study you can master the craft of magic and earn the right to call yourself a magician. With the right combination of personality, skill, and desire, you can go beyond the craft of magic and become a magical artist. No matter whether you be craftsman or artist, whether magic becomes a hobby or a profession with you, may the world of mystery give you the ability to see life, at least at times, through the eyes of a child. And may the practice of magic give you as much pleasure as it has given me.

Index